HOMESICK

by

Mary Minnock

For Mathilde, Nora, Johanne and Ashlinn.

With all my love.

Chapter 1

Peter Lawlor winked at her. Christina ignored it. She had just put up the final slide of her presentation and she didn't want to be distracted. In any case, it was hard to know with Peter if he was being encouraging or condescending.

'So, to summarise.' She paused to take a drink of water. The room was warm but she didn't want to take her jacket off for fear she might look unprofessional. Russell Hunter, the American CEO of their parent company had flown in expressly for this meeting and, despite his casual, unhurried manner, she knew from past experience that very little passed him by. He was a Texan and everything about him was big: his height, his girth, his face, his hands, even his deep, warm voice. Frank, their boss, was hopping around him, anxiously trying to anticipate his every need. The whole senior management team was there: Tony Sheridan from Business Development, Noel Shanahan, Systems Manager, Peter Lawlor who was in charge of human resources, Frank, the General Manager and, of course, Christina, Financial Director.

'I've outlined the main financial implications of the takeover, both the costs and the benefits.' She pressed a button on the remote control and a new slide with two columns appeared. Suddenly, over the seated heads of the other managers, she noticed a movement behind the glass pane in the boardroom door. The face of Aoife, her assistant, appeared, a frown darkening her features. Christina stopped speaking for a moment. Aoife had her hand on the handle of the door, obviously of two minds about whether or not to interrupt the meeting. Christina gave her a barely perceptible shake of the head. Whatever it was could wait until the meeting was over. Aoife disappeared.

'On the whole, I see the benefits of this takeover coming mainly from reduced costs in the form of lay-offs but not from expansion into new sales segments.' She turned back to the screen. 'We could end up letting up to twenty percent of the workforce go. I think we should really consider the impacts of this.'

Peter gave her a quizzical smile. 'What's this? Christina Cavanagh worrying about the plight of the workers?' he said. She stared at him. What did he mean? Of course she cared about making people unemployed. She certainly took that into account but dealing with that aspect wasn't part of her job. Her focus was on preserving the financial health and long-term viability of the company. She dealt with the money; it was his job to deal with the people.

'Lay-offs cost money, Peter,' she said evenly. 'And not just in direct financial terms. You've seen yourself how work quality slides when there's talk of redundancies.'

'Aha,' Peter said with an air of having solved a mystery.

His assumptions needled her. She frowned and continued. 'One last point. CCM operates very differently to us. I'm afraid that we might be underestimating the hidden costs of combining the two companies. What I'm saying overall is that we need to proceed with caution.' She switched off the projector and picked up a pile of papers.

'I have copies of the presentation here if you want to examine the figures in greater detail.' She gave each of the men a stapled bundle and sat down. She glanced back at the door. There was no sign of Aoife. She thought about excusing herself for a moment. Her assistant wasn't one for making a fuss unnecessarily.

'That was a very interesting presentation, Christina.' Russell stirred, making his seat creak loudly. 'It's an important decision and I'm glad that we are looking at it from all sides before we make it.'

'Indeed, indeed,' Frank said. 'We are all anxious to do the right thing here, Russell. We'll definitely be considering all the angles before we move forward. Now, I think Tony has arranged to take you to visit a couple of our biggest customers, isn't that right, Tony?'

Christina stood up. 'I might leave you then. If anyone has any questions, you know where I am.'

On her way out, she heard Tony making a point. 'Christina's done a great job but, honestly, I think she's being pessimistic. I think we can make this work. Buying CCM would mean that we'd be the market leader in the sector.' She closed the door before she heard anyone respond.

When she got back to her office, Aoife had her head down, working at her desk. It was a good sign. Her son had been seriously ill six months earlier. If he had had a relapse, which was Christina's first thought on seeing Aoife's anxious face, she would surely have left already.

Aoife stood up and rushed towards her as soon as she saw her. The frown was back on her face.

'Is everything all right, Aoife?'

'There was a phone call from your brother Mark during the meeting. It's your mother.'

Her heart thudded against her ribcage.

'He said that she had a stroke. She's in hospital.'

Adrenaline flooded her veins and she froze.

Aoife continued. 'He said to say that she's stable at the moment but for you to call him as soon as you can.'

The relief that she was still alive was immense.

'Thank you, Aoife. I'll call him now.'

'Is there anything I can do?'

'No, I'm fine.' She turned to go to her office but then stopped. 'By the way, thank you for your work on the presentation. Well done.'

At her desk, behind the glass panels that separated her from Aoife and her other work colleagues, she took her mobile phone from the top drawer. She had left it there so she wouldn't be distracted during the presentation. There was a missed call from Mark. She hesitated a second, took a deep breath and pressed redial. He picked up at the first ring.

'Hi, Christina. Did Aoife give you my message?'

'Yes, I heard. Tell me, how is she?'

'She's stable. She's in hospital in Galway; they have her under close observation in case she has a second stroke.'

'What happened?'

'She wasn't feeling great when she went to bed, Dad said. Then, during the night, she got up to get a drink of water and fell in the hall. Luckily, Dad heard it and called an ambulance immediately. They took her to Galway. We were lucky they got her there as quickly as they did.'

'Have you seen her yourself since?'

'Yes, I was just in with her earlier. She's better than I expected; able to sit up in the bed and talk although she's slow and very tired. A bit groggy too although it's hard to tell how much of that is from the sedation and how much is from the stroke.'

'What do the doctors say? Is she going to be OK?'

'It's early days. They haven't finished running all the tests but I get the impression that they're positive enough. She's in good health generally and she's being monitored closely. Hopefully, she'll recover fully from this.'

'It's Friday. I can drive down after work this evening.'

'I don't think there's any need to do that, Christina. It's a long drive in the dark. If you head off fresh in the morning you'd be here by lunchtime.' He paused. 'I know she'd love to see you.'

'OK, I'll be there tomorrow. Tell her I'll come to see her directly. Thanks, Mark.'

She was about to hang up when his voice held her back.

'Hey, it's your birthday tomorrow, isn't it? It's a big one too. We should mark the occasion.'

'Thanks but don't mind about that, it's no big deal. See you.'

She hung up and stood staring out the big window behind her desk. She was on the fifth floor and she could see the expanse of Dublin Bay extending off to the horizon over the top of the lower reception building below her office. The cold February sun glinted on the water creating a carpet of diamonds.

You have to make it, Mam, she thought. You have to be OK. It can't end like this. She took a deep breath and counted the cars passing by on the road below until her heart rate slowed down.

She'd forgotten her birthday. She was supposed to be going to dinner with Steve the following night to celebrate. Now she'd have to cancel. She hoped he wouldn't mind. He was far keener to make a fuss of her fortieth birthday than she was. Birthdays had never been important to her. It was only a day like any other. It seemed like a silly thing to celebrate: being in the world another three hundred and sixty-five days. Maybe it was because there had been little celebration around birthdays when she was a child. With nine of them in the family, they were simple events in her house. Her mother would make a Swiss roll and after dinner, everyone would sing 'Happy Birthday' and that was about the height of it. In Steve's family, birthdays were a big deal, an occasion for a party with decorations and presents and extended family and friends being invited. Was this how things were generally done in

Birmingham or was it specific to their family? There was only him and his sister so they had the time and money to organise these kinds of events.

In any case, Steve, normally so easy-going, was determined not to let this birthday pass unmarked. It was her second birthday since they had started going out and the first since he had properly moved into her apartment. Maybe it was just as well that she had a good reason to opt out. That way, she wouldn't disappoint him if she didn't react the way he wanted her to. This whole relationship management business was new to her and she suspected that she wasn't very good at it.

She was pulled out of her thoughts by a knock on the door. She turned around. Frank entered, followed by Russell.

'Everything all right, Christina?' Frank asked.

'Yes, of course. Sorry, I thought the meeting was over. Did you need me for something?'

'I know it's short notice.' Russell placed one of his meaty hands on her shoulder. 'We just called in to ask if you might be available to join Frank and me this evening for dinner with Nick Roche from CCM. You had some interesting ideas at the meeting and I'd like to get your take on things.'

'No hassle if you have other plans, but it would be good to have you there,' Frank added.

She hesitated. It wasn't that she had definite plans for that evening but it would mean not seeing Steve at all for the weekend. On the other hand, it would keep her busy and she wouldn't have to discuss family matters with him. Steve was great but she wasn't quite sure if she was ready to let him find out about the messiness that was Cavanagh family life.

'Sure, I think that would be fine. I'd be happy to go.'

'Great. I'll get Susan to give you the details.' Frank said.

'Well then, I'll see y'all later on. Many thanks.' Russell hitched up his trousers to loosen them and reduce the strain on his braces. The two men left her office and she got back to work.

There was something surprising to Aoife at the idea of Christina having a mother, never mind a brother and a whole family somewhere in the West. She was so self-contained and solitary that Aoife couldn't imagine her doing the normal, ordinary things that people did in families, or at least in families like hers. When she had given Christina the news about her mother's stroke, she had been inscrutable. Anyone else might have said that she didn't care but Aoife knew her boss well enough now to know that she had been shaken. She had gone to her office to phone her brother and after the phone call was over, Aoife had seen her through the glass panels staring out the window, motionless. This wasn't like her. Normally, she never stopped for a minute, she was always busy working on her computer or talking on the phone or examining papers, pen in hand. She was a powerhouse of energy. Nothing escaped her. She could zone in on the key figure in a table or find the one error in a chart after just a quick look. She personified efficiency to an extent that used to be intimidating when she started working for her first – not that she was entirely at ease with her now. But at least now, she knew better what was expected of her and, although she might not be the warmest or friendliest boss in the world, Christina was always fair, and that was good enough for her.

After Frank and the American manager left, she was struck by the lost expression on Christina's face. She had never seen her like that before and her heart pinched in sympathy. She tapped lightly on the door of the office before opening it. 'Christina, is everything all right?'

Instantly, the shutters descended and her usual expression of poised cautiousness returned. 'I'm fine, thank you, Aoife.' She quickly switched on her computer and settled in behind her desk. 'We'd better get back to work. All the time we put into preparing for this meeting means that we fell behind a bit with the day-to-day stuff. We still have to get the monthly sales figures sorted for next week's sales meeting.'

She got the message loud and clear and backtracked immediately. Christina didn't want a personal discussion. 'I'll ask Rory in IT to pull out the data straight away,' she said.

'That'd be great. There were a few issues with last month's figures that I'd like to check.' Christina picked up a blue file from the corner of her desk and opened it.

Aoife backed away quietly and closed the door. She'd been working for Christina for almost four years now and, through trial and error, she had become used to her ways. She kept herself to herself but at least you knew where you stood. When it came to important things, Christina was supportive and helped where she could and she liked her discretion. Like last year, when her son, Cathal, had caught viral meningitis. Her blood still ran cold when she thought about the day the doctor had told her, in that deathly serious voice, to take him to the hospital immediately. She had sat by his little limp body day and night for three days, terrified of losing him. A week later, after the doctors had reassured her that he was out of danger, she went back to work. They needed the money, what with the mortgage on the new house and her dad in the nursing home. But she couldn't settle, fearful every time she had to leave him. As she struggled with the monthly sales report, trying in vain to keep the figures straight in her head, Christina called her into her office. Her heart was in her throat. She was sure that at best she would be reprimanded, at worst, demoted.

'Aoife, I think you should pack up your things and go home and be with your son,' Christina started. She had been just about to beg for her job when Christina continued. 'Take whatever time it takes and come back when he's fully well again. Of course, you'll be paid in the meantime.'

'But what will you do?' She had been close to tears but her boss's cool reserve forced her to hold them back.

'Don't worry. I'll cope,' she said dryly as if the conversation was already at an end.

'Thank you so much, Christina. I appreciate this so much.'

'It's all right. There's no need for that.' Christina shrugged off the gratitude with a trace of a smile. 'It's not as if you're going to be able to do much in the state you're in.'

She gulped and left the office. It was only a while later that she realised that Christina hadn't asked her specifically how Cathal was. It was this ambiguity that kept a distance between them and prevented them from becoming friends but Aoife liked her despite all that and would do anything for her.

She sighed as she pulled out her swivel chair and got back to work. A few minutes later she looked up to see Susan Morris, the chief executive's secretary, arriving, full of her own self-importance. Susan was one of the most irritating people in the company. Her position had obviously gone to her head and in her more illuminated moments she seemed to imagine herself joint managing director of the company.

'Hello, Susan.'

'Aoife. I need to have a word with Christina.' She made it sound as if the two of them had matters of major corporate, if not national, importance to discuss.

'Can I help?'

'Thanks.' She gave her a big smile as if to say, that's a good girl, just tell your mother I'm here. 'I'll just pop my head in and talk to Christina directly. It'll be quicker.'

She pretended to be getting something out of the bottom drawer of her desk to hide her smirk when she heard Christina say 'Ah, Susan, for the dinner this evening, I presume. Just leave the details with Aoife. I'm in the middle of something here. Thank you.'

At ten past five, she, as usual, asked Christina if there was anything urgent that needed doing before she left and, as usual, she was told no. She had no idea what time Christina stayed in the office until but every evening she left her working intently and found her in almost the same position the next morning, just wearing different clothes. She glanced outside at the windy, damp evening, buttoned up her coat and felt very thankful to be going home to Gerry and the kids.

Chapter 2

Christina's car was one of the last left in the car park. It shone a luminous pale grey under the lights. She wedged her laptop bag on the floor in front of the passenger seat and took off her coat. It was already dark and there was enough rain that she needed to flick on her wipers every so often. She put on a CD and music filled the car. She liked being in this tiny, confined world, a bubble of light travelling through the night. She felt safe, untroubled, alone. Sometimes, all she wanted to do was to keep going, driving without thinking, moving without arriving. But she needed to get home quickly. She didn't have a lot of time to get ready.

They were meeting up at the hotel Russell was staying in before going on to the restaurant. She hoped the night wouldn't go on too late. She planned to get an early start on the road the next morning for Galway. A vision of her mother lying motionless, eyes closed, on a white, starched hospital pillow came to her. Stop. No point in worrying when she couldn't do anything about it. There would be time enough when she got there. Like a child picking up a toy train from its track to put it down elsewhere, she forced her thoughts in a different direction. What would she wear tonight? What about that blue and green dress that Steve had admired on her?

As she parked in her numbered space, she glanced up to see if the lights were on in the apartment. They were: Steve was home. She sighed as gathered up her things. She would have to go up and explain the change of plans for the weekend to him. He would understand, he always did, but he might ask her more questions than she was prepared to answer right now.

It was yet another thing that she had to adjust to ever since they had started living together. It was hard to be specific about when Steve had properly moved in. It had been a gradual thing. When he had finally embarked with the last of his belongings and given up his room in the house he shared with the lads about six months earlier, it had been a natural progression rather than a big decision. Apart from sharing a poky flat in Fairview with two girls during college, she hadn't lived with anyone else since leaving her family home and, although she hadn't made a conscious decision about it, she had started to presume she never would. But then Steve had come into her life.

Before, if someone had asked her to describe the man she would end up with, he would not have resembled Steve at all. She might have imagined a smart, ambitious, successful man, a businessman, someone a bit like herself. But as the years passed and she progressed in her job, this fictional man faded away and disappeared.

Steve was nothing like this man. He was tall and big, with a full beard, younger than her by almost four years. He was an aspiring musician who worked as a technician in a biscuit manufacturing company to fund his music. He dressed for comfort in jumpers and jeans. He was English, a Brummie, as he said himself. He was easy to be with, warm and accepting of everyone and people liked him instantly. Because they were so different, their friends often found it hard to hide their surprise when they were introduced.

Sharing her living space with someone else took some getting used to. Before, when she came home, she would change into something comfortable, listen to music, cook, watch TV before going to bed, often without speaking a word to anyone. She had a few close friends but she liked to be able to choose when to spend time with them.

The first time she had invited Steve back after a night out, he had almost literally swept her off her feet. His gentleness and his obvious interest in everything she had to say completely disarmed her. After he stayed that night, it was easier to be together in her apartment rather than in the house he shared with three other guys. Eventually, he spent so much time there that moving in fully just happened.

She turned the key in the lock and through the open door she heard the soft strumming of Steve's guitar. He looked up when she came in and smiled. He kept playing while she hung up her coat and took off her shoes.

She curled into the opposite corner of the sofa, listening to him. Finally, he stopped and leaned across the top of his guitar to kiss her briefly on the lips.

'That sounds good,' she said.

'Getting there,' he said. 'How was your day?'

She took a breath. 'Not good,' she said. 'I got a phone call from my brother to say that my mother had a stroke during the night.'

Instantly, Steve's pick froze. He stared at her and put his guitar to one side. 'Oh, Chris, that's awful. How is she?' he said. He was the only one who called her Chris. In the beginning, she had tried to correct him and tell him that her name was Christina but no one in his family had managed to hang on to their full name so he never seemed to remember and now she was getting used to it.

'She's in hospital in Galway. I think she's doing OK but I'm going to drive over there in the morning to see her.'

'You poor thing. Do you want me to come with you?'

'No, it's OK,' she said. She had enough to come to terms with without having to deal with introducing Steve to her family as well.

He scratched his beard. 'And it's your birthday tomorrow.'

'I know. I'm sorry. We can go out for dinner next weekend if you like.'

'Don't worry about it. Look after your mother. How long do you think you'll be gone?'

'Oh, I'll probably just stay overnight. It's a bad time to be out of work.'

'Don't let work even come into it, Chris. Stay if your mother needs you. She should be your priority at the moment.' He moved over closer so that he could pull her against him.

She was irritated with him. She would decide what her priorities were, not him but she said nothing.

'Is everything all right between you and your mum?' he said after a while. 'I get the impression that there's something you're not telling me.'

'Everything's fine. Not all families have to live in each other's pockets, you know.'

'I know. It's just that I only met her once since we've been together, that time we went for lunch with your parents when they came to Dublin for Christmas shopping. But you don't talk about your family much and I wondered if there was something up.' He was treading carefully.

'No, not at all. I'm just busy with work and don't have time to go home much.'

'Hmmm,' he said.

This was exactly the kind of conversation she was trying to avoid. 'Steve, I'm not trying to avoid bringing you to Kilnalough. We'll go soon, when the weather is better but not now.'

'Hey, I'm not trying to impose but I don't want to go just to play the tourist.'

'Fine, fine, we'll find a time.' She stood up abruptly.

They stared at each other before Steve relented.

'Why don't I go out and pick up something to eat and a bottle of wine. We'll have a quiet evening and celebrate your birthday here.'

'I can't, I have to go to a work thing.' She looked at her watch. 'I'd better run, I'm meeting Frank and Russell for dinner. I have to get ready.'

'Really? You never mentioned this before.' He was obviously exasperated with her.

'It only came up this afternoon. It's important. I have to go.' She turned to go to the bedroom to get changed. She quickly put on her dress and freshened up her makeup. She could hear him still playing the guitar and softly singing.

'What'll you do for dinner?' she asked when she came back into the sitting room.

'Don't worry about me,' he answered shortly, keeping his eyes on his strings. 'I'll find something in the fridge, one meal less probably wouldn't do me any harm.'

Steve often made comments about his weight even though she liked him exactly as he was. His extra kilos suited him.

'Sorry to leave you like this.' She hovered on the doorstep.

'I might go out for a pint. I think the lads are meeting up in Coughlan's later on.'

She left.

Conversation over dinner about the impending takeover was animated but her mind wandered and she had to make an effort to stay focused.

'I'm flying back to the States in a few days, Christina,' Russell said as they went their separate ways afterwards. 'I'd like to get a chance to talk to you before I leave.'

'I'm going away this weekend but I'll be around next week so call in to my office whenever it suits.'

'Enjoy your weekend. You deserve a break. Would you like us to drop you home?'

'Not at all, Russell. Thank you. I'll take a taxi. It's no problem.'

After Christina left to go to dinner, Steve was restless. His plans for the weekend: the special dinner he had booked at the restaurant, chosen after much research, followed by drinks with a few of Chris's friends in the pub were not possible anymore. He understood very well her reasons for pulling out and he didn't want to be so petty as to object but the problem was that he got the impression that it suited her to cancel. He didn't want to pin her down, especially with everything happening, but she always seemed to back away when he got too close as if she had some kind of sensitive alarm system set up around her innermost self. The problem was that the perimeter was invisible to him and he never knew when he might step into a no-go area. He shook his head and decided to go out for a pint.

'Hey, Steve. We weren't expecting to see you here tonight. I thought you had the whole weekend booked for birthday plans with Chris?' Alan said as Steve arrived in Coughlan's.

'Yeah, well, change of plans. She's got work stuff on tonight.' He used to share a house with Alan and Shane before moving into Chris's place. He still enjoyed spending straightforward, uncomplicated time in their company.

'Does she ever stop?' Shane said.

'What are you having, guys?' Steve didn't want to get into it.

He went to the bar for a round and looked around the pub as he waited to be served. He liked this pub. It was a comfortable, relaxing place. At the weekends, they had live music sessions, mostly with local talent, and it was here that he had met Alan playing the guitar on the first occasion when he had wandered in for a drink one of the first few weeks after he'd moved to Ireland. He'd remained a loyal customer ever since.

He returned with three pints and put them down on the table.

He took a long mouthful and wiped off the foam from his moustache. 'Alan, remember you asked me to do that gig with you tomorrow evening. Well, if it's still on, I can do it.'

'I thought you had plans.' Alan reached over to take his pint.

'That's changed. Chris has to go to Galway. Back to her homeplace to see her mother. She's in hospital.'

'Anything serious?' Shane asked.

'I don't know. I think she had a stroke. But she seems to be doing OK.'

'Sorry to hear that.'

Alan looked at him through narrowed eyes. 'Everything all right with you two?'

Steve nodded. 'Yeah, sure. Just sometimes, it's hard to figure out what's going on in Chris's head.'

'I know what you mean. She plays her cards close to her chest, doesn't she?' Alan said. 'Anyway, that'd be great if you were up for it. We can include all the new stuff we've been practising lately.'

'I have a couple of new songs I'm working on that I wouldn't mind you hearing.' Steve became more animated as the conversation moved onto music.

Finally, after all the musical arrangements had been discussed, he looked at his watch. 'I won't stay too late. Time for a last one and I'll head. Same again?'

Outside, he checked his mobile phone out of habit to see if Chris had rung. There was nothing. The air was cold but dry. He took his woollen hat out of his pocket and pulled it down over his ears. He stuck his hands in his pockets and walked towards their apartment. He wondered if Chris was home already.

Despite their occasional communication difficulties, Steve was reasonably confident in his relationship with Chris. He loved her and she loved him. It would just take time for her to realise it. It was as simple as that. He was in no rush, he had all the time in the world.

From almost the first night that they'd met at Tom and Rita's engagement party, he'd been sure that they were good together. It had held in a private room over one of the pubs in town. Tom was a drummer he had met through Shane and Chris was friends with Rita through a French evening class they'd taken together. It was one of those parties where the women sat around together chatting at tables while the men gathered at the bar, an invisible line drawn between them. She gave the impression of being confident but when he caught her eye she looked flustered and broke eye contact. The contrast appealed to him so when the woman beside her got up to go to the toilet he seized his chance and crossed the room to sit beside her. Everyone looked surprised to find him among the femininity of their table.

'My name's Steve,' he said. 'I thought I'd come over and say hello.'

She looked wary, as if she suspected him of ulterior motives. She glanced around at the other women before replying.

'Well, hi,' she said. 'I'm Christina.'

'Nice to meet you, Christina. Can I get you a drink?'

The other women exchanged knowing looks and turned towards each other, edging their chairs away to give them space. He couldn't remember what they had talked about but they were still sitting there when the barman came to clear off the last of the abandoned glasses. They looked up to see that they were among the last few left in the room.

On the pavement outside, he asked her if he could see her again. She hesitated as if she might say no but then said, 'why not?'

And that was how it had started.

Steve was already in bed with the lights out when she slipped in beside him. She could tell from his breathing that he wasn't asleep yet. She didn't want to get back into discussing her mother, her family and going home. She wanted to forget about it and go back to talking about ordinary, everyday things. She heard him take a preparatory breath, ready to talk, but he let it out without saying anything. Under the duvet, she reached across the space between them. She slipped her hand under his T-shirt and caressed the abundant hair on his chest. She moved her hand downwards and although he didn't move, she could sense him reacting. His penis unfurled to meet her hand. She snuggled in closer to his large, warm body. He was lying on his back so she pulled herself up to kiss him on the lips and lean on his chest. She could tell he was hesitating to accept her peace offering but, after a second, he relented and kissed her back. She wriggled out of her T-shirt. He ran his hands along her back and pulled her on top of him, his face buried in her hair, and nuzzled her neck.

Afterwards, he whispered to her in the dark. 'I hope your mother recovers quickly. You can tell me all about it when you get back.'

'I think she'll be fine,' she replied, with more hope than confidence.

She wondered what he expected of her. She had warned him from the beginning. She didn't want marriage or babies or even to make long-term plans. What they had at the moment was enough for her but she could understand if he got impatient and wanted something more out of his life than this.

Chapter 3

On her way to Galway, her stomach churned and contracted as if she hadn't eaten for days even though she'd had breakfast before she left. To calm down, she put on a CD by a Spanish group, La Oreja de Van Gogh. She didn't speak Spanish but when she was troubled, she liked to allow the music to fill up the car and listen to the soft, lisping voices, latching on to the odd word that she understood.

When that didn't work, she tried to regain control over her galloping emotions by making each movement a deliberate one. She became conscious of the muscles that controlled each gesture, in her hand and arm as they gripped the gear stick and pushed it in a direction, in her leg when she pressed on the clutch, even in her neck when she tilted her head to look in the rear-view mirror. She made a mental calculation of the impact on the company's bottom line if the new product launch was successful. She worked out how much it would take to cover the cost of their debts if there was an increase in the lending rate. She even estimated the percentage of the journey that she had already covered and the rate of fuel consumption but none of her usual tricks was working. She was going home. She didn't know what to expect and there was nothing she could do to take away the jitters.

She was always nervous when she headed west, but this time more than ever. She kept her visits to Kilnalough short and sweet and if that meant allowing a certain distance between her and her family to grow, then she accepted that this was how it had to be. This time, however, she suspected it might be more complicated.

It was midday when she arrived in Galway. Her family home at Kilnalough was twenty miles further out of the city along the Lough Corrib road. She would go there later after she had seen her mother. She entered the foyer, her steps making loud, resonant clicks on the marble floor, each one taking her closer to her sick mother. She knew it was illogical but as long as she stayed away she could imagine that what had happened was nothing major, that people were making a big fuss out of nothing, that it was something easily resolved by the doctors. However, once she came face to face with whatever the situation was, she would have to accept the reality and all that that would entail. She tried to swallow the lump in her throat before asking at the information desk where she might find Mrs Cavanagh.

When she pushed open the door of the ward, her first impression was that it was full of people. There were four beds. The room was big and bright. A large window stretched the length of the room with a view over Galway with the sea in the distance. Her mother's bed was near the window. Although she couldn't see her yet, she could tell it was her bed because of all the familiar faces crowded around it. Mark was sitting on the side, his two little girls on the floor playing with tiny dolls. Aidan was standing on the other side of the bed, arms folded. At the foot of the bed, Louise was asking their mother what she wanted her to bring in, using sign language for the benefit of Nuala who was watching the exchange intently. They looked up when Christina walked in.

'Hello, stranger,' Aidan said, but not in a nasty way.

'Hey, you're here,' Mark said.

'Hello, everyone.' She forced a smile onto her lips as she looked around at them but her first priority was to see how her mother was. She looked beyond them to see her mother lying in the bed, her head propped up against pillows. She was wearing a new blue floral nightdress and her hair had been recently brushed but one eye was a little more open than the other and Christina could see from the way her hands were placed on the bed cover that something was wrong. She leaned down and kissed the soft, loose skin of her cheek and breathed in her familiar perfume.

'Hello, Mam,' she said quietly.

'Good – to – see – you, – Christina,' her mother said and attempted a lob-sided smile, although her name came out more like Kissthina.

'How are you feeling?' she asked.

Her mother made an expressive face that said both 'not so good' and 'could be worse'. The stroke had affected her facial muscles and Christina hated to see how contorted her expression was.

She was struggling to say something so Christina leaned in closer.

'Happy – birthday – sweetheart,' she said.

'Oh, don't worry about that. You just concentrate on getting better,' she replied.

'Oh yes, it's your birthday, isn't it?' Louise said. 'Happy birthday!'

They all chimed in but it made her uncomfortable. Celebrating didn't feel right in the circumstances.

She held her mother's hand and looked around at everyone. 'Well, is there any update? What do the doctors say?'

'I got talking to one of the doctors yesterday but I didn't get much from him. It was all a bit manic. It's hard to get someone to talk to, especially since it's the weekend. There was a doctor here doing some tests this morning, Mam said, but none of us was here at the time,' Mark said.

'We'll try and catch someone and get an explanation this afternoon,' Aidan said.

'Is Dad here?' She looked around again, just in case she had missed him in the crowd.

'He's at home. He was here earlier but he'll be back in again this afternoon at some stage,' Louise said.

'I have to go,' Mark said. 'I have to take the girls home but I'll come up to the house later. Come on, Amy, Sinead, give Granny a kiss, we have to go.'

'I should go too.' Aidan reached for his jacket. 'I have to get back to the shop. One of the girls is out sick and we're understaffed. See you later, Mam.' He leaned in to kiss her and she reached up to pat his cheek.

Christina bent down to help her nieces gather up their toys. Already, they seemed more grown-up than when she had seen them last. Amy, always affectionate, gave her a big hug.

‘Are you staying for long, Christina?’ Louise asked.

‘I don’t know. It all depends. I’ll see how it goes.’

‘Nuala and I are going shopping. There’s nothing in the house. If that’s OK with you, we’ll let you sit with Mam for a while. We’ll get a cake to celebrate your birthday this evening,’ Louise said. ‘See you at home for dinner.’

‘Sure. I’ll stay here for a while. See you back at the house,’ Christina said.

‘Are you ready to leave now?’ Louise signed the words to Nuala.

‘Yes, let’s go,’ Nuala signed back. She turned to Christina. ‘Good to see you. How was the journey?’

‘Journey OK. Glad to see Mam. Worried,’ Christina signed awkwardly, her hands a little stiff from lack of practice.

Nuala gave her a quick hug and then stood back. ‘I’m glad you’re here,’ she signed quickly.

Christina found herself alone with her mother. She pulled a chair to the bedside and sat down.

‘Hard – to – believe – it’s – forty – years – since – I – had – you. – Doesn’t – seem – so – long,’ Kate said.

Christina smiled, not trusting herself to speak.

‘How’s – work?’ Kate asked.

‘Good. Busy.’ She was alarmed by the effort it took for her mother to talk. ‘Maybe you shouldn’t talk, you’ll tire yourself out.’

Her mother had always been slim but in recent years she had gained some weight. She had always seemed young and dynamic to Christina but now she looked every one of her sixty-six years. Her skin had a grey tinge to it. She had no makeup on and she looked exposed, vulnerable. Her deep blue eyes hadn't changed though.

She reached across and put her hand on Christina's. 'Good – to – see – you, – love. – We – don't – see – you – often – enough,' she said with long spaces between the words.

Christina's heart inflated like a balloon until it pressed against her rib cage and threatened to explode. She wanted to cry.

Instead, she looked down at the bed and squeezed her mother's hand. She stood up.

'Here, let me prop you up a little bit more,' she said. 'You don't look very comfortable there.' While she was helping her mother to sit up in the bed, a nurse came into the room and approached them, wheeling a blood pressure monitor ahead of her.

'Well, you must be Kate's daughter. There's a strong resemblance there.' She smiled at both of them.

'This – is – Christina, – my eldest,' her mother replied before Christina could answer.

'I'm sorry but I have to run some tests on your mother now. In any case, I think it might be good to let your mother rest for a little while,' the nurse said. 'She's had a lot of visitors today and she needs to take it easy.'

'Of course,' Christina said. 'I'll come back this evening.'

'See – you – later,' her mother said. As she sank back into her pillows, Christina could see the effort she had been making until then.

She left the ward, unsure of what to do next. She wasn't ready to go back to Kilnalough straight away but she didn't know where else to go. She followed the signs for the hospital restaurant and ordered a coffee. She took her mug to a corner table away from people.

Looking out the window, she was suddenly hit by a memory from when she was about twelve. Vivid and real, it bubbled up and she lived it again in that instant. She was curled up on the sofa reading. In the armchair beside her, her mother was watching the nine o'clock news while she polished their shoes for school the next day. It must have been a Sunday because she always did that on Sundays. Christina was allowed to stay up a bit longer than the others because she shared a bedroom with the baby and couldn't turn on the light to read when she went to bed. For a second, her mother's hand stopped moving to better concentrate on what was being said on television, one hand inside a black shoe, the other holding the polishing brush. Christina looked up at her serious face full of concern at the news being presented and was struck by a sudden realisation, so obvious that she found it hard to believe that she hadn't thought of it before. No matter how long her mother lived, she would be the child who got to be with her for the longest because she was the eldest. She felt a guilty pang at this immense privilege which was hers purely by chance. Her mother looked across at her and smiled. 'Is your book good?' she asked. 'What's it about?'

Christina shook herself out of her daydream and stared out the window. She took a sip of her coffee and realised that she'd forgotten the sugar. She stood up and was on her way to get a sachet when she stopped suddenly. Coming into the restaurant was a familiar face. She didn't recognise it straight away, it was as though she was seeing a famous person whose face she had seen a thousand times before on television, but now she was looking at it in the flesh. Her instinctive reaction was to flee, to avoid being seen. She turned away, managing to do it slowly enough to avoid drawing attention to herself, although, in any case, the woman coming towards her seemed engrossed in conversation and oblivious of her.

'…it's not as if the night-shift pay is that great, especially when you think about the stress levels involved in ICU…', she heard her say to the other woman as she passed by. She was dressed in a white nurse's uniform with a navy cardigan over it. She was wearing glasses: she never used to before. She had a plumper, more womanly figure and her hair was shorter and straighter now, but, even after twenty years, she could tell without a doubt who it was. It was Lynn.

Christina sat down again, her knees weak. She held her coffee cup in front of her face as she watched Lynn join the queue to order food. When she felt she could trust herself, she stood up and slipped away. With each step she took towards the exit, she feared that Lynn would look up and see her, her eyes like two bullets searing through her back, felling her in her tracks as surely as with a gun.

1986

They were both fifteen when they first met. It was the year Lynn's parents had moved to the area from Dublin. They had bought the old house that used to belong to the Jamesons about a mile down the road from the Cavanaghs. Throughout the summer, Christina had seen the workmen renovating and decorating the house but it was only when she went back to school in September that she discovered that the new girl in her class lived there. From the first day, she could tell that Lynn was different. For one thing, she managed to make her school uniform look as if it wasn't one. The uniform was a navy skirt for the girls, navy trousers for the boys with white shirts and navy jumpers or cardigans for both. Lynn's skirt was slightly on the short side and she wore cute pumps or white high-top runners with laces in different colours that she changed regularly. She wore chunky pastel socks that she scrunched down to her ankles. Since socks and shoes weren't specified as part of the uniform, she took full advantage of that loophole in the regulation to maximise her style impact. She had a huge array of earrings but the ones she liked to wear best were super large hoops that gave her a bohemian look. She even wore a zip-up navy cardigan instead of a button-up one but Christina imagined that even the teachers were so impressed that they didn't dare mention it.

Within a few days, it was obvious that Lynn was amazingly relaxed (amazing to Christina, at least) with the boys in the class. One day, she even sat beside Peter Kennedy in class, grabbing the first available seat when she arrived late for history, flashing him a big smile as she sidled across in the seat. Caught unawares, he blushed bright red and knocked his book to the floor. She also knew more than anyone else in the class about sex. She had two older brothers which probably was why she was so competent in both of these areas. Even though makeup was not allowed in school, Lynn wore bright pink lip gloss. When Miss Connolly, the English teacher, challenged her about it, Lynn told her calmly that it was just a balm to prevent chapped lips. It was the first time Christina had ever seen a teacher outmanoeuvred and silenced by a pupil and the extent of Lynn's power and self-assurance awed her.

All of this made it even more incredible that Lynn would choose to be friends with her. They took the same bus in the mornings and evenings, and when, one evening, Lynn sat into the empty seat beside her and dazzled her with a smile, Christina was tongue-tied with shyness.

'You're Christina,' Lynn said. 'I heard you're the best in the class at Maths. I was wondering if you could explain one of the problems we have to do for homework.'

'Of course, I'd be happy to. Which one?' Relieved at being on familiar ground, she could hear that she was being a bit too effusive but Lynn didn't seem to notice and pulled out her maths book.

Lynn was like that with everybody. Instinctively she homed in on the things that people were comfortable with and talked about those. She took no notice of any awkwardness or gaffes as if they had never occurred, her friendly chatter pouring oil on troubled waters. Within weeks she was hugely popular with both the boys and girls, all hoping that some of her worldliness might rub off on them. She was pretty but not stunning which made her approachable. She had curves where Christina had none and she made the most of herself, blow-drying her hair into soft curls and wearing as much jewellery and makeup as she could get away with while remaining just barely inside the school uniform rules.

One Friday, at lunchtime, Lynn strolled over to Christina who was reading something on the notice board and invited her to come to her house that weekend. She said this in a casual voice as if it was nothing much. Christina waited a strategic moment to avoid seeming too eager. 'I'd love to,' she said. 'When?'

'Saturday afternoon?'

She nodded. She'd get through all of her jobs in the morning and then she'd be free for the rest of the day.

'Great, we'll have fun.' Lynn squeezed her arm, gave her a smile of complicity and walked away. She had a sudden glorious vision of herself and Lynn being best friends who told each other everything. Since she had started secondary school she had no one special friend who stood out from the girls in the class, no one to whom she could systematically turn at break time, no one who would be entirely on her side against all the injustices of home and school. At home, Mark, Aidan and Enda were fun to play with at times but there were other times when they were just annoying little boys. Nuala was glued to their mother all the time and Louise was only a baby. She had always thought of her mother as her best friend but now she was starting to concede that there were limitations to mothers as confidantes.

On Saturday, she rode her bicycle to Lynn's house. It was a big two-storey house with thick ivy growing across the front. Since Lynn's parents had moved in, they had made a lot of improvements. It was a lovely old house but it had become dilapidated over the years. Now, they had spent money on it and given it back its elegance. The changes on the outside were subtle. It had been given a new coat of paint and the overgrown shrubs in the garden had been chopped back and tamed.

Inside though, the old house had been revamped entirely and to Christina, whose home was plain and practical, it was the height of luxury. They went in through the back door into a laundry room and then into a shiny modern kitchen with a wide breakfast bar and high stools. On the other side of the bar were big, squashy armchairs and a sofa. Lynn called this part the family room.

'Let's get some stuff and take it to my bedroom,' Lynn said as she opened the door of the fridge and gazed inside. Lynn's mother wandered in, cradling a large mug of coffee in one hand, a lit cigarette in the other. Her cigarette created a haze around her and she looked glamorously absent-minded. She said a vague hello but didn't seem particularly interested in Christina, or even in Lynn for that matter, who was poking around in the fridge.

'There's nothing nice to eat here, Mum,' she said.

'I'm going shopping tomorrow,' her mother said before drifting out of the kitchen. This level of freedom was a revelation to Christina. In her house, she was not allowed to take food without asking her mother first, and, if she brought someone home, her mother would have asked ten questions by now in a friendly but nosy way. Everything about the way Lynn lived was so different that she wondered how much they could possibly have in common.

'We'll take enough for Emily as well,' Lynn said, taking a large bottle of Coke and a packet of biscuits. 'She should be here soon.'

Christina tried to hide her disappointment at not being the only chosen one, at having to share her with someone else. From the kitchen, they went into the front hall which was almost as big as the Cavanaghs' whole sitting room.

'Hold on a sec, I need to get something here for Emily.' Lynn opened a door and, from the hall, Christina could see a thick carpet with a pattern of roses on it and a large cream-coloured sofa. She was amazed at the luxury of being able to choose such an impractical colour. It wouldn't have stayed clean for five minutes in her house. There were all kinds of things, paintings, ornaments, lamps, all of which seemed to be there only to decorate and she was awed by the fanciness of the room. Against one wall was a long cabinet in dark wood. Lynn opened one of the doors and took a record out.

'Emily asked me to lend this to her.' Lynn casually waved the album at her. The lurid graphics showed a red background and an airbrushed motorcycle revving up at an angle. It looked like something edgy and exciting from a dangerous world she knew nothing about.

Lynn's bedroom was very girly and personal with a pink bedspread and what seemed like hundreds of stuffed animals on the bed and the floor. It had a tall window with wooden shutters that folded back into recesses in the walls on either side. It had a window seat with tasselled cushions. She couldn't help comparing it in her mind to her own basic, serviceable room full of Louise's baby things.

The only chair in the room was a high-backed wicker one, too covered in soft toys to contemplate removing them, so they sat on the bed. The doorbell rang. It was Emily. It was obvious that she had been there before, judging from the familiarity with which she came into the room and hugged Lynn. They sat in the opposite corners of the window seat, their knees under their chins, mirror images of each other, while Christina stayed on the bed. She had nothing against Emily, in fact, she got the impression from the little she knew of her that she was quite nice. She was friendly and chatty with an easy laugh, but they had never managed to strike up much of a rapport before, possibly because Emily had no interest in anything academic and gave the impression that anyone who did was a complete bore.

The conversation between Lynn and Emily was light and easy, full of inside jokes. Christina would have liked to join in but it was like eating froth, she tried to bite down on it but it was impossible to get a solid grasp on anything. After a while, Lynn jumped up and suggested that they go to the sitting room and listen to some music.

Feeling left out, Christina tried to think of something to say.

'What music do you like, Christina?' Lynn asked her eventually, her hand poised in front of the huge collection of LPs.

'Whatever. You choose.' She didn't want to admit that she knew very little about music and didn't own any album personally. All they had at home was an old second-hand record player her uncle had given them and a few traditional Irish and folk albums which had never attracted her interest.

'How about this? I just got it last week. Let's practice slow dancing,' Lynn held up a single and pulled it out of its sleeve. She put it on the player and carefully placed the stylus in the right place. The smooth, aching sounds of the singer's plaintive voice filled the room. Christina knew the song from the radio but she couldn't remember who sang it. Lynn joined in on the chorus. She had a good singing voice but what was even more impressive was her confidence in it.

'So, who have you kissed, Christina? Which of the boys?' Lynn asked conversationally, as easily as if she was asking her favourite colour.

Christina blushed bright red and Emily giggled.

'Go on, tell us.'

'No one.' She could feel herself burning up inside. She wanted to lie but she knew she could never pull it off: she didn't know enough to fake it.

'Are you serious? You've never kissed anyone? Anyone at all?'

'No.'

'I bet you don't even know how to, then. Do you want me to show you?' Lynn grabbed her hand and pulled her to her feet. She swayed to the music and put her arms on Christina's shoulders. She moved closer so that their faces were too close for Christina to focus and see her features anymore. Christina could feel her warm breath getting closer. Emily giggled. Just as her lips grazed those of Lynn's, she broke away and ran out of the room. Behind her, the two girls burst out laughing. She was fumbling at the front door when Lynn caught up with her, still laughing. 'Christina, I was just joking, come back.'

'I have to go, my mother's expecting me.'

'Don't be silly about it. Can you not take a joke?' Lynn touched her arm. 'Come on back.'

'I'm fine, it's OK. Really. But I do have to go now.'

On the way home, she cycled as fast as she could so that the wind might cool down the burning of her cheeks.

Chapter 4

She sat in her car in the car park, unsure of what to do next. Seeing Lynn had rattled her completely. She contemplated driving home, back to Dublin, but then she remembered Steve was there and, for a moment, she was annoyed with him for taking away her refuge. If she went back, he would ask her questions and, even if he didn't, his enquiring eyes would be looking for answers. No, it was better to stick with the original plan and go through the motions so that nobody would notice anything, and then, as quickly as possible, she would get away and go back to her normal life.

She took the road out of Galway away from the sea towards Lough Corrib. The suburbs thinned out as she left the city and took the familiar road home. The impact of the wind as a sculpting force of nature became more obvious in the slanting trees. After a while, she left the main road and took the small departmental road into the village of Kilnalough. She continued past the post office and its only shop and then took the first turn on the right, onto a road so narrow that there were no road markings anymore. She drove on between the stone wall on the right and the hawthorn ditch on the left, alert for the arrival of another car in which case she would slow down and they could manoeuvre past each other. She crossed the small stone bridge close to her home and remembered the numerous times in her childhood that she and her brothers had dared each other to go all the way underneath, through the water, from one side to the other.

It had been like stepping into a different, parallel world; it was cool where the real world was warm; it was ominous and oppressive where the real world was open and expansive. The change was instantaneous. Once you crossed the line between light and shade, the sounds of laughing and teasing faded, and you were alone. A chill of anticipation ran through your body as you took a step forward, half-afraid, half-fascinated by what you could make your body do.

The arch of stone was too low to stand upright and you were forced to hunch your shoulders. It emanated coolness and yet it was slimy and green so you didn't want to touch it unless you had to. But you didn't want to bend too low either. The water was usually at the level of your knees but after a wet spring, it might reach even higher, almost up to your thighs. The soft silky mud squeezed up through your toes and you wondered what kind of creatures could choose to live in such a place. Through the water, long, slippery water weeds flowed and rubbed against your legs like eels wanting to be petted.

As you moved slowly forward through the long, dark arch, reality relaxed its grip and it became possible to imagine that some kind of underwater monster might grab your legs and drag you below. The water restricted your movements and emphasised that this was not your element and certainly not one where you could win any battle. Every time you lifted a foot and put it down, your throat prepared itself to scream if it made contact with anything unexpected. Until you reached the halfway point, you told yourself that you could always turn back but you knew you wouldn't. This was the darkest point, bright light tantalisingly out of reach on both sides. You could hear your own breathing echoing back to you.

There was a hole in the arch of the bridge at the halfway point where a stone had fallen out. Once you reached it, you would speed up to get out quickly except that the flow of water was now pushing you away from where you wanted to go where before it had been encouraging you to turn back. If you went too fast you might have to reach out and touch the algae-smeared walls to prevent yourself from falling into the water. Just the idea of falling made your heart beat faster. When you finally came out the other side, the warmth of the sunshine hit your head and shoulders and it was like being blessed. You looked up to see the grinning faces of the boys waiting for you to make it. Their cheers and teasing made you grin back; there was no way you could prevent that smile from breaking out, you were so relieved and thrilled at having succeeded.

The smile came back even now as she slowed down to cross the bridge. Through the car window, she stretched her neck up to try to see over the stone wall to the river below. It looked smaller and more overgrown than she remembered through her child's eye.

She took the next right and, around the corner, her family home appeared, an old pebble-dashed farmhouse with a mishmash of extensions. The original house was a small rectangular bungalow with a green front door and two small windows on each side. Between the front of the house and the low wall that separated the house from the road was a strip of lawn. On the part nearest the house, someone had planted tulips and daffodils, green spears piercing the soil that would flower in a few weeks. Mam must have more time on her hands these days, she mused, before cutting off this thought and driving into the yard separating the house on the left from the farm buildings on the right.

At the back of the house, a two-storey extension had been built in the seventies and in recent years a utility room and conservatory had been added onto the kitchen. There were several cars already parked in the yard although only Nuala and Matthew lived at home now with their parents. She took her small suitcase from the boot of her car and went to the back of the house through a glass-paned door that led to the utility room and then, into the kitchen.

Louise was standing by the kettle waiting for it to boil. 'Hi,' she said. 'How was Mam when you left?'

'Tired. The nurse asked me to leave so she could get some rest.'

'What did you think of her?' she asked, anxious to hear what Christina had to say.

Christina looked quickly at her. What did she mean? How could she have an opinion? It wasn't as if she had spoken to a doctor or as if she had any particular medical knowledge. The old gossamer threads of responsibility were latching on to her and reeling her back in.

'I'm sure she'll be fine. At least, I hope so. Where is Dad?'

'He's in the sitting room. He's a bit shaken.'

'I'll go and say hello.'

Jim was sitting by the fireplace, an open newspaper on his knees but he didn't look as though he was reading it. The fire was lit and Nuala was sitting on a big cushion on the floor beside it. She was rubbing down the cat curled up on her knees who was purring loudly, his constant hum underlying the commentary of the match Aidan and Enda were watching on the television.

'Hello, Dad,' Christina said and leaned down to kiss him on the cheek. He looked up, more aged than the last time she had seen him. He seemed vulnerable and confused. His relief at seeing her bothered her. She wanted him to be the independent, quiet, hard-working man of her childhood, not an old man who needed support. He folded over the paper and took off his glasses.

'Well, Christina, you're back from the hospital? What did you think of your mother?'

What was this with everyone? What did it matter what her opinion was? It meant nothing more than the opinion of the tea lady. She wanted to snap at him, I'm an accountant, Dad, not a doctor, but she didn't. Instead, she answered his question with one of her own. 'Have you been talking to the doctors lately?'

'I was talking to them yesterday but I don't know what they're saying half the time. They all seem very cagey, it's very hard to get a straight answer out of them.'

'I suppose they're telling you what they know. They can't give guarantees.'

Louise came into the room with a tray of tea things and put it on the coffee table in the middle. Aidan moved along the sofa to make room for Christina to sit down.

'Everyone help themselves,' Louise said as she poured the tea into the various mugs.

The door opened and Matthew came in. He was wearing jeans that had a veneer of several days of wear and an orange t-shirt with a black silhouette of Bob Marley on it.

'Hi, lads,' he said before spotting Christina on the sofa. 'Hey, sis,' he said, giving her his familiar ear-to-ear grin. He leaned down and kissed her cheek. His stubble scratched.

'Hi Matthew, how are you?' she said.

'Oh, great stuff! You're an angel, Louise,' he said and pounced on a mug of tea. 'Well, I have to admit, I've had better days.' He glanced at his father before continuing. 'I chucked in the job today.'

His father sat up. 'Matthew! What on earth!? Why did you do that?'

'I've had it with that place. Olly Wallace was bugging the shit out of me. You'd swear he was Bill Gates the way he takes the whole thing so fuckin' serious. I got in a bit late this morning and he was on my back the whole day. In the end, I took off my Wallace's Hardware jacket and threw it at him. I told him he could stuff his job wherever he liked.'

Jim winced at the violence of the language. 'Matthew, that's your third job since you finished college. You can't throw up every job you get as soon as something doesn't suit you.'

'Yeah, well I don't see why I should put up with that shit either. Don't worry, I'll get another one.'

'There's not an endless supply of them, you know. What'll you do now?' Despair and confusion could be read on Jim's face, aggravated by the fact that he believed that the highest compliment he could pay anyone was to say that they were a good, reliable worker.

'Don't worry about me. I'll sort something out and get out of your hair just as soon as I can.' He stormed out of the room.

Jim looked around at everyone and no one in particular. 'What am I going to do with that fellow? He can stick at nothing. What's going to come of him?'

'He'll be all right, Dad.' Enda said. 'He's a bit fed-up because he got out of college two years ago but can't get a job in his field. He'll settle down. We've all been through it.'

'I don't think any of you were like him. Christina there now was a great girl. She never gave us an ounce of trouble.'

'Well, I'm not sure that's exactly the point though.' There was a sharp edge in her voice that she hadn't meant to come out. She tried to soften her tone. 'I mean, it's not entirely his fault. It's a different environment now compared to when I qualified nearly twenty years ago. The recession means that it's tough to get a decent job.'

'I know but he could hold on to the job that he does get while he's applying for other things.' Jim leaned forward and put a spoonful of sugar in his tea.

'Matthew is his own worst enemy. Somehow, hassle always finds him,' Enda said.

She held her mug to her lips, determined to say no more. She was hardly half an hour in the house when she was already being sucked into an emotional family whirlpool. All her life, she had had to be the one who 'never gave a bit of trouble'. Well, it wasn't true: she had had trouble. Just nobody had bothered to understand or share it with her. Even as she shrugged off the flash of anger that had flared up in her, she realised that she wasn't being fair. This wasn't their fault.

She stood up. 'I'll be back in a minute,' she said. She needed a breath of fresh air. She avoided looking anyone in the eye as she left the room.

Jim Cavanagh could see that Christina was upset over something. He had no idea why. Had it been something he said or was she just worrying over Kate? With Christina, it was hard to know what she was thinking. She kept a lot to herself. She was his daughter, his firstborn, and he loved her but she was a puzzle at times.

He knew that her job was a high-powered one and that she had a lot of responsibility; maybe that explained why she had become so remote. Although he loved seeing her, there were times when he wasn't sure how to talk to her. She had become a mystery to him. It was strange: how had that happened with his own child who had once been so easy to please, so good-natured? He couldn't pinpoint when she had changed but then, he had never been all that involved in the day-to-day business of his children's lives. Maybe Kate would know.

It had always been very clear who dealt with what between himself and Kate, so clear that it never had to be discussed. Theirs was a partnership, a perfectly satisfactory one, where she dealt with the house and everything to do with the children and he worked on the farm to provide for them. Although he didn't see much of the children as they were growing up, especially the girls, he knew they were there, his reason for being. He saw them for dinner in the evenings after the milking was done but he wasn't a big talker. He enjoyed the hustle and bustle of family life around him, but he didn't feel the necessity to get involved in the detail. In any case, Kate was so much better than he was at dealing with all that. When the children were all in bed, he and Kate would sit in the sitting room with a mug of tea and then she would bring him up to date with any of the important events in the children's lives and he'd get her thoughts on any new investments or changes to the farm. This arrangement had seemed a good, natural one at the time. Each of them was master of their own domain, but imperceptibly the world around them had changed and their choices didn't seem to fit with the ways of today. Young people now were obsessed with equality, with obliterating the lines of demarcation. No wonder there was so much divorce.

Until recently, he had always considered this to be a flaw in modern society, another proof that the old days had been better, if poorer. But now, ever since Kate had become sick, he wasn't so sure. If anything happened to her, how would he cope? This was not a sentiment he was comfortable expressing, even to himself. It might be selfish but deep down, he was scared, not only of losing her but also scared that some of the choices they had made might not have been the right ones, that maybe he should have been more involved in their children's lives. He looked around at the four of his children that were still in the room. He loved them, everything he had done, he had done for them, but he wasn't sure that he knew them. They were unexplored islands and Kate was his bridge to them. She was his bridge as well as his interpreter of a language he feared he was too old now to learn by himself. If Kate wasn't there, would the heart of their home be cut out? Would they all drift away from each other, leaving him to a lonely, pointless old age?

He had never been one for introspection so this overdose of rumination made him uncomfortable. He stood up to go out and check on the sheep. Nuala, who was sitting on a cushion on the other side of the fire, leaned across and squeezed his hand. She gave him a small smile of sympathy and he wondered at the irony that, in recent times, his deaf child had become the one with whom he had the least communication difficulties.

As he put on his coat, he remembered how Kate used to worry about her although she had never talked much to him about it. When Nuala was a baby, she used to go into screaming fits of frustration in a way that the others never had. But at other times, she was a particularly silent baby and both excesses had bothered Kate. She took her to the doctor several times until eventually, he sent them to a specialist and when Nuala was a year old, they discovered that she was profoundly deaf. Kate made sure Nuala got all the support and help she needed. She took her every week to Galway to a special school for the deaf. Making those kinds of arrangements was Kate's job and she took it all in her stride or at least, he thought she did at the time. In reality, they had never really talked much about it.

In that way too, they were out of sync with the ways of today. Nowadays, people believed in talking endlessly about things but their way had been to deal with problems silently, refusing to give them too much power by acknowledging them. Nuala's deafness had never been a major subject of discussion within the family, merely a fact that everyone adjusted to. They all knew that special care had to be taken with Nuala near the road, that she needed to be protected from insensitive outsiders and that they had to talk clearly and directly to her face when she was around but these things came instinctively rather than being taught. They had all learned sign language to a greater or lesser degree but he had just learned the basic words he needed to get by and hadn't made a huge effort beyond that. Kate always insisted that Nuala should help out like everyone else in the family and not be treated as handicapped. She expected her to contribute as much as the others and it was a philosophy he silently agreed with but now he wondered if he should have asked for more details and tried to better understand the difficulties that Nuala faced. When Kate got better, he'd do that.

It was cold outside and he put on his cap as a last thought. On his way across the dim yard, he spotted Christina, her arms wrapped around herself against the cold. He hurried into the shed and was greeted by the bleating of the sheep and lambs. The shed was divided into sections, several pens for the sheep who had already lambed and were feeding their young, another for the sheep who had still to lamb and the last one was for the lambs who, for various reasons, couldn't or wouldn't suckle their mothers and needed to be fed by hand.

After checking on the sheep yet to lamb, he turned his attention to the motherless lambs. He was filling the boiler with water to make up their milk when the shed door opened slowly and Christina came in.

'Do you want a hand?' she said. She was wearing an old anorak of Kate's and a pair of wellies she had borrowed from the back door.

'You can help me feed these little fellows if you like. Bring over that mixing stick by the door.'

He measured the substitute powdered milk into the buckets. While they waited for the water to heat, the little lambs crowded around them. The one that had been born the week before with a deformed leg was being pushed out by the others in their eagerness to get fed. Christina noticed and made space for him. Jim had considered doing away with him after he was born but, for some reason, he hesitated. He'd wait and see how he coped.

'Why do these need to be fed by the bottle?' she asked.

'Various reasons,' Jim said. 'Some of them are twins or triplets and the mother didn't have enough milk for them all. Others were rejected because they are too weak or too crippled to survive.'

'Poor things. What age are they now?' she asked.

'The oldest of them is about four weeks old.'

'They're cute.'

‘Hmm, I like sheep. Dairying was getting too much and in any case, there’s no money in it anymore. They need a lot of attention around now but for the rest of the year they’re no trouble.’

‘Does it not bother you though, to send them off for slaughter?’ She picked up the damaged one in her arms and scratched his tightly curled wool.

‘Well, that’s the way of the world. It’s a business: they wouldn’t exist at all if it wasn’t for the lamb market.’

‘Will they get to go outside and run around in the fields at least?’ Christina said.

‘I’m not sure if that fellow will survive but the others will get out for a few weeks, as long as the weather doesn’t stay too cold.’

Jim filled the now-boiling water into a plastic measuring jug and poured it on top of the powdered milk in the bucket. Christina stirred it, making sure that the powder was dissolved properly. While they waited for the milk to cool down, they rinsed out the teats and bottles and lined them up in preparation on the partition wall between the pens.

‘How are you getting on in Dublin?’ Jim asked awkwardly.

‘Fine, work’s going well.’

‘You’re still an accountant with that American company, are you?’

‘Actually, I’m Financial Director now.’

Jim gave a low whistle, although, in reality, he didn’t fully understand the distinction. More money, more stress, he supposed. Was this what she wanted out of life or was there some aspect he was missing?

‘With all that work I can understand that it must be hard to find the time to come back home.’ He poured the milk into the bottles while Christina attached the teats. He picked up two bottles and passed them to her.

'How much will I give them?'

'As much as they'll take. They'll let you know when they've had enough.'

Three lambs tumbled over each, falling to their knees and scrambling up again in their eagerness to get to the bottles. She laughed at their antics and he was glad to see it.

'Will we go to Galway together to see Mam this evening?' she asked when they had finished feeding the lambs.

'That'd be fine,' he said.

'We'll have something to eat quickly and then go. I'll go in and see if I can give them a hand with dinner.' She glanced around the shed at the lambs before leaving.

'Right so,' said Jim. A ewe in the next pen caught his eye. She seemed to be limping so he went to investigate.

Chapter 5

As she took off her boots in the utility room, Christina could hear Nuala setting the table in the kitchen. 'Hey.' She waved and smiled at her through the open door. Nuala gave her a wry smile back while she continued to lay out the knives and forks. One of the good things about being with Nuala was that there was never any pressure to talk. It was OK just to be together, doing things in parallel.

'What's for tea?' Christina signed.

'Vegetable soup and brown bread. Not very exciting but it'll do,' Nuala signed once her hands were free.

'I'm going to take Dad to the hospital to see Mam after dinner. Do you want to come?' she signed back but enunciated the words clearly as well so that Nuala could lip-read, just in case her rusty signing wasn't understandable.

Nuala shook her head. 'No, thanks. Give her my love though. I'll see her tomorrow.'

Christina nodded. She opened the sitting room door and made a general announcement that tea was ready for those who were hungry.

After supper, she drove Jim to the hospital, their anxiety as material as a third passenger in the car. The evening atmosphere of the hospital was different from how it had been earlier that day. Earlier, it had been a bustling professional place full of trolleys of medication, nurses until pressure, medical teams having serious discussions. Now, there were visitors wandering around bearing flowers and boxes of chocolates as it wound down towards night-time. She took a deep breath and prepared herself for a possible encounter with Lynn. Every time a white uniform approached her or passed by, her whole body tensed for the possibility that it might be her.

Her mother was sleeping when they entered the ward, although how she could with all the commotion was a mystery to Christina. There were at least ten visitors in the room creating a loud hum of talk and laughter but nobody was at her mother's bedside. Looking at her mother's still face, her mouth slightly open, her breathing audible, that lethal cocktail of emotions churned up inside her again and threatened to explode. She and her dad looked at each other and nodded in unspoken agreement that they would allow her to sleep. Christina indicated the empty chair beside her mother to her dad and he sat down. He picked up the newspaper on top of the bedside table and opened it to the sports pages.

She turned away and looked out the window. From the fourth floor, the near view was of the backs of old, shabby council houses with their tiny gardens and ugly sheds with corrugated roofs. Night was blurring their edges and yellow squares of light pierced the dark, dirty blue which gave them a homely appeal that they didn't have in daylight. Further out, the sea stretched to the horizon. She turned, although she hadn't heard anything. Her mother was awake. She turned her head towards her two visitors, a faint, crooked smile on her lips. She inched her hand across the bedspread towards them. Her husband folded the paper over, put it on his lap and pulled his chair closer to the bed. He placed his hand on top of hers.

She blinked her eyes to greet him.

He nodded abruptly and Christina could tell that he didn't trust himself to speak.

Kate looked up at her daughter. 'How – are – you?' she said.

A hiccup of ironic laughter escaped Christina. 'How am I? Fine, just fine. It's you we should be asking.'

'I'll – be – OK. Takes – a – lot – to – get – rid – of – a – bad – thing.' Her mother's voice was slow and almost a whisper. 'How's – Steve?'

'He's well. He sends his regards.'

'A – nice – lad. He's – good – for – you.' Even though she had only met him once in Dublin, Christina knew that she meant it. It wasn't an idly mentioned comment. A painful silence fell.

Kate looked at her husband. 'The sheep?' she said.

He folded the paper and put it back on the bedside table. He took a deep breath and sat up straighter as if he had been asked for an official update. 'Fifteen left to go. Should be out of it after this week. Not a bad year, all in all.' She nodded and he continued. 'That little fellow, the one with the gammy legs. Haven't fully made up my mind about what to do with him. He's lively enough. He gets around just fine on the knuckles of his front legs. I don't know whether to leave him the way he is or break his legs and splint them. Might not be worth it for the sixteen weeks he has ahead of him.'

'Doesn't – stop – him – getting – his – ration.' Kate smiled as she remembered the damaged lamb.

'That's what I was thinking.'

Christina looked from one to the other. Somehow, a joint decision had been made although the question hadn't been asked or answered.

'I'll go on out for a minute,' she said. 'Do you need anything, Mam?'

Her mother made a slight movement with her head to indicate no and Christina left the room.

She walked down the corridor and stopped by the window of the TV room. Inside, a young nurse was standing beside an elderly woman in a wheelchair. She had one hand on the handle of her chair and held a TV remote control in the other. She was flicking through the channels to find something for her to watch. When she reached an old black and white movie with Katherine Hepburn, the old woman said something and the nurse put down the remote control. She patted the woman's hand and left the room.

Lynn would make a good nurse, Christina thought. She knew how to do those little things that made people feel at ease, those things that made you feel special. She remembered how warm Lynn's approval had made her feel. Her smile was like the warmth of the sun coming out from behind a cloud.

Shortly after she joined the class, Lynn got into the habit of dropping in to Christina's house after school, often to ask for help with her homework, sometimes just to chat. She charmed her parents, and even her little brothers thought Lynn was cooler than any of her other friends. She even persuaded Christina's parents to allow her to go with her to the Christmas Teen Disco in the local hall.

'Don't worry, Kate,' Lynn said. Christina never used adults' first names. If she had to, she said missus or mister but mostly she avoided saying anything at all. 'The whole class is going, it'll be great. It really motivates us to work hard knowing that we have that to look forward to.' Lynn always knew what to say to parents.

In the weeks leading up to the disco, they spent ages discussing what they would wear. She didn't have anything remotely suitable so, in the end, Lynn lent her a purple top with a V back and batwing sleeves and a denim mini. They were in Lynn's bedroom examining and trying on everything she had in her wardrobe, which was a lot. Christina didn't feel totally at ease about wearing the mini but Lynn persuaded her that she should.

'It's perfect on you. You have such thin legs. I wish I had.' She sighed and raised her legs in front of her to examine them. 'You're lucky, you have such a good figure. I wish I had no boobs and small hips like you.'

This comment amazed her. Until then, she hadn't given the shape of her body much thought. She was filled with a sense of delight that Lynn might admire or even envy something about her but she wasn't entirely convinced that she deserved it. For a start, she wasn't sure what she thought about her breasts. Most of the others had full, obvious boobs that filled out their jumpers but she had barely enough to justify wearing the smallest bra size. Only the previous summer, her nipples had felt like small hard buttons inserted under her skin. Months went by and they weren't getting much bigger. They did nothing to lift her top out from her chest but she wasn't sure whether she wanted them to or not. Breasts meant being more like the other girls, venturing into a new unknown world full of sophistication and boys, but it also meant leaving the world she knew by heart, the familiar one occupied by her parents and little brothers and sisters.

'Yes, definitely wear the mini,' Lynn said. 'I think I'm going to wear the black drainpipes.' She lay on her back on the bed and took a large breath in. She stopped breathing, holding her stomach in as she wriggled into the jeans and struggled to pull up the zip. Afterwards, when she stood in front of the mirror, her legs looked as though they had been spray-painted black. She held up her fair hair and turned her head to one side. 'Oh, in any case,' she said. 'It's more important to have a pretty face than a good figure. If the boys have to choose, that's what they prefer. At least I have that advantage.' Her comment, although it wasn't entirely clear if she was referring to Christina and what she said before, had the effect of erasing all the confidence her previous compliment had given her.

Back then, she had assumed that it was a throwaway comment but it had hurt all the same. Now, twenty-six years later, knowing what she knew, she wondered if Lynn had intended it to hurt. Funny how that self-conscious, inexperienced fifteen-year-old self was still there, in the centre of her, as if she had grown up around her instead of evolving into someone else. Someone stopped behind her and spoke. She jumped in fright. It was her father.

'Sorry, I didn't mean to startle you,' he said.

'I was lost in my thoughts.'

'I think your mother is tired. I don't want to wear her out. Do you want to say goodbye and we'll go?'

She stopped at the door of the ward. She could see her mother's head on the pillow with her eyes closed and decided not to disturb her. She and her father walked to the car.

'I was talking to one of the nurses there. She said that she can't tell me much but she said I should talk to your mother's doctor on Monday to find out what is going on with her. She said he's off for the weekend but he'll be doing his rounds at 11 or so on Monday morning.' He was walking more slowly than usual, not looking at Christina. 'I thought you might like to come with me. You'd know all the right questions to ask.'

She instinctively wanted to say no. Powerful undercurrents tugged at her, destabilising her.

'Dad, I have to get back to the office. I'm sorry but why don't you ask Mark? He's nearby. It'll be easier for him.'

'I'll do that,' Jim said slowly.

She was now annoyed with him for accepting her refusal so calmly but a cool voice in her brain told her that she'd probably be just as annoyed if he'd pressed her to stay. Only here at home, did she find herself ensnarled in this kind of illogical reasoning. It was crazy-making, like trying to argue with shadows.

She was the first to hear the banging on the door in the middle of the night. She was a light sleeper but it still took her several seconds to recognise where she was when the harsh sounds broke through her sleep. The bed was unfamiliar; it was too soft and sagged in the middle. In the dark grey light of the room, she could make out an unfamiliar, imposing dark shape at the end of the bed. It was only when she reached out and her hand touched the tasselled lampshade of the bedside lamp that she realised that it was the big mahogany wardrobe in her old childhood bedroom.

There was another flurry of bangs on the front door. Her heart raced. Was it news about her mother? What was wrong? Surely they wouldn't send someone out to the house though. They'd phone, wouldn't they? She couldn't make out the time on her watch. She jumped out of bed and went quickly down the stairs, pulling on her cardigan as she went. As she opened the door, her father arrived behind her, dishevelled and grey-faced.

Matthew stood on the doorstep, propped up on either side by two of his pals. One of them was very tall with wiry red hair. He had a familiar look: she could tell he was one of the Egans. His older brother had been in class with her at school. The other was smaller, pudgy, with a red blotchy face. Both of them looked the worse for wear, probably only a pint or two behind Matthew. Although when she took a closer look, she could see that he was completely out of it. His eyes were almost closed, his face was flushed and his hair was wet with sweat, slicked down against his head.

'Come in,' she said impatiently and stood back into the hallway. As they stepped under the hall light she could see that his hair was not wet, it was soaked in blood. She gave an involuntary gasp.

'My god, what happened to him?' Jim asked.

'It's not as bad as it looks,' the smaller guy said. 'He tripped over in the car park and banged his head against the bumper of a car. There's a fair bit of blood but he'll be okay.'

She glared at him.

'Sorry to wake you up,' the young Egan lad said. 'We could have used his keys to let ourselves in but we wanted to make sure he was all right. He's had a bit to drink.'

'You don't say!' she said. 'Bring him in here so that I can take a look at his head.'

As they shuffled Matthew into the sitting room, he roused himself and opened his eyes. He caught sight of his sister and father hovering over him, groaned and closed his eyes again. His two friends dropped him onto the sofa without ceremony and took a step backwards towards the doorway. They glanced at each other and it was obvious that they were keen to be gone. She touched Matthew's head and tried to part his hair to see the extent of the damage but he flinched away from her.

'We'll be off then if that's all right,' the young Egan lad said.

'Right, right,' Jim said and went to the door to let them out. She wondered for a second if they had any intention of driving. She hesitated to offer to drive them home but then decided to let it go: it wasn't far and life was complicated enough at the moment.

'Why don't you go to bed, Dad? I'll look after him,' she said when he returned. She went into the kitchen to get what she needed from the medicine drawer to dress Matthew's wound. When she got back, she could see that Jim was hovering, unsure of what to do, while Matthew sat, head bent into his chest, squirming with embarrassment.

She put a towel around Matthew's shoulders and, then, not overly tenderly, dipped a wad of cotton wool into the bowl of warm water and tried to clean the area where the blood was thickest.

The ticking of the clock on the mantelpiece was clearly audible. She turned to her father. 'Go on, Dad, go to bed. There's no point in even attempting to talk to him tonight.'

'You'll need me to get him up the stairs.'

She snorted. 'He's not that bad. Don't worry, he'll walk up the stairs himself or he can stay on the sofa. Don't waste another minute's sleep on him.'

Jim left reluctantly, anxious to do something but not sure what. The despairing slope of his shoulders as he made his way to the stairs caused her to dab even harder at Matthew's head wound. She could see it was only a superficial cut although it had bled a lot.

'Hey,' he said. 'Take it easy.'

'What the hell got into you? Especially at a time like this?'

'Since when do I have to ask anyone for permission to have a few drinks on a Saturday night?'

'A few drinks? Give it over, Matthew. You're plastered. You really upset Dad and he has enough going on at the moment. After the shock you gave him earlier, you could try to be a little less selfish.' She applied some antiseptic spray to his head and gathered up the debris from her ministrations.

'Selfish? For fuck's sake, who are you to talk? You couldn't give a damn about anyone but yourself and your fuckin' high-flying career. When was the last time you went out of your way to come to see Mam or Dad?'

'This isn't about me, Matthew.'

'Well, pity about you, but it isn't up to you to decide what this is or isn't about. Just mind your own fuckin' business! That's something you normally do very well!'

'It's pointless talking to you when you're like this. Can you get to bed by yourself? I hope you're not going to go and get sick during the night or anything stupid like that.'

He gave her a withering look. 'Oh, if you hear me choking in the night, whatever you do, don't bother to come running. Leave me to it.'

She shook her head. 'I'm going to bed anyway. Good night.'

Matthew's words echoed in her head as she made her way through the silent house to her bedroom. It's late, you're tired, she told herself, this is not the time to read meaning into angry, drunken talk. She knew it was foolish to have said anything but she had been annoyed.

Yet, what he had said hurt as only the truth could. She stopped outside the closed door of her parents' room and her heart pinched as she wondered what her father was thinking about on the other side of it.

The dream came back that night. It had been a long time but it was exactly as before.

As usual, she was alone, walking on the beaten path along the cliff-top. It was night-time but her way was lit by frequent flashes of lightning. Below her, the sea crashed powerfully against the cliff face. Despite the storm, she wasn't frightened or cold. Underneath her feet, the grass was soft, absorbing her steps. She wasn't going anywhere in particular, just moving forward, one foot moving through the air, following the other one in a mindless, smooth motion.

The wind blew across her bringing the first whisper with it. She shivered in fearful anticipation. She knew what was coming. The voice became louder. There was nothing to see, she could only hear the disembodied voice. The whisper was louder than the storm, it filled her ears. A wave of terror lapped the shores of her heart. This persuasive, whispering voice was calm and rational and made her internal tumult seem silly and contemptible. She strained to hear what it was saying. She couldn't make out the exact words. She didn't know if it was because the words themselves were unintelligible or because of the rushing panic in her ears. Even without hearing them, she was sure it was trying to persuade her to walk over the cliff towards the sea below. She knew she would fall if she did but how could she explain this? In the face of its implacable certainty, any argument she might possibly formulate was empty and pointless. Better to run away. Her legs speeded up in response, efficient well-oiled pistons accelerating to comply. But it served no purpose, the voice was just as present, neither louder nor weaker. It was the voice of a god, everywhere and nowhere, reduced to a whisper to make it bearable for her ears.

Her body became heavier and clumsier. She held her hands up in front of her face. They were now huge, her fingers so swollen and massive that she could only barely move them. She opened and closed them trying to make them go back to normal but they were so out of proportion with the rest of the world that she could no longer touch, grasp or feel anything with them. As it did every time, the usual sense of horror filled her. She knew she was dreaming and, with a tremendous effort, she forced herself to wake up.

Her heart was pounding. She sat up and, although she knew it was ridiculous, she held up her hands in the dark to check that they were normal size. She imagined that the last traces of heaviness were seeping out of them. She tried to calm down, to allow the adrenaline to drain from her system. It's only a dream, she told herself. You've had it before. But somehow her body remained unconvinced.

Chapter 6

When she woke up the next morning, it was still early. She lay still, listening. She could hear no sound in the house. Her watch told her it was only seven. She clambered out of the hollow in the middle of the mattress. Her back hurt. She decided to go down to the kitchen and have a coffee by herself before having a shower. She crept downstairs, remembering to walk on the outside of the steps so that they wouldn't creak. When she pushed open the kitchen door, Nuala was already there. She was staring out the window, absorbed in her thoughts. As Christina moved into her line of vision, she jumped.

'Sorry,' Christina signed. 'I didn't know you were up.'

'It's all right, I couldn't sleep,' Nuala said in words. Her voice was thick with effort, like a person talking underwater. She never liked speaking when she could sign and Christina knew that she was only doing it to show a willingness to meet her halfway. The kettle bubbled to a boil and switched itself off.

Nuala put her two hands together and made the sign for coffee, raising her eyebrows in question.

Christina nodded. 'How are you? You look a bit pale and tired.' she signed. 'Did the ruckus last night wake you up?'

Nuala looked surprised. 'No. What happened?'

'Oh, it was Matthew. He got drunk and had to be carried home by some of his pals. He had a bit of a fall and cut his head.'

'Is he all right?'

'Oh he's fine, I'm sure. Although he'll have a headache this morning. I'm not sure how Dad took the whole episode though.'

'I saw him on his way out to check on the ewes earlier on. I thought he looked a bit stressed but I thought it was because of Mam being in hospital.' She shook her head.

'Don't worry too much. I think everything will turn out fine. We're all on edge at the moment so the timing isn't great.'

Nuala passed her a mug of black coffee. As she took it to the table to sit down, she noticed the local newspaper open on the property page. She twisted it around and saw that some of the ads had been ringed in red pen. She looked up at Nuala.

'Is this yours? Are you thinking of moving out?'

'No, not really. Just looking to see what's available.' Nuala folded the paper over and pushed it aside. 'You never know; I might get my own place one day.'

'But do you think you'd be able to manage by yourself?' As soon as the words were out, she regretted them.

Nuala hated to have her deafness referred to as a disability. Her expressive face closed in, showing that her pride had been hurt. 'I don't see why not,' she signed.

'Sorry, I didn't mean it that way. I'm just surprised, that's all. I thought you were happy here.'

'But how would you know?' Nuala didn't ask the question aggressively, she genuinely wanted to know, but now it was Christina's turn to be hurt. Nuala's comment was too close to Matthew's of the night before for her to dismiss it without thought.

'You're right, I suppose I don't know.' She stared into her coffee.

'Are you going back to Dublin today?' Nuala signed after a moment.

'Yes, I didn't take time off work and we have a big sales meeting tomorrow. I think Mam's going to be fine. It's just a matter of time before she gets her strength back and, in any case, I'll come back next weekend.' Her calm, measured words belied her true fears and she busied herself buttering a slice of bread in case they were visible in her eyes. 'After lunch, I'll call in to see her on my way back to Dublin.'

Nuala was about to say something else when the door of the kitchen opened and Matthew appeared. He was holding his head in his hands. His hair was matted into spikes and there were traces of blood in his ear. He looked awful.

'Good morning,' Christina said. He grunted at his two sisters without looking directly at either of them.

He pulled open the medicine drawer and rummaged around in it until he found what he was looking for. He gulped back three tablets with a mouthful of water.

Eventually, he looked at Nuala with a quick sideward glance at Christina.

'Don't ask,' he signed. His hand movements were quick and fluent.

'I won't. I was told and even if I wasn't, I could imagine,' Nuala signed back. Christina had trouble keeping up with her and realised that Nuala had been slowing down her gestures for her but that she didn't need to do that for Matthew.

He put his arm around Nuala's shoulders and peered into her mug.

'Coffee. Would you like some?' she asked, turning to face him.

His grin of gratitude answered her question.

'All right then. I should let you suffer but just this time I'll help you out of your misery.' Nuala flicked the kettle back on to boil. She put a mug of steaming coffee in front of him.

'Any chance of some milk?' he pleaded with a helpless grin. 'A bit of -' Then, he then made a sign Christina didn't recognise. He made a gesture as if he was gliding his hand in front of this face followed by the sign for milk. Nuala frowned and then, after a moment's hesitation, laughed a harsh seal bark of a laugh. Matthew laughed too, pleased with the impact. She looked from one to the other. Nuala noticed her confusion and pointed to the word 'pasteurised' on the milk bottle. Christina was still puzzled.

Matthew made the same sign again. 'Past your eyes milk,' he said for her benefit.

'Good joke. I like it,' she said and smiled but the moment was over and she had not been part of it. She drained her mug and took it to the sink to rinse it.

She left Nuala and Matthew at the table chatting in what looked to her like accelerated sign language and went upstairs to have a shower.

Afterwards, she decided to go for a walk to get out of the house and clear her head. She noticed two texts from Steve, one from the night before and another even more concerned one sent early that morning asking how things were. She should have called him. She had texted him briefly the previous evening while she was at the hospital but she knew he would want to hear from her. She rang him but it went through to his voicemail. She was relieved. If he guessed from her voice that something was wrong, he would quiz her up about everything and putting it into words was scary. She left a message telling him that she expected to get home around six after she had called in to the hospital that afternoon on her way home. She put away her phone and picked up her pace.

Instinctively, she turned right, in the opposite direction to Lynn's old family house, although she didn't imagine that Lynn lived there anymore. The day was sharply cold but the sun was shining and she started to enjoy the old familiar country sounds, the absence of traffic, the brisk one-two of her steps, the cold air lining her lungs. The drivers of the few passing cars gave her a wave and she wondered if they had recognised her or if it was just the habitual acknowledgement of anyone they crossed on the road.

She continued to walk, taking the familiar route the school bus used to take every day to school. Less had changed than she would have thought. The huge stone at the side of the road just before the hump-back bridge was still there except that it looked so much smaller now to her adult eyes. Before, as a child, climbing to the top had made her feel as though she was scaling a rock face but now, as she stood beside it, the top of it barely reached the level of her eyes. Had her perspective changed so very much since then? A mad urge to climb up and balance on it, arms wide apart, seized her, but she wasn't a child anymore. She continued walking and crossed the bridge. She walked past Flanagan's pub which had been repainted and was looking much smarter. She remembered the poster of Bobby Sands and the other hunger strikers in H Block pinned to the telephone pole outside it. She could see their faces on the poster from the bus to and from school. Each time one of them died, the poster was replaced to include the additional face. After a while, there were so many she could no longer make out each individual face from the bus window. They became just small dark blobs and she was glad to be far enough away from them so that she didn't have to look into their eyes, see their expressions and imagine how they felt.

She turned back for home. How many times had she taken that bus, praying for it to arrive quickly so that she could get off? What had started it all? The first specific incident she could remember was about the shoes.

1986

Her mother had come home from Galway having bought her new shoes in the sales. They were great value, her mother said, less than half-price, good sturdy shoes that would last all year. Lucky they had them in your size, she said. They were heavy and black with thick laces. They had a swirling pattern of tiny punched holes in the top layer of leather and a ridge around the outside that made her feet look even bigger. They looked like men's shoes. She hated them, but she wore them anyway. They were only shoes after all and it was pointless asking her mother to buy her another pair. She knew only too well how little money there was available at home. At school, she was hanging up her coat in the cloakroom when Lynn spotted the shoes.

'Hey, Christina, are they new shoes?' she asked.

'Mmm.' She didn't want to talk about them.

'Emily, Fiona, Ger, come here, you have to see this,' Lynn called. 'Come and see Christina's shoes, they are the funniest things.' Her laughter attracted the others who came to see what had triggered it.

'Where did you get them?' Lynn asked. 'My god, I can't believe those shoes.' Her laughter became louder. It was contagious and several others became infected and joined in. Christina was hemmed in, unsure of what to do next. Her cheeks were burning. She hated the shoes but walking away would take more courage than she had.

'Go on, tell us, where on earth did you get them?' Lynn could barely get the words out through the laughter.

'My mother got them for me,' she said in a small voice.

Lynn could hardly speak. 'Who did she think she was buying them for? An elephant that was taking up the hornpipe?'

By now, Christina was the only one not laughing. She had no idea how to deal with this situation. Should she pretend it wasn't happening or get angry or even laugh along with them? Except that she couldn't laugh, it was all she could do not to cry.

The door of the cloakroom opened. Miss Doherty's head appeared around it. 'What's going on in here? The bell just rang. Hurry up, girls, you'll be late for class.'

The rest of the day was a misery. Everywhere she went she was conscious of her shoes. They were now enormous on her feet, impossible to ignore. Several times she saw girls and boys whispering and laughing in the corridors and she was sure that they were pointing at them out, telling the story of what had happened in the cloakroom.

As they waited for the school bus that evening, she resolved to ignore Lynn, no matter what she said. She would stay as far away from her as possible and let her understand how hurt she was by chilling her out. But Lynn just nudged her and said blithely, 'You're not *still* annoyed, are you? We were only having a laugh. Don't be such a baby about it. Come on, sit with us on the bus.' She linked arms with her and tugged her. It would have been churlish to stay angry.

She got off the bus and on the short journey to her house she fired herself up to ask her mother to buy her new shoes, assembling all the arguments necessary to convince her. When she walked into the kitchen, her mother was folding a pile of clothes she had taken in from the line. Nuala was playing with a doll on the floor beside her. Christina picked up a towel and started to fold it while she considered the best way to approach the subject. Nuala stood up and tugged at her mother's skirt until she looked down at her. She pointed at her doll and then rubbed her own tummy. She was saying that her doll was hungry. She made a sign of peeling the lid off a tub, her personal made-up sign for yoghurt.

'No, Nuala, you can't have a yoghurt and neither can Dolly. It's almost dinner time.'

Nuala made the peeling sign again.

Her mother shook her finger and made a gesture as if she was eating with an imaginary knife and fork.

'I thought we weren't supposed to make signs, Mam. Didn't the doctor say that we had to talk to Nuala all the time so that she would learn how to talk?'

'Easy for him to say! There are times when all I want is to get through the bloody day and stay sane,' Kate snapped.

She was shocked. Her mother never spoke to her like this.

Nuala didn't understand. She insisted again with the peeling sign and when that had no effect, she opened the door of the fridge. Kate pulled her away and closed it again. She bent down to ground level and tried to explain again that dinner would be ready soon. Although she was insisting on the word dinner,

Christina had the impression that 'soon' was the one that Nuala was having difficulty in understanding.

Nuala gave an ear-piercing shriek of frustration. She put her hands to her ears and pulled out her hearing aids. Before Kate could stop her, she threw them with force to the other side of the room. She applied her considerable five-year-old strength to push past her mother and opened the fridge door again.

'Nuala, stop it,' Kate screamed and burst into tears. She pushed her away from the fridge. Christina was frightened, she had never seen her mother this upset before. She pulled out the furniture in search of the aids and found one beside the radiator. Eventually, she could see the second one in the gap between the cooker and the wall. She poked it out with the handle of a wooden spoon. Gently, she put them on the table in front of her mother and waited for her reaction. Her mother sat in a chair with her elbows on the table, her face buried in her hands. Nuala became upset at her mother's refusal to keep eye contact with her and continued to tug at her mother's sleeve. She didn't even know that she was the cause of her mother's despair.

'Come here, Nuala.' Christina tried to distract her with her doll but Nuala wanted her mother's attention.

'What is it, Mam? What's wrong?' Christina asked timidly.

Her mother gave her eyes one last wipe and took her hands down. She pulled Nuala onto her knees and hugged her. 'I'm sorry for getting annoyed, love. I've just had a hectic day. I suppose I can tell you now, you're a big girl. I'm pregnant, I'm going to have another baby.'

She smiled but her eyes were sad. She didn't look very happy.

'Are you not pleased about that?' Christina said.

'Of course I am,' her mother said. Christina examined her face for the truth.

'It's only that Nuala already takes up so much of my time. And it's not easy to find the money for everything. Another baby won't be easy at first but I know we'll cope. We always do.'

'I can help you more. What do you want me to do?' In an internal act of sacrifice, she decided to forget about her shoes and say nothing.

'You already help me a lot. What would I do without you, Christina? You're a great girl. Don't worry about anything, we'll be fine.' She pulled her closer and squeezed Christina's shoulders. Suddenly, the weight of her sacrifice lightened.

Chapter 7

On her return, Christina saw that Mark and Deirdre, his wife, had just driven into the yard before her. They were opening the back doors of the car to let their little girls out.

'Hello, Christina, how are you?' Deirdre said. 'I brought over a chicken casserole for lunch for everyone. Somehow, I doubt that you are all eating properly'

'Thanks, Deirdre.' She smiled, glad to see her bossy, motherly sister-in-law. She took the dish from her hands to allow her to look after the children.

While she was setting the table and Deirdre regulated the oven to heat up the casserole, Matthew wandered into the kitchen. 'Hi, Dee,' he said.

Deirdre looked up at him. 'Well, you've seen better days. Out on the tear last night, were you?'

He made a face at her and picked out a piece of chicken from the casserole to eat.

'Stop it,' she said and slapped his hand lightly. 'You'll eat properly, not like a savage.'

'Oo, you're a hard woman, Deirdre.'

'Is your headache gone?' Christina asked.

'More or less,' he said. There was a sense of awkwardness between them as though they both wished last night's exchange hadn't happened. Deirdre sensed it and glanced up curiously at both of them but before she could speak, the phone rang.

'I'll get it,' Matthew said.

'Yes, this is her son Matthew,' Christina heard him say from the hall. 'Do you want to talk to my father?' Then, Matthew listened, and in that silence, she stopped moving so that she would be ready to hear the next thing he said. An inner chill spread through her body as her blood suddenly dropped in temperature. She put the plates down on the table and moved to the doorway to see Matthew's expression. He had turned pale. 'We'll be in straight away,' he said. Another silence. 'We'll come in anyway.' He looked at Christina, eyes wide. Inside, she started to bargain desperately with fate, please no, please no, please make her not be dead.

'Thank you,' Matthew said and hung up.

'What happened?' she said.

'Mam just had a heart attack. They've resuscitated her but they're taking her to theatre now. I said we'd go in although they said that it might be a few hours before we can see her.'

Nuala tried to catch someone's attention so that they would explain what was happening. One of the little ones started to cry.

The babble of noise became frenetic. She recited a mantra in her head, over and over. Hang in there, Mam,

I'm coming, we're all coming, don't go, hang in there, we need you, stay, stay, I'm coming.

Matthew started to cry.

'Stop, don't do that,' she said, sharply. 'Wait until we go and talk to the doctors. I'll go and tell Dad.'

He was in the yard talking to Mark when she got to him.

'Dad, we got bad news from the hospital.' She glanced at Mark in a silent request for support. 'Mam's had a heart attack. I think they've stabilised her but we should go in as soon as we can.'

Jim's mouth sagged. He stared at her. He walked away from his son and daughter towards the gate near the road. A neighbour passed by on a bicycle. 'Howaya, Jim. Best regards to Kate,' he called out. Jim raised his hand in silent greeting.

Mark joined him and took his arm. 'Come on, Dad, let's go.'

At the hospital, they were sent to the Intensive Care waiting room. Louise and Aidan were already there, standing in the corridor outside. They hugged everyone for comfort. Christina had rung them on their mobiles to tell them the news and, as they were closer to the hospital, they'd arrived first. Matthew had sent a text to Enda's mobile but it was switched off.

'Is she in there? In intensive care?' Mark asked, indicating the door. Access to the unit was more complicated than it was to the normal ward where they had come to see her before. There was a buzzer and a large sign with 'ICU SILENCE' in large red letters at the entrance to the unit. The atmosphere was heavy and ominous.

'Not yet,' Louise said. 'She's still in theatre. They'll bring her here afterwards. That's what one of the nurses told us but she couldn't tell us how she was. They won't know until the operation is over.'

'How long will it take?' Christina asked. She noticed that her father seemed not to be listening. He looked distracted, as though he had retreated into another world.

'She didn't know that either. She expects her to be brought here shortly. She told us she'd tell us as soon as she had any more news.' Aidan's eyes were red, his hands jammed deep into the pockets of his jeans.

'Let's move into the waiting room so we don't block the corridor.' Louise indicated the door opposite.

It was a small room with one long, narrow window with a blind. It was sparsely furnished with stacks of cardboard boxes containing medical supplies in one corner. Beside them were a kettle, a box of teabags, a jar of instant coffee and some disposable cups. There was upholstered seating in an L shape against two walls with a brown Formica coffee table in the middle. The idea of sitting in a circle around that table, forced to watch the drawn faces of her family and being watched by them was unbearable.

She went to get a bottle of water from the vending machine downstairs. She stood staring into the machine, mentally working out the square roots of numbers one after the other. She felt like a child avoiding standing on the lines of the pavement for fear of causing something terrible to happen until a man behind her lost patience and told her to speed it up. After walking up and down the corridor a few times, she returned to the waiting room. Enda had arrived in the meantime. Now they were all there. Mark indicated the empty chair beside him in case she wanted to sit down but she shook her head.

The tension in the room was tangible. They spoke in voices that were almost whispers when they spoke at all, but, on the whole, they stayed quiet, waiting. Eventually, the surgeon came to the room accompanied by a nurse. Their serious faces didn't do anything to calm her racing heart. It pumped blood to her ears, preventing her from properly hearing what the doctor was saying. She took a breath and examined their expressions for any clues of hope. The surgeon was a tall man of about fifty, overweight, with plentiful grey hair that stuck out from under his disposable cap. His bright blue eyes and full lips were cast in an expression of grim resolution. The blond-haired nurse by his side was young but she looked confident and unflappable.

'Mr. Cavanagh?' The surgeon looked around for him in the room.

Jim's eyes drifted up to meet his. 'Yes,' he said.

'I'm not sure how much you've been told but your wife suffered a heart attack earlier this morning. Luckily one of the nurses was close at hand and she was treated very quickly. We took her to theatre as soon as she was stable and I hope we have done what it takes to allow her to recover.'

'So she will recover then?' The hopefulness in Louise's voice rang out.

The surgeon looked at her for a second before answering. 'It's much too early for us to be able to say. I'm afraid it could go either way. The next few days will be critical. This ordeal has exhausted her. We've put her in an artificial coma for the moment to help her body to heal itself but there are no guarantees. All I can say is that the operation has stabilised her and she is not getting any worse.'

Christina wasn't sure if she was relieved or not. She was worried, worried sick, but at least her mother was still alive. As if she could ever be dead! And yet, the reality of death had never felt so close before. The word echoed in her head like the sound of the slamming of a heavy door in the distance.

'Can we see her?' Nuala said but the surgeon didn't understand her. He looked to the others for a translation and Nuala glanced at Louise in embarrassment. 'She asked if we could see her now?' Louise said.

'Of course. Sorry,' the surgeon said. He turned to the nurse. 'I think that would be possible. Perhaps you could explain the formalities?' He turned to leave. 'I hope all goes well for your wife and mother.'

'My name is Jackie,' the nurse said after he had left. 'You have to keep in mind that all the patients in ICU are seriously ill so, to reduce disturbance, a maximum of two people are allowed in at any one time. I suggest that, today, you don't stay too long. I'll go through the hygiene procedures with you in the prep room. Mr Cavanagh, perhaps you'd like to go in first?'

Jim stepped forward as though his name had been called in a roll call.

'You go in with him, Christina,' Mark said. The privilege of the eldest. One that she would happily have relinquished in that moment. She had been hoping to be able to sneak in alone but that wasn't going to be possible now, not unless she made a scene and she wasn't going to do that.

In the prep room, she did what she was told. She scrubbed her nails and hands until they were sore, she pulled on the plastic overshoes, the hair bonnet and put the mask over her mouth and nose and then followed the nurse through the door.

The first thing that struck her was how noisy it was. All around, machines were beeping, buzzing or ticking. Three doctors were doing their rounds and a group of nurses followed them, listening to their instructions. They were speaking in low, authoritative voices but not in whispers. Christina and Jim followed the nurse to a bed where Kate lay. She wanted to run to her, bury her face in her ample chest and cry but instead, she held back, hesitant and cautious. She hadn't realised that she would be on a respirator so it gave her a shock to see the tube leaving her mouth, to see it taped to her cheek. It ran all the way to a machine which blinked green fluorescent numbers and pulsated as it pumped each breath into her lungs. She stood back to allow her father to reach the bedside first. He leaned heavily on the edge of the bed with both hands. She walked around the other side to take her mother's hand. It was only when she tried to hold it that she realised that she had knocked off a clip attached to the index finger. She recoiled instinctively, fearful that she was interfering with some machine function critical to her mother's well-being. A nurse quickly arrived and reattached the clip, explaining that it was merely to monitor her blood pressure.

Her mother's face was devoid of any pinkness, instead, it had a yellowish tinge. Her hair was plastered back from her face against the pillow. She looked so feeble and helpless that Christina wondered how any of these people who were caring for her could possibly understand how important she was.

'Mam,' she said gently. 'We're here, it's me, Christina. Dad's here too. You gave us a fright but everything is under control now.'

There was no reaction, not that she had expected it.

She rubbed her mother's arm. She was still wearing the blue, paper surgical gown. Her skin was clammy. What if she didn't get better? A surge of panic overtook her. It took an enormous effort of willpower to quell it.

Jim cleared his throat. 'Kate.' He stopped. He tried again. 'Kate. Get better soon.'

Her father didn't look very steady on his feet and there were no chairs around. 'Would you like to go now, Dad? We'll let the others see her and if you want to come back in again at the end, I'm sure the nurses would be okay with that,' she said.

As they were leaving, she was conscious of her father's frailty but she hesitated to hold his arm. She didn't want to embarrass him but, if she was honest, her real reason was that she didn't want to think that he needed her as his crutch. In the prep room, as they removed their masks and shoe covers, the external door opened. She looked up to see Lynn coming in, examining something on a clipboard. Strangely, for the first time almost since she had come home, Lynn had been far from her thoughts.

Lynn looked up from her clipboard. She stopped, her face furrowed in an effort of recognition before brightening. 'Christina Cavanagh! I don't believe it. I haven't seen you in years.' Then she collected herself as she realised that the reason Christina was there couldn't possibly be a happy one. 'Who are you here to see?'

'My mother. She was just moved here. She had a heart attack earlier today,' she said stiffly.

'Oh, no, I'm so sorry.' Lynn then noticed her father. 'Mr. Cavanagh, Jim, that's dreadful news about your wife but please don't worry too much, we'll be doing our best for her.'

'Thank you…,'

'Lynn,' she prompted him.

'Ah, I remember now, I knew the face was familiar. You're a friend of Christina's. Were you in school together?'

'Well, we used to be friends but we haven't seen each other for years.'

'So you work here then?' Jim said.

'Yes, I've been in ICU for nine years now.'

'Well, it's a great relief to me to know there's someone here from home, someone who knows Kate.'

'Don't you worry, when I'm on duty, I'll ask to be assigned to your wife but all the staff here are very good, she'll get the best of care.' Lynn leaned across and patted Jim's arm.

Christina winced. She hadn't changed, she still had that same ingratiating manner. It was strange to notice that she was still afraid of her. Why had that not died away? They were equals now, there was nothing she could do to her anymore. It was an instinctive defensive reaction by her body in the presence of an old familiar threat, even if that threat no longer had any power to cause new hurts.

'Let's go, Dad, the others will be anxious to see Mam,' she said abruptly. She knew her rudeness would be excused in light of her mother's illness but she didn't care what anyone thought, especially not Lynn.

Chapter 8

Christina was trembling when she left the unit. Already destabilised by her mother's heart attack, this encounter with the past had shaken her to her core and she didn't want her family to notice.

'I'll be back in a little while. I'm going to phone Steve. He's expecting me back today. I just want to let him know that I'm staying on,' she told Aidan in the corridor, walking away from him as she spoke. She went outside and switched on her mobile. On the front steps of the hospital was a group of hardened smokers, undeterred by the cold, some of them in dressing gowns or attached to drips. She took a few steps away from them. Life around her was surreal, hard to reconcile with what was going on inside the hospital. She wanted to cry but all her tears had hardened into a solid block lodged in her chest.

Once again, she was trapped. Except that this time she was an adult. She wanted more than anything for her mother to recover and once again Lynn was in the role of gatekeeper. She should have more control over her life. For the past twenty years, she had done everything she could to ensure that she would never be in the same position again, that her life would remain sovereign, governed by her alone.

So many times Lynn had tricked her back into friendship, so easily that she came to believe each time that she had imagined or exaggerated the previous torments, that it had been her own fault for being so sensitive. Each time, she drew her into the magic circle of her popularity only to throw her out again, merely because she could. Each time, wallowing in humiliation, she had sworn that the next time she would resist, but the draw of Lynn's smile, the warmth of her friendship, had fooled her yet again.

1987

By Easter of her first year in the school, Lynn had become the unrivalled queen of coolness. Everyone wanted to be in her gang, even the boys, in fact, especially the boys. She was daring, exciting, confident and she made her cohorts feel the same way. When the weather got better, Lynn started stealing cigarettes from her mother and bringing them to school. A wink or a nod of Lynn's head indicating the direction of the basketball court was a thrilling invitation to join her behind the wall at the end of the court. There, they gathered to smoke, chat and laugh, feeling like adventurers and rebels, thumbing their noses at authority. Even the ones who didn't smoke wanted to be there.

Christina was eating her sandwiches by the climbing frame, on the outskirts of a conversation between Helen Spollen and Cliona Brady, hoping for an opportunity to join in, when Lynn sidled up to them.

'Coming for one?' she said quietly to Helen and Cliona, on the alert for teachers.

'Sure,' Helen said and threw a questioning glance at Christina to check if Lynn wanted her to come too. For months now, Lynn had been toying with her, sometimes mocking her but mostly excluding her and sometimes, when she felt like it, being friendly. It was one of those times when Lynn was ignoring her but there were hints that she was softening up.

'OK, fine, you can come too, then Christina,' Lynn said dismissively before turning back to the others. 'Just let's split up first, girls, we don't want to get nabbed. You two go round by the old bicycle shed, we'll go the other way towards the back gate.'

Christina hesitated, inclined to refuse but the thrill of being included as an accomplice and the hope that this might be a turning point towards better things were too strong. She sauntered nonchalantly along beside Lynn, trying not to attract attention, but her heart was beating faster. They slipped between the wall of the basketball court and the hedge until they reached a point where the gap between the two widened. Colm Flynn and Brendan Duffy were already there. Colm was small and skinny with red hair but he had a knack for making everyone laugh that made up for his lack of good looks. Brendan was very different. He tried to be funny but it was always obvious that he was trying too hard. He was tall with blond hair, cropped short and a muscular body. He was a boxer and doing well. His dad was training him and he'd won all kinds of junior medals.

Helen and Cliona arrived almost at the same time from the other direction followed by Emily.

'Sorry, guys, I don't have enough for everybody. You'll have to share,' Lynn said. 'She only had one pack. She doesn't mind if I take an odd one but she'd skin me alive if I clean her out altogether.'

Christina was relieved: she'd have a good excuse to refuse now. She had never smoked before, she didn't know how to and didn't want to be put to the test in front of everyone. Her heart sank when Brendan took a new pack of ten from the front pocket of his jeans and waved it at them. He pulled off the plastic wrapper and the foil paper, crumpled them up and threw them on the ground beside him.

'So girls, what'll you give me in return?' He looked around the circle with a leer.

She could feel herself blushing but was saved by the distraction of a high-pitched squeal from Cliona. Colm had picked a long feathery stalk of grass and was tickling the inside of her knee with it.

'Colm!' Lynn said. 'You eejit. Stop making her squeal. They'll hear us.'

'Don't worry, it's Miss Phelan on yard duty today. If she catches us, I'll say:' He joined his hands together and put on a pleading expression. '"Please, Miss Phelan, give me detention. Oh yes, keep me back after school. Just you and me. Together. In the science lab. To the light of the Bunsen burners."'

Everyone giggled and Colm pretended to look offended. 'What? Everyone knows she has the hots for me. I can do no wrong.'

'So who's got the matches?' Helen said.

'Shit, I thought I had some.' Lynn was searching her pockets.

'Brendan's our man, there's a bit of a caveman about him. Go on, Brendan, rub two stones together there.' Colm nudged him and knocked him off balance.

'No need,' Brendan said and took a squashed box of Maguire and Patersons out of his pocket.

The cigarettes were passed around. She didn't take one.

'Go on, Christina, have one,' Lynn said.

'It's not fair to take all of Brendan's cigarettes, he'll have none left.'

'Oh, Brendan doesn't mind. Do you, Benny? In any case, he's smoked enough of mine in the past. Unless of course, you don't want to.'

Christina noticed Helen and Cliona giggling together privately and was immediately convinced that they were laughing at her.

'Well, OK then.' She pulled one out of the pack and held it between her fingers, watching the others closely. When it was her turn to light up, she took in a deep breath as she had seen the others do. The smoke hit the back of her throat and made her feel sick. Her nose tingled painfully. She was seized by an uncontrollable fit of coughing. Everyone laughed but quickly muffled it so that the teachers wouldn't hear them.

'Brendan, there's only one thing for it: I think you're going to have to give her the kiss of life,' Lynn said.

'Oo, yes,' Helen said, although she didn't look all that relaxed with her own cigarette. Lynn, on the other hand, was leaning back against the wall, casually blowing smoke rings towards the sky. She looked at Brendan. 'So?'

'No way,' he said.

Colm started tapping Christina on the back. When she managed to stop coughing, she held out the lit cigarette to him. Colm reached to take it but Lynn stopped him. 'No, leave her. Go on, Christina, try again. You can't give up like that.'

'No. Thanks. I don't really like it.' She was fighting against a wave of nausea as the smoke swirled into her nostrils.

Lynn laughed. 'No one ever likes it the first time. Go on, have another drag.' Something in her voice had changed, this was no longer an invitation, it was an order, a challenge. The others sensed it too. They were all looking at her with detached curiosity, wondering how she would react without feeling personally involved.

She attempted a small laugh and tried to give it to Colm again. 'Maybe I'll like it better next time then.'

Colm hesitated and glanced at Lynn but she was looking directly at her. 'Maybe there won't be a next time. Go on, Christina, don't be such a sap. Do it.' The hard steel running through Lynn's voice frightened her. Her head was spinning and her stomach was churning but whether it was from nicotine or fear she could no longer tell. She felt the hard detached eyes of the others on her. They might have been watching a scene on television instead of a real person.

Her fingers trembled a little as she brought them closer to her lips. She tried to keep them still. Her lips were dry and stuck to the filter of the cigarette. 'A proper drag,' Lynn commanded.

She drew the smoke into her lungs. Her stomach heaved. She forced her body to control itself and retain its contents inside. She withdrew the cigarette and blew out the smoke with only a slight splutter.

'You see, you'll be a smoker yet,' Lynn said. When the bell rang, she took two quick puffs from her cigarette and then crushed it underfoot. Emily handed around a pack of chewing gum.

'I'll go first,' Helen said. 'I'll let you know if someone's coming.' She stood by the gate so that she could see both the staff room and the yard. The others left one by one and sauntered towards the open doors where Miss Phelan was ringing the bell.

She had History next but she couldn't concentrate. Instead of focusing on the Easter Rising, her mind was a swirl. She knew she should have stood up for herself and not let Lynn boss her around but, even now, after the event, she couldn't figure out how she might have handled the situation differently. Should she have walked away? Should she have cried and hoped that they would take pity on her? Should she have shouted at them?

She said very little on the bus on the way home and deliberately sat in the front seat behind the driver. She decided to talk to her mother about it. Even though nothing she said now could change the course of events, she still wanted to feel her support and hear from her that she had not been totally ridiculous.

When she got home her mother was at the cooker preparing the dinner. She was now very pregnant and moved more slowly.

'Mam, there's something I need to talk to you about,' she said and sat down squarely in front of her to show how serious she was.

'Christina, I've so much to do right now. Could we talk about it after dinner?' She sounded tired and worn out. Christina nodded. She was disappointed but tried to hold on to her grievance so that it would still be fresh when they spoke later. Over the next few hours, however, the power of it slipped away and she didn't feel quite so strongly about the incident when eventually her mother sat down in her armchair. She was mending a pair of jeans belonging to one of the boys. How to tell her what had happened that day? How could she make her mother understand when what she really wanted was for her mother to explain it to her? She couldn't find the right words to start. Maybe the best way was to shock her and make her sit up and listen.

'Mam, I smoked a cigarette today. Behind the school. With Lynn and some of the others.' The words came out in a rush as she tried to get them all out before her mother exploded in anger at her. But the explosion didn't come.

Her mother rested the jeans on her knees and stopped mending. 'Was that the first time you smoked, Christina?'

'Yes.'

'Did you like it?'

'No, no, I hated it. It was awful.' She wasn't sure if it was the smoking or something else she was referring to. Her mother leaned over and squeezed her hand.

'It's all right, love. It's OK to try something out once. I'm sure you were curious. You know I wouldn't like you to smoke, it's very bad for you, but one cigarette isn't the end of the world.'

She clenched her jaw in frustration: her mother didn't understand.

'It was all because of Lynn. She made me. I didn't want to and now I feel rotten about it.' She was desperate to get her meaning across but the right words wouldn't come. They swirled around, unidentified and out of her grasp.

Her mother smiled but there was a slight note of reproach in her voice. 'It's not Lynn's fault, you know. There's no need to blame her. Don't worry too much about it, sweetheart, now you know what it's like, you won't do it anymore. I think it's time for bed now. It's late and you have school in the morning.'

She stomped out of the room without kissing her mother goodnight.

Her linen jacket wasn't very warm and she started to feel the cold. She walked around the corner of the hospital in an attempt to escape the grip of the wind. She wasn't ready to go back inside and face everyone. It was surprising that past humiliations remembered could still have this power over her.

She scrolled down to Steve's number and selected it. He answered immediately.

'Chris, honey,' he said and she smiled spontaneously at the warmth in his voice. 'What's going on? I've been so worried about you.'

'Steve, I won't be coming back this evening. My mother has taken a turn for the worse. I'm going to take a few days off and stay here for a while longer.'

'Oh, you poor thing, I can come straight away, if you want me there.'

She was taken aback; it hadn't occurred to her that he might come. He lived in a different world and she didn't know how the two would mix.

'No, it's OK, Steve, thanks anyway. There's nothing you can do here.'

'Is she going to be all right?'

She couldn't answer his question without first composing herself and that tiny silence gave her away. 'I don't know. I hope so. I think it's touch and go.'

'Are you sure you don't want me to be with you, Chris? I hate to think of you so far away at a tough time like this. I wouldn't be in anyone's way if that's what you're afraid of.' She had to blink several times to reabsorb her tears.

'Steve… I have a lot to deal with here. Wait a little bit.'

'OK then. Tell you what, we have a new machine being delivered tomorrow, I'll work overtime tomorrow evening to get it installed and then I'll be able to leave on Tuesday.'

'Let's talk about this tomorrow. She might be on the road to recovery by then and I could come back to Dublin. Don't rush into anything.'

'If that's what you want. But if you change your mind, just tell me and I'll be there as fast as I can.' He paused, as if aware of the weight of the words he was about to say. 'I love you, Chris. Look after yourself.'

'They're calling me; I've got to go. Talk to you tomorrow.'

His talk of love was a weight on her that she wasn't ready to deal with. Right now, love was an obligation, a risk, an impossible paradigm. She couldn't see how it could fit into her complex, fragmented life at the moment. It made her long for freedom.

Steve put the phone down and went back to the sofa where he had been playing the guitar before Chris's phone call. He picked it up and strummed absentmindedly. If he could set his thoughts to music, maybe he would find some kind of logic in them. He could tell that Chris was distressed no matter how controlled she might appear from the outside but he didn't fully understand why. Of course, it was normal for her to be upset that her mother was sick. That, he could understand, but there was something more to it. She was guarded, on edge. She made him think of a wild animal hesitating between allowing him to approach or darting away. He had never been one for analysing his words and actions but this time, he was afraid that a wrong movement might send her bolting out of his life forever. Should he stay in Dublin and leave her the space she asked for or should he go and be with her? She had never been particularly close to her mother, at least not that he had noticed. Chris didn't talk a lot about her, or even about her childhood in general. He had always assumed that came from her desire for privacy but now he wasn't so sure. Maybe there was a more concrete reason why she was so reserved on that subject.

There was a part of Chris he had never seen, one that was unknown to him, like the dark side of the moon. Even when they made love, she didn't let go fully. She was loving and willing but she never let herself lose control. What was on the other side? And, if he were never to see it, would the side he could see be enough for him? He thought it would, but he couldn't give up hope that someday he might get to see the whole Christina.

He stumbled on a musical phrase that fitted the song he was working on and a tingle of excitement ran through him. He picked up a pen to write it down and pushed his concerns about Christina out of his mind for the moment.

Chapter 9

Kate's condition changed little over the next couple of days. She lay immobile in the bed under spotless white sheets, oblivious to the bustle of activity around her in the Intensive Care Unit, unaware of the constant flow of worried visitors riveted to her every movement. Occasionally, she twitched or her eyes rippled under her eyelids and this was taken as an encouraging sign by her family, even if the medical staff refused to show any enthusiasm or commit themselves to an opinion about the future. They remained stubbornly stoic, unwilling or unable to give any definite prognosis.

Christina tried to minimise her contact with Lynn but it wasn't always easy. On the afternoon of Kate's second day in the Unit, she was standing by her mother's bed, unsure of what to do but reluctant to leave because she couldn't shake off the ridiculous belief that her mother's condition couldn't worsen as long as she was there to watch over her. Lynn approached her.

'You could try talking to her, you know,' she said. 'It's perfectly possible that there are moments when she can hear you. Nobody can tell for sure. But we know from a lot of cases we get here that hearing is often the last of the senses to go when a patient is in a coma.'

'Hmm,' she said, still gazing down at her mother.

'There's a stool here if you want to sit beside her.' She indicated one behind a monitor.

'No thanks. I'm OK standing.'

'Or you could try to put some water on her tongue. She is getting all the fluids her body needs through the drip but if you put some in her mouth it keeps it from drying out too much. Use this so that she doesn't get too much and choke.' Lynn passed her a plastic tumbler half-filled with water and a sponge cube on a stick.

Christina dipped the sponge in the water and rubbed it against her mother's lips. The reaction was instantaneous. Her mouth moved to grab the sponge and suck in the water thirstily. An involuntary cry escaped Christina and she almost dropped the sponge. She looked at Lynn, hope fluttering upwards from her stomach. 'Did you see that? She drank the water. Does that mean she's waking up?'

Lynn shook her head. 'I'm afraid that's a natural reflex, you shouldn't read too much into it. She can feel pain and she can feel the relief from discomfort but she's not conscious in the real sense of the word.' She said this with calm authority but hope had arrived like a ghost and refused to leave. Christina wet the sponge once more. She put it into her mother's mouth beside the respiration tube and again her mother gulped the water greedily. She bent down and peered in from the side and could see that the inside of her mother's mouth was dry and cracked like parched land. Suddenly, she couldn't take it anymore. This was too much suffering. She put the tumbler on a stand and rushed away. She went home but over the next few hours, the memory plagued her, making her feel sick and helpless. Each time it did, she tried to distract her brain, pushing it through mathematical hoops so that it couldn't linger on that image.

Being at home was difficult too. Everyone was tense and the same conversations were repeated over again with merely the roles being exchanged. Any snippet of information gleaned at the hospital was examined and analysed until the last drop of meaning was squeezed out of it. The local grapevine had been active and the phone rang frequently with calls from neighbours and friends wondering how Kate was. She found she could cope when the call was merely a request for an update or a wish for a speedy recovery but she found it tough when it degenerated into reminiscences of the past and recollections of Kate's kindnesses in various circumstances. However, early in the morning or late at night, when the phone rang out, it had an ominous sound. They glanced at each other, dread in their hearts, hoping someone else would answer it.

On Tuesday morning, reluctant to spend the morning waiting for her turn to see her mother at the hospital and anxious to get out of the house, Christina went shopping for food. She wandered around the garishly-lit supermarket picking up bits and pieces for dinner that evening. Her brain was operating at quarter-speed and as she stood trying to decide between wholemeal and white sliced bread, she noticed someone nearby with a trolley craning curiously to get a better look at her. She pretended not to notice and picked up a sliced pan to examine the ingredients in detail.

'Christina? Christina Cavanagh, is that you?'

She turned around, no longer able to ignore the intrusion. 'Yes?'

The woman became flustered. 'Sorry to disturb you – it is Christina, isn't it? – but you took me by surprise. I haven't seen you for years. Helen, Helen Spollen. You don't remember me, do you?'

'Of course. Helen! How are you?' In the face of this older woman, she could still see the young teenage Helen through the layers of age. She still had the same turned-up nose with the wide nostrils, the same unmanageable curly hair although it looked thinner and there were touches of grey now. She even

had the same habit of dipping her head to the side as she spoke, as if in half-apology.

'I'm fine. I don't think I've seen you since school. You look great. What have you been doing with yourself?' Helen asked.

'Oh, this and that. I worked in London for a while but I moved back to Dublin five years ago. How about you?'

'I never made it very far. I'm a bit of a home bird, me.' She laughed, dipping her head to the side in that old Helen way. 'I'm married to Peter Flynn. Do you remember him? He was the year ahead of us in school, Colm Flynn's brother. We have three children, two girls and a boy. Do you have any?'

'No.' She paused, wondering if she should add something but there was nothing to add.

'You're as well off,' Helen laughed but Christina could see that she didn't mean it.

'Not at all, I'm sure you're very lucky.'

'Listen, would you like to go for a coffee? I've just finished shopping.'

Instinctively, she was going to refuse but then thought why not, for once she wasn't rushing to be somewhere else.

They left their groceries in their cars and arranged to meet at the coffee shop next door to the supermarket.

As Helen talked, she raised the ghosts of forgotten events and old school memories. It was strange to hear words that conjured up days long past as she looked into this face so familiar and yet so changed. It was as if she had just intersected a parallel world where the young Christina continued to live, go to school and be tormented while the grown-up Christina left her there, unable to save her.

'And remember Mrs Higgins, the religion teacher?' Helen babbled on. 'She had an affair with a Garda from Clifden, her husband found out and went crazy. Can you believe it? After all the lectures she used to give us about remaining pure and the big fuss she made over that dirty picture Colm brought into school one time. What a laugh! Do you remember that?' She giggled afresh.

She was amazed. Did Helen really think that she would remember her school days with fondness and laughter?

'Of course, you were such a brain box at school. You never got into trouble.'

'Not with the teachers, no.'

Helen realised what she was referring to and made an embarrassed face. 'Yes, you had some sort of a run-in with Lynn at one stage didn't you? I think I remember that. You must have had a bit of a hard time around then, but it all blew over fast enough in the end, didn't it?'

'Hmm, I suppose.' She didn't want to show how much damage that episode had caused. 'Lynn wasn't very easy to stand up to, for me or anyone.'

'Oh, we were all very young and it was just a bit of silly messing around anyway, wasn't it?'

Easy for you to say, she wanted to reply but instead, she smiled tautly at Helen and asked her about her children.

As they counted out change to pay for their coffees and gathered up their belongings, Helen said 'I'll have to tell Colm I met you. He'll be so surprised.'

'What's he doing now?' she asked.

'He has his own business, hiring out specialised machinery and drivers for the building trade. Brendan Duffy's in it with him. Do you remember him? He always used to hang out with Colm. Well, he went to live in Cork for a while but he moved back with his wife and kids a few years ago. They built a big house near us so I see him around the whole time.' She rolled her eyes in mock exasperation.

Christina's heart started to beat faster. 'That's nice,' she said, anxious to be gone.

Separating was awkward; it felt rude to leave with no reference to the future and yet she didn't want to suggest any arrangement to meet again. She thanked Helen for the invitation and excused herself as quickly as she could.

As Helen put on her wool coat, it now seemed more shapeless and frumpy to her than it had when she'd put it on to go shopping a few hours earlier. It wasn't that Christina Cavanagh had been wearing obvious big brands or high fashion or anything, but even in black jeans and a blazer, she looked cool and sophisticated. Her blouse fell open at the neck the way it did in fashion magazines, with just the right balance of casualness and elegance. She had certainly changed since they were at school together, although, even then, she had a way of keeping herself apart as if she was too good for the rest of the class. She never said anything specifically, but you could sense it. So, in that way, she hadn't changed. Over coffee, Helen could feel that she was looking down her nose at her, friendly enough, but with a superior sort of air.

While she edged her way forward in the queue at the post office, she tried to recall how exactly that incident between Christina and Lynn had happened but the details escaped her. All she could remember was how they had all ignored Christina for a while, pretending not to hear her when she spoke and wandering off whenever she came near. They didn't do anything to her though. If she was honest with herself, it had been a bit of excitement towards the end of the year when they were getting well and truly fed up with school and restless for the summer holidays - not that she had been proud of herself or anything. It had been Lynn's idea, as everything at that time was, but they hadn't done it out of badness, just boredom. And Christina was always a bit of a lick, getting good marks the whole time and even studying stuff she didn't have to. Helen wouldn't go so far as to say that she was asking for it, but she didn't exactly try to fit in either. In any case, the whole thing had blown over quickly once the novelty of it faded.

She'd turned into a tough cookie now though, not someone you'd want to mess with. Funny that, the way she was the very same in some ways and yet so different in others. She could imagine her as one of those tough-as-nails businesswomen who'd walk all over anyone to get what they want. Her career was probably the most important thing to her; a husband and kids would just hold her back.

Strangely, Helen was a little bit envious of her even though she would normally feel sorry for someone in her position, still single and childless at her age. As she made her way to the dry-cleaners to pick up one of Peter's suits and to the bookshop to pick up a textbook for her son, the thought occurred to her that Christina was free, free to do what she wanted and be who she wanted. And yet Helen hadn't the faintest idea who else she would want to be if she wasn't who she was. It was not something she'd ever considered before. All she knew was that the meeting had reinforced that vague feeling of dissatisfaction with her life. Now that the kids were teenagers, they were moving away from her and living their own lives and they didn't need her as much and sometimes she thought that she lived beside Colm rather than with him. It was probably the effect of meeting someone from the past out of the blue like that. When you were getting on with life and were wrapped up doing all the day-to-day things that needed to be done, you didn't notice how time was passing and how much you had changed since your school days. But then, when you met someone from those times who had taken a different path from you, it came as a bit of a jolt to see how far you had come without knowing it. To shake off her pessimism she cheered herself up by thinking that she'd have something to tell Cliona and Colm when they went out to the pub for a few drinks over the weekend.

Christina was more thrown by the encounter with Helen than anyone could guess from observing her. The mention of Brendan's name had brought back that same old stomach-sinking feeling again. She resorted to her old trick of squaring numbers consecutively until she reached larger numbers that required her brain to focus on that rather than think of other things. It wasn't working as well as usual. She still felt sick. She thought she had managed to move on from the person she was at that time but now her old teenage self had come back to haunt her.

1987

The day the row broke out had started well. Mr Brady, the maths teacher, was a big man with red hair and a red beard. He had a way of commanding respect when he entered the classroom, and when he did, the class became instantly silent and attentive although she never heard him raise his voice or lose his temper. That morning, he walked in, put the corrected papers from their recent maths test on his desk and picked up a piece of chalk.

'I'll hand out your test papers at the end of class. We're going to correct the answers from the test together because it looks as if some of you are struggling. With a few exceptions,' he said. Then, he looked directly at her and nodded. She squirmed under his gaze. 'Good work, Christina. Keep it up.' She blushed. His compliments were rare but when they came, they gave her wings and her heart soared. 'Maybe you could come to the board and take us through your reasoning for question five.' He held out the chalk to her and she stood up. She outlined her solution on the board and when she had finished he gave her a slow, appreciative nod. 'Good,' he said. This was high praise coming from Mr Brady and when she sat down again, she thought that she loved Mr Brady with an intense, hitherto unknown passion.

She was still floating on a cloud of hero worship when the bell rang for Science after the break. Miss Roberts was late. She often was. To kill time, some of the boys removed the central ink chamber from their biros, chewed up bits of paper into pellets and used the outer bit as a blowpipe to aim sodden bullets at the girls at the other side of the room. The girls retaliated and converted their biros into weapons until the room became a blizzard of tiny, saliva-soaked ammunition blown with force and sometimes with accuracy. Miss Roberts opened the door. 'What is going on here?' she shrieked. 'Stop it, all of you, stop it at once.' She was a nervous woman who had difficulty controlling a class on the best of occasions.

Slowly, they calmed down and sat back in their places but there was an undercurrent of mutiny in the air. Just as Miss Roberts opened her mouth to speak again, a white paper pellet hit her on the cheek with an audible splat. She went pale and shook, barely able to control her fury. She rubbed her cheek where she had been hit. 'Who did that?' Her voice was low and intense with anger. The atmosphere changed: this was serious now.

She stared around the classroom looking for the culprit. Something in Lynn's expression caught her eye. 'Lynn Carter, did you do it?'

'No, miss, no, I didn't,' Lynn said earnestly, leaving no doubt as to her innocence.

'Well then, did you see who did?'

'No, no,' she said but this time her protest was less certain.

'You did! Tell me, who did it?'

Lynn's eyes darted almost involuntarily to the next row and looked at Christina before looking back at Miss Roberts again. 'I don't know, miss.'

'I'm not going to let this go. I will find out who it was. I'll be right back.' The teacher turned on her heels and stormed out the door.

Lynn was staring at her. 'Christina, say it was you,' she whispered across the aisle. 'If Brendan gets caught, he's in big trouble, he might even get expelled. He's in enough trouble already for that prank with Mr Halpin's car. Nobody will say anything to you, you're such a teacher's pet.'

'Why should I?' she said.

'Do it,' Lynn said. 'It'll all blow over to nothing if they think it was you.'

Filled with courage from the praise from Mr Brady that morning, she resisted. 'No, Lynn, I won't. Find another scapegoat,' she said.

Miss Roberts came back into the room accompanied by Mr Halpin, the principal. If anything her anger and determination had increased. 'You have one last chance.' Her voice has high and stretched. 'Whoever spat that…that object at me should own up now.' A perfect silence fell on the class. They could hear the voice of the teacher droning on in the classroom next door.

Mr Halpin cleared his throat. 'I am taking this very seriously. This kind of treatment of a teacher cannot be tolerated.'

Lynn glanced at her and jerked her head in the direction of the teacher as if to say, go on. Miss Roberts noticed. 'Christina, was it you?'

'No.'

'Well, then why was Lynn looking at you?'

A crazy suicidal instinct surged through her. She stared at Lynn. 'Maybe you should ask her that.' Her tone was defiant.

Mr Halpin interrupted. 'Let's talk about this outside the classroom. Lynn, come with me to my office. Miss Roberts, I suggest you continue with your class and we'll discuss this afterwards.'

She knew that she was in trouble, that she had declared war against an enemy far more powerful than her. But it wasn't until the next day that she realised that surrender was no longer an option, Lynn wanted annihilation. The exact content of the conversation between Lynn and Mr Halpin never became known but, in the end, when the real culprit could not be identified, the whole class was punished with additional homework and an order to write a letter of apology to Miss Roberts signed by everyone.

There was little over a month left until the summer holidays and this time turned into the worst weeks of her life. Where before Lynn had conducted sporadic guerrilla attacks on her, now this was fall-out warfare. No one in the class spoke to her, they avoided sitting beside her unless ordered to do so by a teacher, they ignored her or disbanded a game if she attempted to join them. There was no overt violence, although she could see that some took more pleasure in her discomfort than others. The treatment was so invisible that not even Mark who was a year below her noticed anything. Each class year was its own little universe, independent of all the other years so it never occurred to her to seek companionship or support elsewhere. She wanted to tell her mother but she was reaching the end of her pregnancy and in any case, she wasn't sure what she could do to help.

One day, after three weeks of solitude, she approached Lynn in the cloakroom. She was with two of the other girls but there was no point in waiting for a better time; there was never an opportunity to see her alone. 'Lynn, can I talk to you for a minute? I'd like to sort this out. It's horrible to be fighting like this.'

Lynn looked at her for a moment as if recalling who she was. 'Fighting? What fighting?'

'I mean this 'not talking'. I'm sorry if I said anything to upset you. What do you want me to do?'

Lynn seemed to be considering her request and Christina hoped that there could be a quick and easy solution to this dispute.

'You mean you want us to be friends? You want us to *like* you, is that it?' Lynn said eventually.

Christina didn't want to speak for fear that it would dislodge the lump in her throat and cause tears to fall. She nodded.

'No can do.' Lynn sat down on the bench and started tying up the laces of her runners. 'Friendship has to be deserved. And you don't deserve to be friends with us.' She said it as if her decision was final, that it gave her no pleasure but justice demanded that this was how it had to be.

Christina stayed for a second, watching her, but then left the cloakroom, defeated and humiliated. After that, she no longer tried to talk to the others in the class. It was demeaning to stand around hoping for a few kind or even neutral words so she stayed away from all of them. She asked for permission to stay in the classroom during lunchtime to do projects, claiming it was impossible to get work done at home. The teachers were delighted at her commitment to work and praised her zeal.

As the holidays approached, the vendetta against her lost its momentum. She still felt physically sick every morning as she got ready for school and she dreaded break times but people gradually forgot that they weren't supposed to talk to her and continued their conversations when she was nearby. Trish Hegarty even asked her for her Biology notes when she got the flu and missed a couple of days. But the experience had changed her. She was both weaker and stronger. She had been tested and her weaknesses had become self-evident. Never again would she allow others to see them. Schoolwork became a cocoon within which she planned her metamorphosis and eventual escape.

Chapter 10

That afternoon at the hospital, Lynn was on duty. She was talking to a colleague by the nurses' station. She acknowledged Christina as she passed by and as soon as she was free, she approached her. 'Are you all right, Christina?' she asked. 'You seemed a bit upset yesterday when you left.'

'I'm fine.' Her concern was disconcerting. 'How is she today?' She glanced down at her mother.

'Nothing new to report, I'm afraid. The doctor's just done her rounds and she thinks that we should consider turning off her respirator in the hope that it will trigger her system to respond.'

A mix of emotions collided in that instant. She nodded in a way that she hoped conveyed that she was seriously contemplating this eventuality and not trying to manage her childish terror of becoming motherless.

'Obviously, there's a risk involved but if the doctors decide to do that then they will have weighed up that risk. They know what they are doing. They could have taken her off the respirator before but they wanted to give her body time to repose and recover. But now it's time. I think they are doing the right thing.'

'When would they do this?'

'Tomorrow, I think.'

'Do we have a decision to make? Or is it up to the doctors to decide?'

'No, it's the doctors' decision. Don't worry too much about it, I think she'll cope fine. At least, I don't think her condition will deteriorate.'

'But you don't think it will improve either?' She pretended to smooth out the washed-stiff hospital blanket stretched over her mother's chest so that she wouldn't have to look Lynn in the eyes.

'I don't know. I'd like to be able to say that she'll make a full recovery but her body has been through a lot in the past week. I don't want to build up false hope either. I don't think anyone can give you a definite answer. It's impossible to know for sure how she will react,' Lynn said in a practical, down-to-earth voice.

Every comment, every word, every facial gesture, every change in tone caused hope to inflate or deflate inside her like a hot air balloon. She had no idea if this hope was false or real, all she knew was that it controlled her completely. So here she was, back at the same point in her life where she wanted to beg Lynn for reassurance, for peace of mind, but this time, as last time, she would not get it.

'She's not in pain, is she?' she asked, remembering her mother's dried-up mouth and cracked tongue with an internal shiver.

‘No, you can be sure of that. She’s on morphine.’ Lynn pointed to a bag on a drip stand. The digital screen showed that it was regulated to deliver two units. She had no idea how much a unit was and didn’t ask.

Lynn had taken a step away when she stopped and turned back. ‘Christina, I’m very sorry to see your mum like this.’

‘I know,’ Christina said, without looking up. ‘Thanks.’

Lynn hesitated still. ‘Is everything all right between us? I mean, it’s been a long time.’

‘Yeah, it’s fine.’ She flicked a glance at Lynn before looking away again. A machine nearby started to beep. An alert. She started to count the beeps in her head. If they stopped the alarm before she got to ten, she would be safe.

‘We were kids. Doing all kinds of silly stuff until we knew better.’

Six…seven.

‘I know, water under the bridge and all that. It’s just not a good time for me right now.’

Nine…The alarm stopped.

‘I can understand that,’ Lynn said. ‘I’d better get back. See you later.’

Christina found a stool and sat by her mother’s side. She held her hand and ran her fingers over the soft, loose skin of her cheek. She kissed her and whispered. ‘It’s me, Mam. Christina. Please get well. Please wake up and come back. I don’t know if you can hear me but if you wake up, it’ll be different. We’ll make things better. I promise.’

She left the ward to allow Enda and Louise their turn to visit. They had all come together so while she was alone waiting for them, she took out her phone and, on impulse, wrote a text message to Steve, 'Come tomorrow? xx'. Her finger hovered over the send button before pressing down firmly.

Less than a minute later, he called her back. 'Chris, are you all right? What happened?'

'Nothing. There's no change. I didn't mean to worry you. Remember you said that you might be able to come here after Tuesday? Well, I'd be happy if you could, that's all.'

In the silence, she sensed that he was at a loss for words and she felt suddenly guilty that he could be surprised by this scrap of attention showing her need for him. She didn't deserve him: he should be with someone who would love him back the way he should be loved. She was on the verge of telling him not to come after all, that she had changed her mind when he replied. 'I'll get out of work early tomorrow and I'll be with you tomorrow evening. I'll take the train to Galway. Can you pick me up?'

'Of course, text me the time.'

'Will do. I miss you, Chris.'

She hesitated. 'Yes, looking forward to seeing you tomorrow.'

Her eyes stung and a tear leaked out. The threads of her life were becoming a tangled mess no matter how she had tried to lay them out straight and keep them separate. The idea of losing her mother filled her with horror and yet she had to acknowledge that for the past twenty years, she had maintained a distance between them, not so much a physical distance as an emotional one. She had always blamed her mother for what had happened to her, for not hearing her and rescuing her in time but now she realised that really she had been waiting for her mother to say sorry, to reach out to her and pull her into her arms. And yet she remembered very well a time when she had believed her mother's presence to be the ultimate safe haven, a place where nothing could touch her.

One of the last times she had felt that unwavering conviction in the power of her protection was the summer before her last year in school.

1987

The baby was born two weeks early. In the soft light of early morning, her father tiptoed into her room, trying not to wake Louise who slept in the same double bed as her. He shook her awake. 'Christina, I have to take your mother to Galway to the hospital now.'

She tried to sit up. 'Is she all right?'

'Shhh. She's fine, it's the baby. It's coming. I'll take her there now. I'll come back as soon as I can. Look after everyone while I'm gone. Good girl.'

She got them all up and dressed, made food for them and even managed to get them all to help out with cleaning the house to make it nice for their mother and the new baby. It all helped to keep her busy as she waited for news. Their dad didn't get back until evening-time. The birth had been a difficult one and he had stayed in the waiting room to make sure that everything went well.

'A little brother,' he told them when they rushed out into the yard as soon as they heard the car. 'A grand little fellow and your mother is doing fine as well. We'll go and see them this evening if you like.'

They were all relieved and cheered loudly. The collective family joy raised her spirits. The worry and the weight of responsibility for her five brothers and sisters fell off her shoulders like a heavy cloak. There was a party atmosphere in the car as they travelled to Galway. She sat in the back holding Nuala tightly on her knees and laughed at her brothers' stupid jokes and sang along with their songs.

Kate was in a private room. She looked tired and pale when they arrived but she found the energy to sit up and give each of them an individual welcome. They admired the baby in the small transparent cot by her bed, marvelled over the tininess of his fingers and touched the tissue paper softness of his ears before crowding around her again. Louise, who was four at the time, made them all laugh when she folded her arms across her chest in her best imitation of an adult pose while she subjected the new arrival to careful scrutiny. 'He's all right,' she said finally. 'I suppose we can keep him. Except… what can he do?'

'I know, love, he's not very good at doing anything yet. It's up to us to teach him,' Kate said, trying to keep a straight face.

They crowded in on either side of her bed and debated what name to give the new baby. The boys argued that they should have priority given that it was a boy and the girls argued hotly against this. In the end, an acceptable agreement was reached and they decided to call him Matthew. Nuala curled up close to her mother with an unwavering smile on her face. It was one of those rare occasions when they were one united family rather than a group of people whose alliances fluctuated depending on the moment.

Kate was radiant with joy to be surrounded by all her children. She caught Christina's hand and looked at her with eyes full of love. She pulled her closer so that she was sitting beside her at the head of the bed and put her arm around her 'Well done, you, for coping all by yourself today,' she said. 'I don't know what I'd do without you, Christina. I'm very lucky to have you.' She leaned her head back on her mother's shoulder.

Her memory of that summer was that it was hot and sunny and stretched on for ages. With hindsight, it was the last summer of her childhood; the last summer that she poked sticks in the melting pools of tar on the road; the last summer she, Mark, Enda and Aidan made their way along the river to find a good spot to picnic and swim; the last summer they picked the damsons from the trees that had run to wild in O'Brien's field and came back late at night, unaware of the time because it was still so bright. That summer, they had tried in vain to nurse a hedgehog they had found injured on the road back to life. She had cried bitterly the day he died and her father took the little prickly body out to bury him in the field. With hindsight, it was only a tiny blip in an otherwise tranquil but full summer that almost healed her wounds and made her forget what awaited her in September. As the days got shorter and the last days of August got cooler, she started to feel the inexorable pull of time and dread the return to school.

In the car on the way home, her mobile phone announced a text from Steve. She glanced at it while she drove, holding it so that Enda who was sitting beside her couldn't see. He hadn't wasted any time finding out about the trains. 'In Galway at 6.50 pm tomorrow. Call me anytime if u want. xx' She pressed the button on the side to close it down and put it in the compartment beside her seat.

'Did the nurse tell you that they may take Mam off the respirator tomorrow?' she asked Louise and Enda, glad that she was obliged to keep her eyes on the road.

'No. What does that mean?' Louise asked them from the back, leaning forward between their two seats. 'Is that a good sign or a bad sign?'

'I'm not sure. I got the impression that they thought it might jolt her back to life. The nurse wasn't sure if it would work but she seemed to think it was worth trying.'

'The nurse? Do you mean Lynn Carter?' Enda shifted in his seat and looked at her.

'Yes, I was talking to her earlier.'

'It's funny that you refer to her like that. Weren't you friends at school?'

'Yes, but it was such a long time ago. I think of her more as Mam's nurse now.'

'I was talking to her earlier. I think she's very good. We're lucky to have her.' Louise slumped back in her seat. 'God, I hope Mam pulls through. It's awful to see her like that.'

'You'll probably have to go back to work soon, Louise,' Christina said.

'No way. I'll go back when I'm ready. I work hard enough in that place. If they don't understand that I need time right now, then that's their problem.'

'What about you, Christina?' Enda asked.

'I'll stay until the weekend. If there's no change by then I'll probably go back to work.'

‘I don’t understand how you could get any work done with things the way they are,’ Louise said.

‘I’ll manage,’ she said.

‘I’m sure you will,’ Louise said and Christina could sense that her sister’s frustration and upset was being directed at her.

‘I’d rather be working,’ Enda said. ‘I think I’d go crazy if I didn’t. Mind you, the kids in this year’s class are driving me crazy too, but it’s a better sort of crazy to have to deal with than this crazy.’ Neither Louise nor Christina laughed as his tone was inviting them to.

A silence descended in the car.

Louise didn’t like the feel of the leather seats in Christina’s BMW. They were cold and stiff. Just like their owner, she added mentally. She felt a twinge of guilt at that narky observation, even if it was just an internal one. It was a pity that she and Christina had grown apart over the years. It didn’t help that she was so irritatingly perfect. She was always in control, her life running to schedule like the Swiss train system. Beside her, Louise felt disorganised, sloppy and fat. She made numerous resolutions to be more diplomatic, to stand back more from situations, to go on yet another diet but immediately afterwards she would forget and throw herself body and soul into the next situation she found herself in, whether that was a discussion about the environment, a problem at work, or a friend asking for advice.

It was a way of being that had got her into hot water before and even though she would love to be more like Christina who always seemed able to sit back, listen calmly and steadily until she was asked what she thought and then say something terribly logical and profound that you couldn't disagree with. She had tried to talk about this to her boyfriend, John, once but he had laughed and said he didn't particularly want her to be different; she was fine the way she was, even if she had a special talent for driving him nuts at times. He said that there was nothing wrong with a bit of passion, especially when she kept plenty in reserve for the bed and, in any case, he liked his women with a bit of flesh on them, he found Christina was a bit on the bony side. She loved it when he said things like that. Someday, she would have to marry that man.

Strangely, the ten years between her and Christina stretched wider now than when they were younger. She used to think that as she too became an adult, this growing equality between them would have brought them closer but this wasn't what had happened. When she was a little girl she remembered her as a big sister who never minded reading her stories at night or answering any of her random questions about snakes or stars. 'You're so lucky to have two mothers,' her friend, Elaine, an only child, had said to her once when they were about five and she came to play. 'Oh, Christina's not my mother, she's my big sister.' She had laughed at Elaine's mistake but she did feel lucky.

Now, they seemed to talk different languages, although, on the surface, it looked like they should have more in common now. Seeing how unperturbed Christina was over Mam's illness made her feel even more agitated. Deep down, she was sure that she did care but she was so sensible, it drove her nuts. She did the right thing all the time: visiting Mam, helping out at home, but she never got worked up about stuff because she couldn't see what good it would do when she had no control over what would happen. She was right of course, but try as she might, Louise couldn't be like her: she couldn't help but react and let it all out in a burst of panic or excitement.

It was at moments like this that she was glad to be part of a big family. They might have their disputes but at least each one of them knew what the others were going through in a way that an outsider couldn't. She loved John: he was great but he didn't fully understand, not in the way Enda or Nuala did, for example. Although there was something different about Nuala these days; it was as if she had turned in on herself and wasn't paying much attention to what was going on around her. Louise had always seen herself as the one closest to Nuala, the one who understood her best but she sensed that something was bothering her, something she didn't want to talk about. She had tried to talk to her about their mother's condition, in case that was the reason, but Nuala still didn't open up.

That was another reason she hoped her mother would get better and come home. It would be tough for Nuala to live alone with their father at home. Matthew was there for the moment but that wouldn't last forever. He was twenty-five now and he needed to move on. This business of skipping from job to job and getting drunk at the weekends was all very well when he was going to college, but it couldn't go on. She loved her dad but it was obvious that he was not at all equipped to help Nuala to get her life sorted. Or Matthew either, for that matter.

Financially, Nuala might be reasonably independent with her job in the local candle factory but she didn't earn a lot and her deafness limited her in ways she'd never admit to. Louise admired Nuala's insistence that she was not restricted and her determination to live a completely 'normal' life was wonderful, but still, there were times when she worried about her sister and her future. It wasn't always easy to get by in the world when you were 'different'. What would happen if her father couldn't give her the kind of support she needed?

She would have liked to talk about this with Christina who, as their sister, should be equally as concerned but somehow there was something that prevented her from bringing it up. It wasn't that she wouldn't listen or be sympathetic, but, when they talked, it was as if she stood a few steps back from the problem, examining it objectively for ways in which it might be diminished or dismantled. She wasn't *in* the problem in the same way that Louise felt herself to be. It was as if she treated personal issues in the same way that she would tackle and resolve business ones. It might be that Christina's approach was a more constructive one but it was one that kept Louise at arm's length instead of pulling her in close and involving her. The difficulty was that there was nothing specific she could complain about, nothing she could pin down and discuss with her. Oh well, she thought, as she watched Christina's perfectly cut, mid-brown hair sway with the movement of the car at just the right length above her collar, it was something she would just have to live with.

Chapter 11

All too aware that the respirator would be turned off the next day, everyone was on tenterhooks that evening. To escape the tension in the house Christina went outside after dinner to help her father feed the lambs again. Again she borrowed an old anorak and a pair of wellies at the back door and ventured into the cold, crossing the yard to join him in the shed. After they had fed the lambs, Jim went to check on the last few sheep still to lamb. He had put them in a pen by themselves. Christina followed him.

One of the ewes had isolated herself from the others in one corner of the pen. She looked a bit dazed and her head was hanging low. She walked around in a tight circle before lying down again and then standing up and making another circle.

'She's ready,' Jim said. 'She should be all right; it's not her first time. I'll wait here though and watch over her but you can go on to bed if you want.'

'I'd like to stay,' she said.

'It might take a while. You must be tired.'

'It's not as if I'll sleep anyway.'

'No,' he said and his voice trailed off.

The ewe, tottering on unstable feet, turned her head towards her hindquarters as if in surprise at what was going on back there. She began to make soft sounds not quite of pain but as if she was already communicating with her young lamb yet to be born.

Jim approached her for a visual examination without touching her. He stepped back. 'The water sac is starting to show. So far, so good.' He spoke quietly, watching intently what was going on. What looked like a large water blister appeared under her tail. It expanded. The sheep lay down but struggled to her feet shortly afterwards and circled again.

'Poor thing,' Christina said.

'Oh, you don't need to worry about her. This is all very natural and normal so far.'

The sheep moaned to herself and to her lamb. She pawed the ground and swayed a little. Raised on a farm and living in the country, Christina had always been surrounded by animals, but here in this cold barn, there was a different connection with this animal that was almost personal.

With a sudden gush, the water sac broke. Christina started, surprised by the strength of the flow. When it slowed to a trickle, she could see a dark patch with white tips emerging from the sheep's enlarged vulva.

'Ah, here come the front legs,' her father said. 'That's good, that's good. He's in the right position. I'm not too worried now.'

Within minutes, a small nose appeared, resting on the tiny hooves. The progress was slow enough to be able to see the closed eyes of the lamb as he emerged, his slicked-back wool darkened to a bumpy shine by the liquid surrounding him, and finally his ears, the tips of which stuck out at an angle to the sides. The ewe steadied herself on all four legs and continued her labour. The shoulders edged out and then, in one quick rush, the lamb slithered out and landed on the straw at the sheep's hind hooves.

Christina gasped involuntarily and took a step forward but her father put his hand on her arm to hold her back. The remaining liquid flowed out and poured over the dark, motionless mass on the ground. The ewe turned around and nudged the lamb. She licked his nose, his face, all the while making little noises at him. Tears of release prickled Christina's nose. She was filled, not exactly with joy, but with a sort of awe at life. She blinked back the tears, afraid to look foolish in front of her father who must experience this scene fifty times or more every year.

When the lamb's face was clear, the ewe started on the rest of his body. He stumbled to his feet and she pushed him with her head towards her udder. His wool was still damp and matted but it was drying quickly. His first steps were hesitant; he tripped once but quickly pulled himself up again and continued to search for what instinct taught him to seek. Throughout the process, the ewe lowed at her young, in what could only be interpreted as a love song of reassurance. She was licking the tiny lamb around his tail.

'That's to show him how to suck.' Her father's voice was imbued with emotion. Surprised, she examined his face. 'You never get used to it,' he said. 'There's something amazing about it every time.' He cleared his throat, embarrassed. 'We'll give her a drink and something to eat now. She deserves it.'

He passed Christina a bucket and asked her to fill it with water while he grabbed an armful of hay for the ewe. They stood for a moment and watched the two of them together. The lamb became frisky and excited as if he had just found out how great it was to be alive but the ewe was having none of it. She bumped him gently with her head as if to calm him down before allowing him access to her udder again. A smile came to Christina's lips.

'I'll wait until the lamb dries off a bit more. I have to mark him with the number of the ewe so that I know who he belongs to. You go on to bed now if you want.'

'No, I'll wait with you.'

When they entered the house a little while later all was quiet and dark. She glanced at the kitchen clock. Two and a half hours had passed since they had left but time seemed to have travelled at a different speed than usual. She put tea on for both of them without asking if he wanted it. She was reluctant to speak. She didn't remember ever spending time like this with her father and she didn't want to break the moment. His quiet confidence and control over the situation had been in stark contrast to his fearfulness and hesitation since Kate had been taken to hospital. They drank tea and ate biscuits to the sound of the ticking clock. There was nothing that needed to be said with words.

'We'd better get to bed,' she said finally. 'We have a hard day ahead of us tomorrow.'

Her father nodded. 'Thanks for your help. Good night.'

The following morning, she arrived downstairs to find her father, Louise and Nuala having breakfast. Aidan, still wearing his black leather jacket, was standing with his back to the sink, a mug of tea in hand.

'Are you not at the shop today?' she asked him.

'The staff can handle it. Not much point being my own boss if I can't take time off for something like this.'

'Enda rang to say that he can't miss school today but he'll keep his mobile on so that we can contact him,' Louise said. 'And Mark will nip out from work for an hour or so. His branch is not too far from the hospital.'

'Is Matthew still in bed?' Aidan asked.

'He got in late last night,' Louise said. 'And from what I heard of his entrance, I doubt if he'll be up any time soon. I'll go up later and ask him if he wants to come.'

'I can take a few of you with me, and if Christina takes the rest, I think we can squeeze into two cars.' Aidan put his mug in the sink.

'I'm not going to go in this morning.' Christina said, holding her arms across her chest in a tight hug. 'But you're welcome to take my car if you want.'

She walked to the kettle, lifted it and took off the lid to check the water level. She had her back to her family. Nobody said anything but she could feel their surprised disapproval in the air.

'Steve is coming this evening.' She turned around to face them. 'He's getting the train. I'll go to the hospital before I pick him up at the station. It'll save me a journey.'

'Oh, optimal time management above all,' Louise muttered into her mug.

She let it go. There was no point in trying to explain. She was anxious enough about her mother without having to deal with it inside the pressure cooker of that tiny waiting room with her whole family around her. Her being there would achieve nothing.

'So the famous Steve is on his way,' Aidan said. 'We're eventually going to meet him.'

'Well, he's welcome anyway. Will he stay here?' Jim asked.

'If that's all right with you, Dad,' She put her palms flat on the counter top behind her and leaned back against it.

'Of course, of course.'

'Well then, I suppose we'd better get going.' Aidan clapped his hands together in a rallying call to efficiency.

'I'll go and wake Matthew.' Louise's chair screeched as she pushed back from the table.

After she left the room, there was a moment of uncomfortable silence. Nuala stood up and put the lid back on the butter tub.

'Leave everything. I'll tidy up when you're all gone,' Christina signed.

'Right so. Dad, do you want to come with me then? You and Nuala, maybe?' Aidan said.

Louise returned, opening the door with more force than necessary. 'He couldn't be bothered coming either. Forget it, he's too hungover to get any sense out of him.'

She decided to ignore the 'either'. She waited for them to leave. 'If you'd like to take my car, it's no problem,' she said to no one in particular.

'No, it's all right. I'll drive my car,' Louise said. 'You never know, you might need to come to the hospital if something goes wrong.'

'I hope that won't be necessary,' she said, keeping her voice as peaceable as possible. 'But ring me and let me know either way.'

'Of course, we will,' Aidan said.

Louise said nothing on her way out but Aidan raised his eyebrows at her in silent sympathy. They were followed by Jim and Nuala who wore anxious expressions and seemed too preoccupied with their own thoughts to get involved with other people's.

After they left, she tidied up the kitchen. She made a pot of tea for herself and while it was drawing, she took down her briefcase and laptop from upstairs. She laid out her papers on the table and worked for an hour. It helped to focus on something she knew well and it stopped her from looking at her watch every minute. She analysed the sales figures from the previous month and jotted down notes for the next sales meeting presentation. She sent a quick email to Aoife asking her to look into the detail of the increased packaging costs.

Matthew entered the kitchen while she was putting on the kettle for another cup of tea. His shoulders were hunched and his eyes were half-closed as if to protect himself from the aggression of the bright daylight. He looked surprised to find her there. 'The others are all gone then?' he said in a voice that was little more than a croak.

'A while ago,' she said.

'Why didn't you go?'

'I could ask the same of you.'

He didn't reply. He opened the fridge door and stared inside without seeming to register what was in it.

'Do you want tea? I'm making another pot,' she said.

Matthew grunted and she took that as a yes. She gathered up her papers and closed her laptop. Matthew put three Weetabix in a bowl and poured milk on top.

'So what were you up to last night? Getting to be a bit of a habit, isn't it?'

He looked up at her, wary of her intentions. 'Yeah, the pub at the weekend. It's the latest rage, you should try it sometime.' He cast a sarcastic eye over the printout of the spreadsheet in front of her. 'Mind you, with all the exciting occupations you have, I'd understand if you gave it a miss.'

She tried again. She wanted to have a normal conversation with him, not nag him.

'I'm not saying you shouldn't go to the pub. I'm only suggesting that you don't go overboard with the drinking while Mam is in hospital. Dad's got enough on his plate at the moment.'

'Yeah, right, thanks for the advice.' He glared at her.

'I know it's none of my business but I'm concerned about you. I don't think it's a good idea to drink so much. It probably wouldn't do any harm to cut back a bit.'

'If you don't mind, I think I'll pass on the lecture.' He stood up, bowl of cereal in his hand. 'I think I might check out the telly-shopping channel for a bit of company. Don't worry about the tea. I'll make myself a fresh cup later.' He left the room without closing the door. She put her hand over her mouth and took a deep breath. Everything she said was wrong.

Matthew was annoyed. Christina was so perfect herself but judgemental of everyone. Easy for her, with her great job, plenty of money and a flat in Dublin. He went into the sitting room, but even there, he didn't feel right. In fact, he didn't want to stay in this house for a minute longer. He went into the hall, pulled his leather jacket from the hook and put it on. His boots were at the bottom of the stairs where he had taken them off the night before. He thrust his feet into them and laced them up roughly. He put on his helmet, got on his motorbike and revved it up noisily before careering off down the road. He could imagine Mrs Dolan complaining to her husband about the noise, but he didn't care. What he needed right now was a drink to calm down and get rid of the hangover. He glanced at his watch and almost veered off the road in the process. No problem, it was well past opening time. He'd nip down to Flanagan's for one.

Sean was behind the bar watching Sky Sports and emptying the dishwasher.

'A pint and a Bushmills, thanks Sean,' Matthew said, hoisting himself onto a barstool. 'What are you watching?'

'Fly fishing.' Sean poured the pint without removing his eyes from the television.

Matthew laughed. The idea of Sean in thigh-high waders casting his line out over his enormous belly tickled his sense of humour. 'I didn't know you fished.'

'I don't, but I'm thinking of taking it up.'

'Well, let me know if you do.'

'I'll switch over if you want.' Sean took the remote control from under the counter and flicked through the channels at random before settling for one. The change of scene was dramatic. The programme seemed to feature some busty girls drinking beer in a swimming pool under a hot Mediterranean sun and getting carried away in the heat. One of them removed her bikini top under the water and swung it like a lasso over her head, slapping it in the face of a tanned, muscular man, leering at her from the side of the pool.

'What's this?' Matthew asked.

Sean checked the Teletext. 'Ibiza Uncovered,' he said. He poured a measure of whiskey into a glass and put it in front of Matthew with a loud thump. He finished topping off the pint and slid it over to him. 'You're out early today.'

'Couldn't hack it any longer at home. The place is overrun ever since the ma went into the hospital.'

'I was sorry to hear about your mother.'

A second customer came in and Sean went to serve him.

Matthew drank half his pint in one gulp and sat back to watch the holiday antics. He was still annoyed with Christina but the beer was taking the edge off his irritation. She might be his sister but they had about as much in common as Eminem and the Queen did. It couldn't be good for the system to be so much under control, everyone had to let off steam every so often.

But if he was honest, the real problem wasn't Christina, it was Amy. He'd been uptight ever since she'd broken it off with him three weeks earlier. He hadn't thought it would get to him so much. She had become a right pain, a nag, all she wanted to do was stay in or else do cosy-couple stuff together. It was as if, just because they'd been seeing each other for two years, she felt she owned him and could make him do what she wanted. But he liked going out with the gang: if you couldn't go out for a pint and have a laugh with the lads at the weekend, what was the point? Anyway, the past few months they'd spent most of their time fighting and, as often as not, Amy would end up in tears, so he wasn't surprised when she finally said she wanted out. Secretly, although he told her that he was sorry about her decision, he had been pleased to get his freedom back. At the time. But maybe freedom wasn't all it was cracked up to be. He picked up his shot glass and knocked back the whiskey.

He waved his glass at Sean. 'Same again, Sean, and then I'll be on my way. Bit of Dutch courage to face up to the music.'

Sean was equally as absorbed by Ibiza as he had been by fly fishing. Two girls in very skimpy bikinis were kissing a man on a lounger and fondling his chest. He glanced at Matthew. 'You sure? You're on the bike, aren't you?'

'Listen, Sean, it's broad daylight and I'm two miles down the road. If I can't handle a couple of pints, then it's a sad day.'

'Right so, it's your look-out.'

Matthew drank the whiskey in one gulp as soon as it arrived and pushed the empty glass back at Sean. That was better: he was more himself. His edginess disappeared and he was at ease with the world. So what if Amy wasn't around anymore? If she didn't know how to have a good time, then he was better off without her.

'Shocking, isn't it, the stuff that goes on in those foreign places? A crying disgrace, I say,' Sean said.

'Oh, I don't know, Sean. It's doing a good job of selling Ibiza to me. There was none of this advertised in any of the travel brochures I ever looked at.'

He drank back half his pint. He felt the liquid filling up the empty spaces inside him, making him fit snugly into his skin. It made him more content with who he was. He knew he should go home - he didn't have a mobile on him and they didn't know where he was – but he was reluctant to go back.

Chapter 12

It was twelve thirty when the phone rang eventually. She watched her hand tremble as she reached out to answer it. She paused, steeling herself mentally for the worst before picking it up. 'Hi, how are things?' she asked.

'Christina, it's Mark.' His voice sounded worried. She thought she was ready but her body told her she wasn't. How would she feel if she was told that her mother was no longer part of her life?

'Hello? Are you there? Christina?'

'Yes, I'm here, Mark. How did it go this morning?'

'Well, to be honest, there's not much to tell, either good or bad. They took her off the respirator and she's breathing just fine by herself but she hasn't regained consciousness or anything.'

'But they were hoping that she would wake up, weren't they? Did they say anything about that?'

He paused. 'No, nothing specific. I think they are just hoping that she will turn the corner soon.' He paused. 'I get the impression from them that the longer she stays in the coma, the more worrying a sign it is.'

'OK. I'll be in to see her later on. Thanks for ringing to let me know.'

She sat down at the table and propped her head on her hands. She felt curiously numb about this news. She wasn't able to cry but there was a hollowness inside that needed to be filled with something but she had no idea what.

1987

At the end of the summer of Matthew's birth, shortly before she was due back to school for her final year, her mother dropped her off at the hairdresser's while she did the shopping. All the other customers around her were at ease and relaxed while she felt awkward. After washing her hair, the hairdresser led her to a chair in front of a mirror. 'So, what do you want?' she asked while she rummaged in a drawer for her scissors and clips.

Christina knew exactly what she wanted. She wanted to look pretty, she wanted her hair to be long and soft and wavy. She wanted it to fall perfectly on both sides of her face instead of having to battle with it to lie flat every morning before school. But how on earth did you ask for that? Maybe you had to be born with that sort of hair. 'It kind of sticks out all over the place. I'd like it to be more manageable,' she started.

The hairdresser leaned across to give instructions to an apprentice who was putting curlers in another customer's hair. 'Sorry,' she said when she turned back. 'Just a trim then? Neaten it up?'

'Hmm, yeah…' That didn't seem to quite capture what she was looking for but the hairdresser was already combing and snipping with such efficiency that it was hard to stop her. When she produced an electric razor and buzzed away the small hairs at the back, Christina became nervous but forced herself to believe that she was a professional who knew what she was doing. It would all turn out fabulous in the end. Afterwards, looking at herself in the mirror, her heart plummeted with disappointment. It was short and boring and boyish. She had been hoping for something much more feminine and cute, but maybe that was impossible.

Her mother arrived to pick her up just as the hairdresser was spraying a perfunctory jet of hair lacquer over the top of her head. She hated the stiff hard feel of lacquer but she couldn't screw up the courage to refuse. She turned her head to one side and then the other, trying to tell herself that it wasn't that bad but then she caught the reflection of her mother's surprised expression in the mirror. She could see that she didn't like it either. Suddenly, she became aware of just how ugly this new haircut was. She wanted more than anything to go home and stay there for the few months it would take for it to grow back.

'You don't like it, do you?' she asked her mother as they left. Her mother was holding Nuala's hand as they walked along the street.

'No, it's not that. I was just surprised that you got so much off, but it's not bad at all,' Kate said.

'I know you don't like it. I look horrible.'

'Of course, you don't look horrible. It's a little bit short, that's all. But you have a lovely face so you can get away with it. Don't worry, it'll grow.' Her mother said this in a distracted voice as if this was not her main concern at the moment and Christina was secretly pleased by the off-handedness of the compliment which made it feel more genuine. Compliments from her mother on her appearance were so rare as to be precious when they did come. Her mother had little tolerance for vanity, seeing it as a sign of shallowness. Any attention-seeking efforts by her on this front inevitably ended in a put-down.

'How about going for a cup of tea and a bun? I wouldn't mind sitting down for a minute before we go home,' Kate said.

Christina was surprised. She had expected that they would rush home to free Auntie Carol, who was minding the baby and keeping an eye on the bigger ones. And tea out was an extravagant luxury, especially when there was no apparent reason for it.

She found a table in the café and installed Nuala on a booster seat while Kate went to the counter to get the tea and buns. Despite Christina's efforts to keep her amused, Nuala continued to throw nervous glances at her mother as if to make sure that she didn't disappear. She tried as well as she could to explain to her little sister that Mam would be back in a minute once she had paid but, as usual, she couldn't tell how much Nuala understood of what she was saying.

'We saw Doctor Hanlon today,' Kate said, as she poured out the tea. Christina could tell from the careful way she said it that there was something out of the ordinary about this month's consultation.

'What did he say?' she said.

Her mother didn't answer. She was organising her thoughts and seemed a bit anxious.

'There's another mother I talk to sometimes in the waiting room when I take Nuala to her therapy sessions. She has a little boy who's deaf as well. He's a year older than Nuala.' She took a deep breath. 'They use sign language to communicate with each other.'

She wasn't sure how to reply. What answer did her mother expect of her?

'When I see them together, they seem to be having real conversations. They even make each other laugh. She says it's wonderful, that it's the best thing they've ever done,' Kate said.

'So do you want Nuala to learn sign language, is that it?' she asked hesitantly.

'Well, it's not as simple as that. For a start, we'd all have to learn it, it's a big commitment. But the thing that bothers me the most is that Dr Hanlon seems to think it's not a great idea.'

'Oh. Right.' She didn't trust herself to voice an appropriate opinion.

'He says it would hold her back from learning to talk properly and to lip-read. He says if she gets to rely on sign language then she won't bother to make the effort to interpret the sounds she gets through her hearing aids. If we want her to live as normal a life as possible then she needs to be able to talk and understand other people talking.'

'Maybe he's right. Maybe it'll get easier for her to talk as she gets older.'

'But how can she learn if we can't get through to her.' Kate became agitated. Christina was confused. What did her mother want her to say? 'And in any case,' Kate continued. 'I want to be able to talk to her now. Any way at all, any way I can. I don't want to have to wait. I want to tell her I love her now. I want her to know what her name is. At the moment, I don't even know if she does.' She glanced at Nuala who was drinking orange juice through a straw, oblivious to this conversation about her. A tear rolled down Kate's cheek. She looked up one sleeve and then the other for a hankie. Christina glanced around to see if anyone was watching and passed her a paper napkin.

'Am I being selfish, Christina?' Her mother's direct question alarmed her.

'No, Mam, of course not,' she said. The roles between them were reversed. It was her mother seeking reassurance, a reassurance she had no idea how to give.

'I mean; the easy solution would be to learn sign language but maybe I'm only thinking of myself. I don't want to hold Nuala back later in life. Oh God, I just don't know what the right thing to do is.'

'Nuala will be okay, Mam, no matter what you do. She'll be fine. Please don't cry or worry about it.'

Kate looked at her and reached across the table to hold her hand. She dried her tears.

'You're right, love. And I shouldn't bother you with this. You're too young. Let's go home now.'

She was uncomfortable at having witnessed her mother's distress and helplessness, and even if she was glad to have been consulted, to have been treated almost like an equal, she wasn't sure if she had helped in any way. On the way home in the car, her mother talked in an artificial, extra-jolly tone as if she was trying to make up for something. Christina played along.

It was funny to remember this conversation almost twenty-five years later. It was perhaps the first time she had seen her mother as a person with human flaws and doubts like everyone else. It had bothered her at the time because accepting that meant that there was no one who held the answers to life, answers which would be handed over to her at a certain designated time like family heirlooms. With hindsight, from an adult perspective, she could see how alone, overworked and worried her mother must have been but, at the time, she wasn't equipped to help her and found her vulnerability scary.

Chapter 13

Christina packed away the last of her papers, stood up and stretched, stiff from bending over her computer at the kitchen table. She decided to get out of the house, to get away from her family and all the worries that came with them. She scribbled out two notes, one for Matthew, letting him know that their mother had survived the switching off of the respirator and one for the rest of the family telling them that she had a few things to do in Galway and that she would see them later in the evening after she had picked up Steve.

However, instead of driving to Galway, she took the road towards Lough Corrib in search of solitude. She followed the lakeside road towards the north. The sky was overcast, filled with a mixture of clouds varying from pale, translucent white to deep slate grey. The dull steely water of the lake was broken every so often by tufts of tiny green islands. Where the sun managed to penetrate the clouds, the surface of the water became a sheet of shimmering light, corrugated by the wind. On the other side of the road, she passed by small fields enclosed by stone walls and occupied by sheep, heads down munching their way forward through the cold, piercing wind.

She pulled into a narrow laneway and parked her car as close to the ditch as she could so that other traffic could pass. She put on an old pair of runners she always kept in the boot of her car, pulled on a spare jumper under her jacket for extra protection against the cold and walked down the lane towards the lake. She climbed over the stone wall at the end and jumped across a narrow stream flowing into the lake. The ground was spongy and damp under her feet. She walked on, watching the ever-changing and yet ever-constant skyscape. She took in the blue and red paint-splashed behinds of the sheep among the few twisted, stunted tree shapes that persisted in the otherwise mossy-smooth rocky land. A light mist of dampness hovered in the air but it wasn't quite raining. She encountered no one. She walked as fast as she could but she had to watch each of her steps to make sure she didn't slip off an unstable rock and twist her ankle or walk into a disguised pool of water. After an hour or so of walking, she found herself more at peace. The momentum of moving forward tricked her into thinking that she was progressing through her life and not just spinning wheels in place.

She glanced at her watch. It was getting dark. She decided that there was just enough time to get to Galway, visit her mother at the hospital and still be on time for Steve. She stopped to look across the lake before heading back. While she watched, the sun appeared through holes ripped in the ragged grey blanket of cloud and shone in straight rays of light that illuminated the water like an ancient god smiting the world. The islands, untouched by the light, became black outlines in contrast. She was struck by the power of the sun, how such a tiny part of it could leak through and transform the world. She stopped and stared, both empowered and shrunk by the spectacle. The rays of the sun moved across the expanse of water as the wind closed the gaps in the clouds and opened others. She turned away and walked back to the car.

At the hospital, she found her two aunts, Kate's sisters, in the waiting room outside ICU. Auntie Carol was crying and Auntie Anne had her arm around her. Her first instinct was to wonder if her mother had taken a turn for the worse and she had not been told. She glanced at her mobile phone but she could see that no one had tried to contact her. She switched it off.

'Hello, Auntie Carol, Auntie Anne. What's going on? Is it Mam? Is she OK?'

'Oh, Christina.' Carol looked up and, seeing her, found a fresh batch of tears. 'It's so terrible to see her like that. Poor Kate. What a month this has been, what with Tom losing his job and David dropping out of college. And now, Kate, like this, at death's door.'

'I'm sure she didn't mean to inconvenience you,' she said.

Anne glared at her. 'There's no need to be narky, Christina. That's not what she meant.'

'I know, I know,' she said. 'I presume you both have been in to see her already. I'll go on in if you don't mind. I have a train to meet afterwards.'

'Well!' she heard Anne say as she left.

She scrubbed her hands and nails for a full minute. It wasn't butterflies she had in her stomach but snakes, twisting and coiling in a pit. It took all her strength to push open the door and go into the intensive care unit. She didn't want to be there but couldn't leave either.

She walked to her mother's bed, her legs heavy as lead. The unit was relatively quiet: there were no doctors around and even the endless whirring and beeping of the machines seemed to be muted. She looked out for the respirator or, rather she checked for the absence of it. Nothing seemed to have been moved. She watched the green and yellow lines flowing seamlessly across the screen of the monitor. When she arrived by the side of the bed and looked down, she saw that the deeply-lined, yellow-tinged face in the bed was not her mother's. She leapt back in fright and stood on Lynn's foot who was approaching her from behind. Illogical as she knew it was, she felt as though someone had played a particularly nasty trick on her and she wanted to lash out in retaliation.

'Where is my mother gone?' she said to her.

'Sorry, Christina.' She registered the anomaly that Lynn was apologising for a fault that was hers but she didn't feel able to deal with that. 'She was moved earlier this afternoon. She's over here.' Lynn led the way and she followed her white-clad back.

'Why was she moved? Isn't it a bit soon to be shifting her around the place?' she said.

'That other patient is dying. We needed to give her some privacy so she could die in peace. Her husband is in the hospital somewhere. He must have left for a few minutes.' Lynn was calm and in control. Everything was shifting under Christina's feet and she couldn't find solid ground. 'Your mother is here, Christina.'

They stood by Kate's bed. Other than the tube removed from her mouth, she couldn't see any real change in her appearance. Her eyes were closed. She searched her face for any sign that she was rising to the surface out of unconsciousness. Kate's breathing was light, a simple drawing in of air and a soft exhalation barely visible in the movement of her chest. It was only now she became conscious of what she had been expecting: she had presumed that, without the aid of the machine, breathing would have been a more laborious effort. She picked up her mother's hand and squeezed it. How her mother would hate this, to be a helpless, malleable object in the hands of others.

'No change then,' she said.

'No.' Lynn picked up her chart and wrote something on it. 'The doctors will wait and see how she reacts today and if there's no change tomorrow they may consider some form of stimulation to try to bring her out of the coma.'

'So how long is this going to go on for?'

'If only we knew. Even when we think we have the answers, we often get it wrong. The only thing to do is to hope and pray.'

'Well, I hope you medical people are doing a little bit more than that,' she snapped.

Lynn looked at her and placed the chart back on its hook. She left the bedside without speaking.

Christina leaned down to her mother and pressed against her neck. 'Oh, Mam, what is wrong with me?' she whispered. For a second, the comfort of her mother's warmth was enough but then she stood up and hurried out of the unit.

In the preparation area, while she was removing her shoe covers and hair net, Lynn appeared. She had her arms around her waist holding her cardigan tightly closed. She looked upset but her voice was calm and composed.

'Christina, I didn't want to discuss anything in front of your mother in case she could hear us but you obviously have a problem with me. I'd like to sort it out with you.'

'I don't think this is a good time or place to discuss personal matters.'

'So, it is a personal matter then?'

She regretted her words. 'Lynn, I know we knew each other at school but that doesn't mean we have to be friendly now. We've moved on a lot since then.'

'We have but for now, we are obliged to deal with each other. So I'd like to know what's wrong.'

'If you don't know, then maybe it's best not to revive old wounds.'

'Wounds? Don't tell me you're still harbouring a grudge over what happened twenty-five years ago?' The incredulity in her voice hurt her more than she thought possible. That Lynn could dismiss as inconsequential what she had spent most of her life trying to accommodate, brought a red haze of hatred before her eyes.

'Fine, forget about it then.' She brushed past Lynn and marched out of the confines of the prep area.

She didn't stop until she reached her car. When she paused before opening the car door she realised that she was breathing heavily. She stopped and tried to get her respiration under control, spending several minutes mentally totting up the numbers on the registration plates of the cars around her. She had some time to kill before Steve's train arrived. She hadn't eaten since breakfast but she couldn't face any food. She drove to the train station to wait for the train.

When she got there, she sat on a bench near the platform where Steve's train would arrive. She watched a young woman run into the station, looking around until she found the person she was looking for: an elderly man with carefully slicked down grey hair, smartly dressed in a long black overcoat. She rushed over, kissed him on the cheek, took his suitcase from him and apologised for her delay. He smiled and seemed to be saying that he was just glad that she was there now. She also watched a middle-aged woman accompanying three young students to the platform. As they made their way towards the train, she called one of them back and, with a sigh of exasperation, as if to say that this was the very last time, she thrust some money from her purse at him.

The train slid into the station and her heart speeded up, unsure of what she would find. She told herself not to be ridiculous, that this was only Steve, who couldn't have changed beyond recognition in four days but still she created a clear picture in her mind of how he would look as he stepped off the train and walked towards her. He would be wearing his dark-green hand-knit jumper with the fraying cuffs under his navy jacket left flapping open. He would have his guitar in its case slung over his back. He would be carrying a red bag with a Liverpool logo on it containing a spare t-shirt or two, underwear and a toothbrush. His hair would look as if he hadn't combed it that morning. He'd be concentrating on notes playing in his head but when he would see her, his eyes would light up and he would smile.

At first, she didn't see him. The people milled past her and she looked around for him anxiously. After the crowd thinned out, she spotted him standing on the quay by the door of a carriage talking to a girl. He wasn't wearing his green jumper and he didn't have his guitar. He was laughing at something the girl was saying and then turned to walk on. The girl walked beside him. When he saw Christina, he was already smiling, so there was no transformation in his expression.

'Bye, Steve. Nice to meet you,' the girl said with a warm smile. 'Hi,' she said to Christina as she breezed by.

'Who was that?' she asked.

'You're not jealous are you?' Steve put his arm around her waist and kissed her on the lips. 'Who'd have guessed? If I'd known, I'd have used that tactic ages ago.'

'Of course I'm not jealous. You can talk to whoever you like. I was just asking.'

'Well, she's just someone I met on the train. We got talking about music. She sings in a band part-time. Happy?'

'Over the moon.'

'Stop talking about her. How are you?'

'I'm fine.'

'Really? How's your mother?'

'Same as ever. They turned off the respirator this morning. It hasn't brought her out of the coma but she's 'holding her own' as they keep saying.'

Steve's face became serious. 'Well, that's good news.'

'Is it?'

'Well, I mean it could be worse.'

'Yes, she could have died.'

'Chris, can we start over? I'm not sure what the right thing to say is but let me try again.' He shifted his bag to the other shoulder and put his arm around her, holding her against him as they walked. She fitted into the shape of him. She was glad he was there.

'I'm sorry. Thanks for coming, Steve.'

'I'm glad to hear that. I was starting to think you were regretting asking me to come.'

'No, it's not that. It's just hard to cope with everything at the moment. Sorry.'

'Forget it. I'm here now.'

'The car is this way,' she said.

Steve put his bag in the back and sat into the passenger seat. He leaned across and rubbed his nose against her ear. 'So am I worthy of introduction to your family now?'

He was teasing but she responded anyway. 'I never thought you weren't. It's just that I'm not very good at mixing the different parts of my life.'

'That's a funny way to see it. Your life is your life.'

She felt as if her guard had slipped a little and she hitched it up again. What would Steve think if he saw the real her? The very idea scared her.

He put his hand on hers when she put the key in the ignition. He gently put his fingers under her chin and turned her face towards his. He frowned.

'I'm so sorry that you have to go through all this, Chris,' he said. He leaned forward to kiss her. His beard tickled her cheeks and her mouth felt the contrast between the softness of his lips and the wiry resistance of stray beard hairs. One of her friends had asked once if the beard bothered her. She had answered lightly, saying that she didn't have any choice but to put up with it but, in reality, she liked it. It was softer to the touch than it appeared and it made him feel real. Even when he was so close that she couldn't see him anymore, she could feel him. It gave him a contour, a definition. She couldn't say that to anyone, not even Steve, who would laugh at her but it was a comforting part of him.

He kissed her more urgently. She wriggled away. 'Hey,' she said.

'Sorry, I didn't mean to insist. I've missed you, that's all.' He sat back in his seat and put on his seatbelt. 'So are we going to your family home now?'

'Yes, everyone will be there. Don't mind them if they ask lots of questions. They're a nosy bunch.'

'I'm looking forward to meeting them. I'm sure we'll get on fine.'

She had no doubt that he would; it was herself that she worried about.

'I was glad when you asked me to come, Chris. I don't know if there's anything I can do but I'm glad to be with you at a time like this.'

She glanced at him. 'I really am glad you're here, even if it doesn't always seem like it. Thanks,' she said. He watched her while she drove, saying nothing. It made her nervous. 'Stop that,' she said.

'Stop what?'

'Stop looking at me like that.'

'I'm just trying to work out what's going on in that head of yours.'

She laughed. 'If only I knew myself.'

He lay back in his seat and stretched out his long legs in front of him.

She took Steve through the back door to the kitchen. Nuala was absent-mindedly drying some dishes while she stared out the window at the night sky. Louise was sitting at the table typing a text message on her phone and Aidan was opposite her, cradling a mug in his hands.

'Hi, everyone. I'm back. This is Steve,' she said, conscious of her hands and posture. 'Steve, this is Nuala. Aidan. Louise.'

Steve shook hands with each of them. His smile was warm and encompassing.

Jim, hearing their arrival, came to the door of the kitchen from the sitting room.

'Hello, Jim,' Steve said, a hand outstretched. 'Good to meet you again. Although I'd have preferred it in different circumstances.' Steve's calm, unquestioning acceptance of himself and others had the knack of making even awkward situations feel normal and relaxed.

'Nice to see you too, Steve. Come on through to the sitting room,' Jim said. 'Put on the kettle there, Mark. I'm sure Steve would like a cup of tea.'

A twinge in her stomach reminded her that she hadn't eaten. 'I'm going to make a sandwich for myself. Does anyone else want one? Steve?'

Steve flashed her a grateful smile. 'That'd be great.'

When she joined them a couple of minutes later, opening the door of the sitting room, Enda was finishing off telling a funny story. Steve was laughing, a big, open-mouthed laugh. His good humour was infectious.

'So then one of the lads at the back of the class piped up "He's right, sir. I seen him too. He was coming at us, as big as an irosserous."' Honestly, the stuff they come out with – it's hard sometimes to keep a straight face.' Enda said. She had missed the beginning of the story but everyone laughed, even her father, who was listening in over the top of his newspaper. Since she had come home, this was the first moment that resembled normality.

'Here you are, Steve,' she said, handing him a plate and a mug. Mark and Louise followed her in.

Everyone moved along the sofa to make room for the newcomers. Steve, who was sitting on the armchair at the other end of the room, patted the few square inches of space and invited her to squeeze in beside him.

She shook her head. 'You'll need room to eat,' she said and took a loose cushion from the sofa to sit on the floor.

'You should have brought Steve home before, Christina,' Enda said, with a smile.

This was what she hated about introducing Steve. Behind everyone's instinctive liking of him, she sensed surprise that she should have found someone so friendly and easy to be with. It made her feel even less worthy of him. One day, he might even discover that for himself. She pulled her knees up under her chin and balanced her tea on top of them.

That night, as soon as she closed the switched off the light when they were in bed, Steve pulled her towards him and kissed her. He burrowed his nose under her hair. His beard tickled. A desire for sex stirred within her but then, just as quickly, it disappeared. He slipped his hand under her t-shirt and caressed her breast.

'No, Steve, don't,' she whispered.

He stopped. 'You don't want to?' he asked.

She wanted him to hold her, to feel the expanse of his arms around her, to press against his chest and cry out all the poisonous tears blocked inside. But she would never ask him for that. She knew she was being unreasonable but she was irritated with him for wanting sex.

'Not now. Not here.'

'I understand,' he said.

He took his hand back and allowed her to rest her head in the crook of his shoulder.

Within minutes, she heard his breathing change and become deeper and more rhythmic. She turned on her side to look at him. He looked younger in sleep, carefree and tranquil. She envied him. With her finger, she followed his cheek along the coastline of his beard. Gentle, straightforward Steve, who was nothing like her. Her loneliness gaped even wider than before. He stirred in his sleep and moved his arm so that it lay across her stomach. She stared through the darkness at the ceiling above, trying not to move so that she wouldn't wake him.

Chapter 14

1987

For months, Christina attended school quietly, keeping her head down, focusing on her classes but with an eye cast sideways, ready to retreat in case of attack. She was starting to believe that it was over, that she'd been forgotten about. Lynn was by now ensconced in her role as the main source of action and excitement in the class. Christina observed the class interactions warily from a distance. When she went home on the school bus, she sat three or four seats behind the driver, well ahead of Lynn and her gang who occupied the back couple of rows.

One afternoon, Lynn's voice rose above the giggles and chat. 'Go on then, ask her.' She was laughing in a playful, teasing way but Christina's heart shrank into a tight ball. She stared out the window and tried very hard to make herself as small as possible.

'Christina,' someone called out from the back. 'Come here for a minute, Brendan has something he wants to ask you.' It was followed by a snigger.

'Stop it,' Brendan said, annoyed.

She ignored them. She pressed her forehead hard against the window pane and the cold damp condensation seeped into her skin.

At the back of the bus, the voices mingled, a mixture of teasing and laughter while Brendan defended himself.

She closed her eyes and counted slowly in her head up to ten. She followed the momentum of the bus with her body and tried to imagine where the bus might be as she registered the left and right turns and bends in the road. When she got to ten, she guessed that they were at the stretch beside the field with the fairy fort. She opened her eyes and looked up. They weren't: they hadn't even reached the sharp bend in the road with the road sign that said 'Black Spot'. She closed her eyes and counted silently again.

She got off at her bus stop and pretended to adjust the straps of her school bag so that she wouldn't have to look up and see any faces peering down at her from the bus when it turned right and crossed the bridge.

She had escaped this time but she was afraid that it was only a temporary reprieve. And she was right.

The next day, she got on the bus first and sat two seats behind the driver, not so close that he would talk to her, but close enough that he provided some kind of protection. On his way towards the back, Brendan stopped and kneeled on the seat in front of her, leaning over the headrest to talk to her. His body was a barrier between her and the driver. His muscular, boxer's arms were at eye level as he hugged the headrest. She heard a muffled giggle from the back.

'Hi, Christina,' he said, in a friendly enough way.

'Hi,' she said, hoping that her tone was abrupt enough to make him go away. She looked out the window of the bus as if there was something capturing her interest out there.

'Well done on that history test, by the way. You definitely impressed Mr Higgins.'

She glanced at him warily. 'Thanks.' Normally, he had no interest in school stuff.

'I was just wondering. Are you thinking of going to the Christmas disco?'

'I haven't decided yet. Probably not.'

'Would you like to go with me?' He leaned across the top of the seat and grinned at her.

She hadn't expected this. She didn't particularly like Brendan and had no intention of accepting, but despite that, she was flattered. He was the best-built boy in the class and, if you didn't know him, you might find him good-looking, a bit like a more muscly Kevin Bacon. Lots of the girls fancied him although she couldn't see the attraction. But why was he asking her? Did he mean it? Was he just teasing her? Or did he really like her? Would it be rude or hurtful to say a blunt no? She looked intently at him, trying to figure out what was happening inside his head.

'I don't think I'll be able to go, but thanks anyway,' she said.

He smiled the smile of a boy who knew that a no like that really meant yes.

'Come on, it'll be fun. We'll have a laugh.'

Regardless of her opinion of him, she was warmed by the notion of being liked and desired and a tiny smile tried to break out on her lips but she was uncomfortable under the glare of his gaze and had to look away. She glanced across at the seat on the other side of the aisle and caught Orla Fitzpatrick's eye. She was mouthing something at her with her head down, trying not to be seen. It took her a second to work out what it was.

'Say no.' The shapes of the words were exaggerated on her lips.

With a growing sense of horror, she realised that Orla was acting out of pity for her. This was a hundred times worse than being ignored and even worse than being bullied. She cringed and wanted to be sucked into the seat cushion below her.

'No thanks. I won't be able to go, I just thought of something I have to do,' She folded her arms tightly across her chest and fixed her gaze at something outside the window.

Brendan wasn't totally stupid. He knew that something had changed. His quarry had bolted and there was no point in persisting any longer.

'Your loss, Christina.' He sauntered to the back of the bus.

Although she was facing the opposite direction, she knew that Orla's eyes were fixed on her, willing her to turn around and accept a secret smile of sympathy. She continued staring out the window, hardly daring to blink.

The laughter from the back of the bus exploded through her like splinters of ice.

She got off the bus making silent fervent promises to do whatever it took to get her mother to send her to another school. She ran all the way home to get there before her passionate need could cool down. Her mother was making the dinner.

'Just give me a few minutes, Christina. Your dad will be in from the farm looking for his dinner and the boys are starving. Set the table for me, would you?' Kate said. A few minutes later, everyone came in, clamouring for food and there was a flurry to eat while it was hot. Then there was washing-up to be done and the baby to be put to bed. It was hours later before her mother was free enough to listen and even then she kept being distracted by the list of signs she was supposed to learn that week for her sign language class.

'I'd like to change school, Mam.' She went straight to the heart of the subject.

'Why do you want to do that?' Kate was surprised.

'I think I could do better in another school. A bigger school, one with more options.'

'But your results are excellent. I don't know how you could do better.'

'Please, mam. I really need to change.'

'But that's the only school we have a free bus service to. I'm sorry, love. I just don't have the time to take you to school every day and pick you up afterwards. And I don't have the money to pay for the bus fare. What's wrong with your school anyway?'

'Well, maybe it's not the school itself. It's the girls in my class. I don't get on with them. They don't really talk to me.'

'And what makes you think it would be any different in another school?'

'Well, I don't know. But I'd like to try.'

'I don't think that's a good idea at all. You are starting your last year of school. What would be the point in changing now? It would be too hard to join another class and catch up with what they've already covered in the courses.'

'If I change schools, I could repeat the year. I'm one of the youngest in the class anyway so it wouldn't matter.'

'Christina.' Her mother had reached the end of her patience. 'You can't change schools just like that. In any case, don't you think I have enough to do? It's a perfectly good school. Couldn't you try to make it work?'

She hung her head so that her mother couldn't see her frustration and tears. Why was it so hard to make her understand?

Her mother softened. She reached out and squeezed her hand. 'Why don't you invite someone here at the weekend? You know, you need to make an effort too, if you want to make friends in the class.'

She pulled her hand away from her mother's. 'That's right. Blame me for everything. You understand nothing!' She ran out of the room.

'Christina!' She heard her mother call out behind her. 'This is a ridiculous way to behave. Enough now.'

She raced to her bedroom and cried into her pillow, desperate and miserable, but trapped in a situation from which she could see no escape.

Now, many years later, she was lying in the same bed. But this time, she was staring up at the ceiling and the source of the tears was an arid, waterless place. She was so hollow inside, she thought she might float upwards if it wasn't for Steve's heavy arm holding her down.

Chapter 15

'Any news?' Steve came downstairs, a worried look on his face.

'No, nothing new.' She was working on her laptop, drinking a coffee.

'What time is it? Why are you up so early?'

'I couldn't sleep. I'd rather do something than lie there thinking.'

Steve rubbed his eyes and yawned. 'Do you want to go to the hospital?' he said.

'I think Enda and Aidan are going in early before work. They don't like too many of us going in at the same time. Anyway, if I go in later, I think I might have a better chance of seeing one of the doctors and getting some information.'

'Do you want me to come with you?'

'You don't have to. It's not much fun hanging around the hospital all day.'

'I didn't come to have fun. I came to be with you.'

'I know. Thanks.' She stood up. 'Do you want some coffee?'

'I'd love some.' Steve looked out the kitchen window at the cold, icy-blue day outside. 'I'd love to see the farm. Would you show me around?'

'There's not much to see. Dad has cut back a lot and it's not exactly the busiest time of year anyway. Apart from the lambs.'

'I'd like to see it anyway. Funny to think of you growing up here. It's a far cry from our council estate in Birmingham.'

'Didn't you ever go to the country?'

'Oh, sure, we went on a trip to visit a farm with the school once, and every couple of months or so, my mum would pack us all up and we'd go for a hike in the country at the weekend. To stock up on fresh air, I think, was the theory. That's about the height of my exposure to country living.'

She laughed. 'OK then, but don't expect anything amazing.' She handed him a mug of coffee.

He leaned forward to kiss her quickly on the lips. 'I'm not looking for anything amazing. Or at least, not anything more amazing than I've already found.'

She pulled back to look at him and check if he was teasing her.

'I'll have a shower and let you finish off your work. We can go and visit the farm afterwards,' Steve said.

When Steve returned, she was checking the sizes of the Wellington boots under the wooden bench at the back door.

'Here, try these,' she said and handed him a pair.

It was cold and it had rained during the night but the sun was making a valiant attempt to come out. They walked through the yard, sloshing through the muddy puddles to the fields at the other end. The sheep that had lambed earlier were out grazing, sedate and solid beside their lambs who jumped and skipped, shaking out their excess energy. She pointed out the tangle of brambles where, one summer, their neighbour's dog had become ensnared. She had crawled underneath on hands and knees to free him, getting scraped and torn in the process. It took ages to release his long curly hair from the briars and, in return, he had bitten her.

She took him to the small orchard at the far end of the yard where four or five apple trees grew beside a now disused shed. Around their trunks, the first of the daffodils were cracking open. She showed him where she, Mark and Aidan had attempted to build a tree house one summer. All that remained was a half-rotten plank of wood with a rusty nail driven through it.

They crossed the field and made their way towards the sheds. Jim was in the main one, examining the new lambs. He was delighted to find in Steve an interested audience, and an uninformed one at that. He led him around all the sheep, almost introducing each one personally, and gave him enough detail of the intricacies of sheep farming to enable him to start out in the business if he wanted to. Steve listened patiently and was even enthusiastic at appropriate moments. Once, he caught her eye and winked at her. She looked away so that her father wouldn't see her smile, but he was too carried away with evangelical fervour to notice anyway.

Jim stopped talking to examine the swollen udder of one of the ewes and frowned when she recoiled in pain at his touch. 'Hmm, a touch of mastitis here,' he said.

While he was distracted, she took the opportunity to tug Steve's arm and they escaped.

'You didn't think you were going to be taking a sheep-farming course today, did you?' She made an apologetic face at him.

'Oh, there are worse careers,' he said. 'What's in here?' They were passing an open shed.

'That's where Dad keeps the bales of hay and straw.'

'By gum, lassie, summat mighty interesting in thar,' Steve said in a mock Yorkshire accent. He grabbed her hand and dragged her inside with him. He pulled her towards him and kissed her. The weight of him knocked her back against the bales of hay. At first, she kissed him back but, when she felt his hand slip under her jacket and slide around to find contact with bare skin at her back, she stiffened.

'Stop, Steve,' she said. She wriggled a bit to get away.

He wasn't listening. She was imprisoned in the confines of his arms. He started kissing her more possessively. His hand was grappling with her bra strap at the back. A flutter of panic made it difficult to breathe.

'I said, stop. Stop.' Her voice was louder and more insistent than she had intended it to be.

Instantly, he dropped his arms. 'What's wrong, Chris?'

'I wanted you to stop. I don't want this right now.'

His face fell. 'Sorry, I was joking around. I didn't mean to be inappropriate. I missed you, that's all.'

She walked away from him towards the door. She didn't trust herself to speak. 'Let's go back,' she said, in a mangled voice.

'I thought you wanted me here,' he said.

She stopped and looked at him. 'I thought I did too.' She could see on his face that she had hurt him.

Had she given him the wrong message by asking him to come to Galway? Did he think that this meant that she was committed to him, that she belonged to him? This was all wrong.

'Are you saying you'd prefer if I left?' he said.

She paused. Despite her best attempts to sabotage her life, she knew that Steve was good for her. 'No, that's not what I meant. I'm sorry. I don't think I'm handling this situation very well. There's a lot to absorb at the moment.'

They stood looking at each other for a few seconds. 'I'm sorry too,' Steve said. 'I shouldn't have done that. I should have known that this isn't the right time.' He held out his hand to take hers. She took it and they walked back to the house.

Nuala was sitting on the bench by the back door. She was composing a text message on her mobile phone and didn't see them arrive. It was only when Christina sat down beside her to take off her boots that Nuala noticed her. Startled, she snapped her phone away, hastily turning it upside down and putting it on the bench beside her without sending the message.

'Sorry, Nuala, we didn't mean to disturb you.' She signed at Nuala but spoke the words too for Steve's benefit. It was obvious that Nuala was flustered. She was distracted and avoided looking directly at her. She slipped her phone into the pocket of her jacket and stood up. 'Did you show Steve the farm?' she signed. She never used her voice with people unless she absolutely had to or she knew she could trust them. It usually took a while and Steve was too much of an unknown just yet. Christina tried to translate her signs for Steve in a way that included him in the conversation.

'Yes, I got the grand tour.' Steve spoke to her directly with a smile and made a broad, sweeping gesture with his arm to encompass the farm. 'I'm very impressed.' He didn't avoid eye contact or behave as if she were mentally deficient as so many did, and Nuala smiled back at him. Christina was pleased with him, but then, that was Steve.

'We're going to Galway to see Mam in a little while,' she said. 'Would you like to come with us, Nuala?'

'No thanks. I'll take Dad's car. He said it was all right and I have an appointment in Galway later this afternoon.'

'I don't mind waiting for you if you want.'

'No. I'd rather go by myself.' She gave them a big smile to soften her refusal but she was behaving oddly. Nuala went into the house and it felt as if she was cutting short the conversation. Steve looked at her, not having fully understood what the exchange was about. She explained.

'Maybe we could go to the hospital now if that's OK with you,' she said.

'Of course, I'm ready. I'm happy to go with the flow.' Steve looked at her and made a face. As far as he was concerned, their dispute was over.

In the kitchen, when she was alone, Nuala took out her mobile phone again to recompose her text message but, faced with the blank screen, she stopped, lost for words, and closed it down before she had even entered one letter. What was the point? It wasn't as if he would reply. He was running scared. It had been fine when she was just a fling, a pretty girl whose difference made her exciting, exotic. He probably thought he was being open-minded and generous to go out with a deaf girl in the first place. But now, their relationship had changed. In his eyes, she could see that he had no intention of bringing her home to his family, of tying his fate to her defective one.

He was only the second hearing guy she'd gone out with. But she should have known anyway. She cringed to remember how delighted she'd been when he'd asked her out. Was it gratitude she had felt at the time? She hoped not, but she lifted her chin in defiance at the thought. She didn't need the approval of hearing people. But it worried her that her subconscious might have betrayed her.

When he had asked her to teach him a few signs, she'd been happy to. It was a good thing that he wanted to learn her language. She didn't like the way he smirked though when he used a sign. And the way he glanced to the side to check that no one was watching him. He's embarrassed, she thought at the time. It'll get easier when he gets better at it. But he didn't improve.

And the only place there was no discomfort at all was where words were not necessary in either of their languages. He was good at making love, although her limited experience didn't give her many points of comparison. He had confidence and knew what he was doing. He gave her pleasure she hadn't found before with anyone else. She had thought he loved her. But somehow, deep down, she must have known that he didn't, because when she discovered she was pregnant, she'd felt almost sick at the thought of telling him.

'Oh my God,' he had said. The revulsion on his face was instinctive. They were sitting close to the fire in a quiet pub on a Monday night. 'You could go to England, you know.' He didn't say that he was afraid that the baby would be born deaf and damaged. He didn't need to.

She shrugged and pursed her lips together to indicate that she probably would but hadn't fully decided.

'I can help pay for it.'

She shook her head and with a nonchalant wave of the hand, implied that money was not a problem.

'Is there anything you want me to do?'

She shook her head again. She could see that her refusal to talk was annoying him but she didn't want to speak his language whose treachery and wiliness she didn't master. At the best of times, she didn't trust the mangled words that came out of her mouth, the ones she couldn't hear, not to betray her and turn into something else in the ears of those who heard them. When she was upset, like now, it was worse. She forgot all the tricks and exercises she had been taught to keep the volume of her voice even and at the right level. Usually, it was only when people nearby turned to stare that she realised she must be making weird noises or shouting. She hated that.

She pushed her half-full glass away from her, picked up her bag, smiled and stood up to go.

'Nuala, sit down, let's talk about this some more. Do you want another drink? You can't go just like that.'

He looked as though he meant it but he didn't reach out to make her stay. She smiled again, and signed 'Go to hell, asshole'. He didn't understand but something in the gesture must have come across because he looked less sure of himself. She gave him a little wave and left. She didn't cry. She knew a lot about holding things inside and not letting anyone see them.

That had happened three weeks earlier. The day afterwards, he had left a text message on her mobile. 'Call me. We should talk about this.'

Several times she had hesitated to call him back. She almost convinced herself that it had been a shock for him and he needed time to cope. Once he came to terms with it, they'd be able to sort something out. But still, he didn't try again. She checked her mobile at least ten times a day to make sure she didn't miss a message from him.

Now, she needed to decide what to do. It was time. She could ask her family for advice but she hesitated. This was a big thing. And no matter what anyone else said, in the end, the decision was hers. Every choice was fraught with complications. If she kept this baby, could she cope alone? All her life, she had been the dependent one. She wasn't sure that she could suddenly change and become responsible for someone else, especially alone. She didn't earn a big salary, she had no home of her own and now, there was a growing chance that her mother wouldn't be there to help her.

She wasn't sure whether she was more frightened at the idea of having a hearing baby or a deaf baby. She knew about being deaf. She could understand and help a deaf child in a way that her own mother hadn't been able to. She could teach him sign language better than her mother had. She would understand the frustrations and obstacles and know how to get around them.

But what about the hearing things she knew nothing about? For example, she didn't know what music was.

She could see what music was in the faces of the people listening to it. She could feel what music was when she put her hands on loudspeakers and felt the vibrations through them but still, she didn't know it. She wondered sometimes what birds sounded like. She knew from books that they made a sound that signified peace, nature, and tranquillity to those who heard it but she couldn't imagine how their tiny bodies and beaks could produce a noise that could have this impact. Once she had asked Christina to describe this noise and she had told her that it was like a mix of running soft beach pebbles through your fingers and touching the blade of a sharp knife.

If she had a hearing baby, there were so many things she couldn't explain. And the world was a hearing world. Would it be harder for the baby to find his place in it with her as his mother? She didn't want to restrict a child or have him despise or pity her.

And yet, despite all these problems, what if this was her last chance at motherhood? She hadn't meant to become pregnant. This wasn't how she wanted it to be. If she thought about it at all, she imagined that the father of her child would be supportive, capable, confident and, above all, present. Now, not only was she alone, but she feared she was losing her greatest champion, her mother. She could never cope. But just as she approached the decision, her mind backed away at the last second. It tantalised her with a dream of how wonderful it would be to feel this baby growing inside her, to know it and love it and be loved. This was selfish, she knew.

Time was running out. She daydreamed about renting a flat for the two of them. She examined pictures in magazines of mothers and babies looking into each other's eyes as if the answer to her dilemma was in their gaze. A small child stopped and stared openly at her while she signed with a friend and she was reminded of the gap between her normality and the normality of others.

Like two weeks earlier when the salesgirl in the chemist's approached them and spoke directly to Louise, although it was obvious that it was Nuala who was choosing a perfume.

'Oh, it's not for me. It's my sister's perfume,' Louise said. She stepped back to allow the girl to talk directly to Nuala. The girl blushed and avoided eye contact but Nuala needed eye contact. Without it, communication couldn't be established.

'Let's get out of here,' she signed to Louise. She paid quickly for her perfume and they left, Louise still annoyed at the girl. Nuala was sad to have fooled herself into believing she could protect a child when she couldn't even defend herself against a shop assistant. She held back from telling Louise about her pregnancy. Louise was so upset about their mother that this was not a good time. She wasn't very rational these days. She cried often and Nuala didn't want to make her feel worse. She wondered if she should talk to Christina who was much calmer and more unperturbed. Talking to Christina carried its own risks too. Christina would put forward the sensible, logical solution in a sensible, logical way and then, Nuala wouldn't know how to respond. Best to decide alone. If only her mother was able to advise her. She would know what to do, not that she would tell her outright, just somehow she would ask the right questions and make it so that no matter what

Nuala chose, it would turn out to be the right thing to do.

Chapter 16

'You go ahead. I'll wait for you here,' Steve said.

They were in the small, cluttered waiting room outside the ICU. Steve picked up a newspaper someone had left behind and settled into a chair.

'You're not coming in then? They allow two people at a time, you know,' she said.

'I'd rather not. I don't know her well enough. She might not like it for me to see her that way.'

She felt a rush of affection for him and reached out to ruffle his hair before bracing herself to go in. 'I won't be long.'

Lynn was not working today and she was relieved. She could be alone with her mother and not feel that she was being watched. Each time she approached the hospital, she was terrified, her gut in turmoil, that someone might tell her that her mother's condition had worsened. It was exhausting and Lynn's presence added pressure that didn't make it any easier.

She found a stool and brought it to her mother's bedside. 'How are you, Mam?' she said softly. 'I hope you're not in any pain.' Her mother lay motionless on the bed.

Christina examined her face closely for any sign of a reaction, any flicker of her eyelids, a twitch of her mouth, but there was nothing to see.

'We're all hoping that you'll get better soon,' she continued. 'Especially me. I want to talk to you.' She stopped. What would she say if her mother could hear? Would she tell her about Lynn, about everything that had happened during that last year at school? Would she tell her why, for a time, she had hated everything to do with home and why she had needed to get away to survive?

She turned her mother's hand around so that her palm was facing upwards. She picked it up and pressed it against her cheek and closed her eyes. The warm skin, coarsened by a lifetime of work on the farm and in the house, was scratchy against her face. She was invaded by a flood of memories. She remembered, as a little girl, her mother helping her to get dressed, the rough skin on her hands snagging on her long knee socks as she smoothed them up her legs. She gently put her mother's hand back on the bed.

'Just get better, Mam. What counts is the future. I'd like you to get to know Steve better. And I'd like to come home to see you more often,' she said softly into her ear.

The machine behind her bleeped loudly and she jumped up, scraping her stool on the shiny hospital floor. A nurse hurried over to her.

‘Nothing to worry about. Stay where you are,’ he said. ‘That’s only the alarm to let me know that her intravenous fluids bag needs to be changed. I’ll have it done in a flash.’

‘It’s all right, I was about to leave anyway,’ she said. Still, she lingered at the end of the bed, watching him remove the empty bag and replace it with a new one, full of clear fluid. As soon as he was gone, she leaned in close and kissed her mother’s cheek. ‘Bye, Mam, I’m going. I’ll be back soon.’

‘Come on, I’ll take you to a restaurant,’ Steve said when they left the hospital. ‘You need a break.’ She was too worn out to step back into the ring of family life and gladly accepted. They wandered around the streets of Galway examining the menus posted outside and looking in the windows until they found a small Italian restaurant with traditional red check tablecloths and Chianti bottles covered in melted candle wax that served as candle holders. It was predictable and conventional almost to the point of being boring, exactly what she needed.

Steve must have understood because over dinner they talked about everything except her mother, her family and why they were there. He sang a few bars of a new song he was feeling good about. The couple at the next table looked up from their pizzas in surprise. He made her laugh by imitating the new Human Resources manager who was trying to persuade him to sign him up for some management course. They talked about the possibility of going away for a few days hiking in Kerry in the summer. Steve had never been there and Christina had promised to take him to see more of Ireland.

He didn't expect anything of her but he was easy company and kept the conversation going even when she fell silent. As she looked into his kind brown eyes, she was tempted to tell him that she really did care for him, and that if things were different, she might give her heart completely to him but she feared that this might be the wine and the circumstances tricking her into reckless confidences and so, she kept quiet.

When they left the restaurant, he draped his arm across her shoulders and she slipped her hand into the far back pocket of his jeans. It was just the right level of contact, close but uncomplicated. She liked the warmth of his body beside her. She could feel the muscles of his leg tightening and stretching beside hers as they walked.

The streets were not very busy; it was a weekday night and it was too early in the year for there to be many tourists. Steve hummed under his breath and she could feel him resonating against her. That was one of the great things about him: he was alive and constant, a reliably steady presence in her life. As this thought crossed her mind, a smile escaped her. If he knew what she was thinking, he would say that if his being alive was his major attraction, then she wasn't being very demanding. She glanced at him. He smiled back at her but didn't speak.

The door of a pub opened abruptly and a harsh shout carried on the cool night air. Mingled among the sounds of the scuffle were various voices of protest, one of them with a woman's higher pitch. Steve pulled her closer to him and they continued walking.

'I've had it with you. Don't bother showing your face around here again; it won't be welcome.' A burly man in rolled-up shirt sleeves was throwing someone out on the street. He was doubled over and only just managed to regain his balance to avoid falling into the gutter.

'You can go back inside, lady, you'll have no more trouble,' the bouncer said to pacify a woman who was peering past him into the street from inside the pub.

Christina and Steve were preparing to cross to the pavement on the other side to avoid any hassle when the man lifted his head and shouted back at the bouncer, 'Oh, ye can feck off, I was joking. You've no bloody sense of humour.' The door was shut in his face. He leaned against the pole of a street light. 'Bloody hell,' he said, but there was no strength in his curse.

She stopped and stared at him. 'Matthew, what's going on? What are you doing here?' She went to him, slipping out from under Steve's arm.

Matthew looked around, trying to locate the source of the voice. 'Hey,' he said. His eyes were bloodshot and dilated. He was having trouble focusing but his words were surprisingly lucid. 'I dropped in earlier. I was hoping to meet up with a friend of mine here. I was only having one or two before heading home. I made a smart comment to a girl there and she took it up the wrong way. Nothing to worry about.' He winced as he straightened up properly.

'Steve, my man!' he said as he spotted Steve for the first time. He looked back at her. 'Don't mind Bill there. He gets a bit hot under the collar. By tomorrow he'll have forgotten all about it.'

'Do you need a hand?' Steve asked.

'No, just let me get my breath back.'

'How long have you been in there?' she said.

'I don't know. I didn't realise I was supposed to clock in and out with you.'

'Matthew, this is ridiculous.'

'Give me a break, Christina. I was in the hospital earlier. I needed a drink after seeing Mam in that state.'

'Stop it,' she hissed at him. 'Don't you dare blame this on Mam. Leave her out of it. If you get drunk and obnoxious, it's most certainly not her fault.' She could feel her anger level rising. Steve put a protective arm around her shoulders. She shivered. He was right, there was no point in discussing anything with Matthew when he was in this state.

'Oh for Christ's sake, talk about uptight -.' Matthew started when Steve cut him short by taking his arm and guiding him towards the car. 'Here, let's get you back.'

Matthew protested. 'It's all right, I can walk by myself.'

'I'm sure you can but we'll get there faster if I help you. No, it's OK, Chris, I can handle him,' he said when Christina tried to hold him up on the other side.

They bundled him into the back seat and within minutes he fell asleep. They listened to his loud snores tearing through the air as she drove home.

'Sorry about this,' she said eventually. 'He's a disgrace. I don't know what's got into him.' When Steve didn't reply, his lack of reaction bothered her. Instinctively, she jumped to the defence of her brother. 'He's had a tough week; he lost his job. He's still young, he'll cop on with time.' She paused. 'At least, I hope he will.'

'He might need help to cop on,' Steve said tentatively.

'What do you mean?'

'I'm not saying I know much about this, but sometimes a thing like this can get out of control and a person can have trouble getting out of it by themselves.'

'Steve, are you trying to imply that he's an alcoholic or something like that?' She glanced at him before turning her face back to the dark, narrow road.

'No, of course not.' He shifted in his seat and looked out into the night. After a moment, he spoke again. 'Look, I hardly know Matthew, I've only just met him and I'm by no means an expert but I just wonder about his attitude to drinking. He just might need a bit of help if he's to avoid it getting worse.'

Her heart tipped into overload. This was something new. She remembered the chubby baby of her teenage years, how delighted he used to be when she came in from school, how he had taken his first steps towards her. He had always been a little clown, ready to do anything to make them all laugh. Her heart was lined with lead to think of him losing his way in an alcoholic maze but there was a ring of truth in Steve's words.

She glanced at her odometer and tried to calculate the optimum speed for fuel consumption. Steve reached out and squeezed her thigh. She kept her eyes on the winding road to avoid looking directly at him.

Steve hauled Matthew, still fast asleep, out of the car and helped him to the front door. She led the way. Louise opened the door of the sitting room and watched them bring Matthew up the stairs. From where they were sitting, Jim and Nuala peered through the open doorway.

'What's going on?' Louise asked.

'We bumped into him in Galway,' she said. 'He's had a couple too many to drink. He'll be all right in the morning once he's slept it off.' She wasn't ready yet to discuss her new concerns about Matthew with them. She needed to think about it a little bit more.

'You'd think he'd cut back on the socialising these days,' Louise said. Jim looked pale. Christina avoided looking at him.

'A cup of tea?' Steve said when he came back downstairs, made a sign of drinking for Nuala's benefit.

Nuala nodded and went with him to the kitchen.

Over tea, Steve didn't say very much, but his presence as an outsider allowed them to keep away from any difficult conversation about Matthew.

'I think I'll have to get back to work,' Louise said, after a moment's silence. 'My boss is losing patience big time. He wants me back on the road by Monday.'

'Well, I can understand his point of view. I suppose this situation could go on for weeks,' Christina said.

Louise glared at her. 'Oh, right, Miss Big Boss. Of course. The corporate show must go on.'

'Well, you do what you want, Louise, but I'm going back to work on Monday if there's no change between now and the end of the weekend.' She turned to Jim. 'I hope you don't mind, Dad, I can be here in three hours if you need me.'

Steve was stretched back in his armchair while he followed this exchange. He was absent-mindedly smoothing down his beard below his lower lip. Nuala was curled up in one corner of the sofa, cradling a mug of tea in her hands.

Jim rubbed his eyes. 'Of course, of course, Christina, do whatever suits you, that's fine with me,' he said.

The next day, in the hospital waiting room, Matthew was very pale and quiet as they waited their turn to see Kate. Christina hoped that the altercation of the previous night had been a wake-up call, one that would make him see his drinking in another light. He certainly looked as if he regretted it. She didn't raise the subject with him. She wondered if she should. Steve offered to pick up his motorbike from the car park at the back of the pub and drive it home that evening. Matthew accepted without protest. She offered to drive Steve and Matthew there from the hospital.

'How about a quick one in O'Mahony's before we go home?' Matthew said from the back seat on their way to the pub to get the bike. She wanted to say no but she wondered if it might be a good place for them to talk in relative privacy. She glanced at Steve for guidance but his face was expressionless and he shrugged as if to say it wasn't his call.

'Oh, come on, it's too early to go straight home. We'll just have one and then we'll head back,' Matthew said, honing in on the crack of doubt.

Warily, she agreed to go.

It was a Thursday and the pub was busy. The heat, noise and buzz as they entered contrasted sharply with the chilly evening air outside. They squeezed through the crowd towards the bar and, as they advanced, Matthew came to life. A smile appeared and grew into a grin as he recognised and greeted a few people.

'Well, Steve, what's your poison? Christina?' Facing them but leaning backwards over the bar, he was at ease and relaxed. He was no longer the subdued, beaten-down loser; he was the jovial, welcoming and welcomed host. The transformation made her nervous.

'I'll have a Coke, thanks, Matt,' Steve said. 'Have to keep my wits about me for the bike.'

'Arra, have a pint, one won't do you any harm,' Matthew said.

'Coke will be fine.' Steve struck the right balance between firmness and friendliness.

'I'll have a glass of Guinness,' she said.

'Coming right up. See if you can get us seats.' He waved them towards tables on the other side of the pub.

She lingered for a moment. He caught the attention of a barman he obviously knew and ordered their drinks. She noticed him knock back a whiskey in one unobtrusive gulp while he waited for the Guinness to draw. She wasn't sure if Steve had seen it but, if he had, he made no sign.

They found seats but Matthew had trouble keeping his attention on the conversation. His eyes flicked around the pub as if he was being obliged to sit with boring, elderly relatives during a lively party. His pint was almost gone while she still had more than half of her glass left and Steve had barely sipped his Coke. Matthew was getting edgy and she could see that he wanted to go to the bar and get another drink but was holding back. Bar etiquette dictated that it was her or Steve's round.

'Do you really need a drink that badly?' She knew it wasn't the most diplomatic of opening gambits but he was irritating her.

'I don't need one, I'd *like* one. But don't worry, I can get my own.' He was stung.

'That's not what I meant. I'm going to the bar now but maybe you should give some serious thought to the amount that you are drinking.'

'Tell you what? I won't. I'll leave the serious thought to you, that's your speciality. I'm more into trivial thought, myself.'

She glanced at Steve who, as she had grown to expect, was inscrutable.

She leaned forward and spoke so that she wouldn't be heard beyond their circle. 'I'm only saying that it's possible that you are drinking a bit too much these days, Matthew. I'm not saying it's a major problem but maybe you should talk to someone about it.'

'Well, the biggest problem I have right now is that my sister isn't making any effort to go to the bar for the next round.' Matthew turned to Steve and laughed in an attempt to get him on his side. Despite the joking, there was a hard undertone of defensiveness.

'I think Christina is worried about you, Matt,' Steve said.

'Well, there's nothing to worry about. Yeah, I've been drinking a little bit more than usual lately but I've good reason. In the normal run of things, I'm fine.'

Steve looked at her and narrowed his eyes slightly. She could tell he was recommending that she drop the conversation. She heeded the warning. For the moment.

'All right then,' she said and picked up her bag. 'Same again?'

Standing at the bar, she was thinking about Matthew and less aware of her surroundings than she might otherwise have been. At least that's what she told herself afterwards when she didn't instinctively recognise the laugh and the rough voice behind her. She turned and found herself face-to-face with Brendan Duffy. The shock knocked the wind out of her lungs. He had changed, and yet, he was the same. His hair had thinned out a lot and at least half of what was left was grey. He had put on weight too, especially around the belly. His face was reddened and lined from drinking and smoking. He looked much older. It was hard to believe that this was the same boy who had filled her nightmares for months after Lynn's party. And yet she had no doubt that it was he. He had the same crinkled, blue eyes that the girls used to believe reflected mildness, but which she knew was stupidity. He was standing around with a group of men, holding a pint. She saw him before he saw her. He turned in her direction, his open mouth showing his stained teeth, and then his eyes snagged on her face. He had the same slow smile that seemed ominous to her even now.

He frowned in puzzlement for a second before bursting out. 'Christina Cavanagh! I don't believe it.' He looked her up and down. 'You've hardly changed.' A shudder of disgust ran through her. 'Well, I mean you have changed. You look great! But you hardly look a day older. Isn't that mad, after all these years?' His compliments were made even more offensive by his crude dismissal of her younger self. She had always thought that if she found herself in his presence again, she would slap him or spit in his face, but instead, she did the socially appropriate thing and gave him a small polite, tight smile and made a non-committal sound. She tried to escape and get past him.

He was hot and sweaty and his shirt was open one or two buttons too many at the neck. A mixture of grey and fair hairs sprang from pink mottled skin on his chest and curled over the opening of his shirt.

Brendan stood in her path. 'Guys, this is Christina Cavanagh. We were in school together,' he said to the other men who were drinking with him. 'Hey, if I'd known at the time you'd turn out like this…' He left his sentence open-ended implying the wealth of missed opportunities for them both. He moved in too close to her, his pint glass in his hand. She could feel his hot, beery breath on her. 'The good old days, eh?' he said. 'So tell me, what are you up to? Are you married?'

Her throat tightened up. 'I've got to go.' She pushed past him. 'Excuse me,' she managed to blurt out as she stumbled through a group of drinkers to get to the toilet. She pushed open the door and fled into an empty cubicle. She locked herself inside and bent over the toilet. Waves of nausea rolled over her, making her shudder. When her stomach was empty and her throat raw and sour, the revulsion and sickness subsided, leaving her shivering and cold. She hated him as much as ever but she hadn't realised he could still have this impact on her more than half her life later. An impatient rap at the door made her jump. She leaned back against the door, eyes closed.

'Just a minute,' she said and brushed herself down. She opened the door.

In front of the mirror, while she smoothed down her hair and put on some lip gloss, she lifted her head high, her jaw clenched. She straightened her collar and left the toilets.

Steve and Matthew were chatting as she approached them. Matthew seemed to have lost some of his jumpiness and was sitting in the seat she had vacated.

'Do you mind if we go now, lads?' she said, standing over them.

'Christina, I never realised you'd go to this length to get out of paying for a round,' Matthew said. 'Honestly, let me get it then.'

'No,' she said. 'I want to leave. Now.'

Steve looked at her strangely, one eyebrow raised. She didn't like the way he was scrutinising at her. 'Something wrong?' he asked.

'This place is too crowded. I just want to get home. It's been a long day, a long week in fact. How many reasons would you like?'

He held up his hands in mock self-defence. 'No sweat, we can go. Come on, Matt, let's get that bike of yours.' On the pavement, he looked at her intently before putting on Matthew's helmet, pulling down the visor and starting the engine.

At first, in the car, Matthew tried to talk to her as they drove back home but he soon lapsed into silence when she showed no interest in pursuing the conversation. She knew he thought it was because of his drinking, but her annoyance and concern about that had been washed away for the moment by her meeting with Brendan. Even his name rolling around in her head, unuttered, tasted like something bad in her mouth. She wanted to spit it out. She stared fixedly at the road ahead of her, gripping the steering wheel tightly. She counted the number of broken white lines in the middle of the road ahead of her until they disappeared and it became the unmarked road close to home.

In bed that night, she turned her back to Steve and edged away from him towards her side. He put his hand on her shoulder. 'Come here, Chris,' he said.

'Leave it, Steve. I'm tired, I want to sleep.'

'That wasn't what I meant,' he said and she knew she had hurt him again. Deliberately, this time.

She replied with a little grunt. She tucked her arms in so tightly that her elbows dug into her stomach and hurt her. She forced her breathing to slow down and deepen so that Steve might believe that she was asleep and eventually she even fooled her own body and sleep came.

Chapter 17

1988

During biology class, the note arrived on Christina's desk, folded over so many times that it was now almost as thick as it was wide. She quickly put her hand over it and slid it towards the edge so that it would fall into her lap and she could open it without being seen. 'R U going to the Easter disco? (Brendan wants to know.)' it said, After the word 'know' there was a little love heart with an arrow through it. She flicked her gaze left and right, conscious of who might be watching out for her reaction. She wished she could remain cool and unperturbed; she knew the more she reacted, the more interest they had in continuing the game but it was stronger than her. She wanted to shout at them all that she knew fine well that she was being set up. Their plan wasn't very subtle: they wanted her to accept Brendan's invitation so that he could then laugh, saying of course he wasn't serious and then they would mock her 'notions' that Brendan might possibly fancy her when all the girls in the class were mad to go out with him. Even if she said that she wasn't in the least bit interested in Brendan, her protests would backfire, looking as if she was rejecting what she couldn't have anyway.

'What do you have there, Christina Cavanagh?' Miss Farrell's sharp voice made her jump.

'Nothing, miss,' she said and managed to slip the note under her bum.

'Don't say it was nothing to me. I'm not blind. Do you think I can't see you passing notes?'

'Sorry, miss, but I didn't pass any notes.'

'Don't lie to me, Christina. I don't like to be taken for a fool. Where is that note?' Miss Farrell's anger was growing, fuelled by the barely concealed giggles breaking out in the class.

Christina didn't answer. She stared down at her biology book and the drawing of the cross-section of an earthworm swam before her eyes.

She heard Miss Farrell's heels clip smartly towards her desk. 'I asked you a question, Christina. Stand up.'

Her heart was beating far too fast. She put her hand on the seat beside her to catch the note as she stood up but she missed and it fell to the ground.

'No note, eh.' Miss Farrell was triumphant. 'Give it to me,' she said, although it lay on the ground between them both.

Christina picked it up but kept it in her hand. 'It's private, miss.'

'Not if it's in free circulation in my class, it isn't. Hand it over.'

She delayed as long as she could.

‘Hand it over, I said.’

Finally, she gave it to her. The teacher opened it and examined it before handing it back. ‘Do you really think that the middle of my biology class is the best place to organise your love life?’

Warmth flooded her face until it was on fire. The laughter in the class broke out in earnest now.

Miss Farrell whirled around. ‘And who sent this note? Was it you, Brendan Duffy?’

‘No way.’ Brendan sat up straight and blushed red which made everyone laugh even harder. Someone threw a pencil at him.

She wanted more than anything else for the world to blow up around her, for something so awful to happen that her own predicament would be forgotten in the light of it.

‘Right, settle down, everyone. That’s enough, let’s get back to work.’ Miss Farrell made her way back to the front of the room. She knew that she was no match for this guerrilla warfare.

Christina breathed a sigh of relief and bent her head to stare at her book again.

After class, she found herself in the cloakroom with Cliona and Helen. ‘Miss Farrell is a real bitch, isn’t she? Sorry you got caught,’ Cliona said. Helen hung back behind her and rolled her eyes in sympathy.

It was the first time in a long while that someone in school actively tried to be nice to her so it was hard to trust them. Also, it annoyed her that they were keeping their voices low and that they had waited until there was nobody else in the cloakroom to do it.

'Oh well,' she said and pretended to focus on the knot in the lace of one of her runners. 'I don't care. There'll be something else to laugh at tomorrow.'

'So, are you coming to the Easter disco?' Cliona asked.

'I don't know, I hadn't thought about it at all,' she said although she had already decided she wasn't going.

'You should. It'll be fun. Come on, come with us.' Cliona turned to Helen to back her up.

'Everyone's going. You should come.' Helen joined in.

She glanced up at both of them to check if they meant it. A bubble of optimism swelled up in her. She wanted friends so much and here, friendship had come looking for her.

'I'll see. I'm not sure if I'll be allowed to go,' she said.

'Try,' Cliona said.

The door of the cloakroom opened and they looked up.

'Let's go, Cliona.' Helen tugged her arm.

They ran away and while she finished getting ready for PE, she was even able to smile despite the dire biology class.

'There's a school disco at Easter, Mam,' she said gingerly, testing the water with her mother. She wasn't sure if she wanted to go and more than half-hoped that her mother would say no so that the decision would be taken out of her hands.

'And you want to go, I suppose?' Her mother was only half-listening as she measured out flour to make pastry.

'Hmm, yes. I was thinking about it.'

'Well, I don't see why not. You haven't been out for ages. It might do you good to get out with your friends.'

'I don't have anything to wear though.'

'Your black jeans?'

'They're too short now and in any case, there's no way I'd wear them. They're so old-fashioned, way too loose. Everyone wears drainpipes now.' She cheered up. She was in the clear. She had a very good excuse to stay at home.

Her mother placed her floury hands on the worktop and paused to look at her properly. 'We could go and buy you something new to wear to the disco. It's true that you've grown out of most of your nice clothes and you've worked so hard this year.'

'Oh, forget about it, I know that you don't have much money. It doesn't matter. I'll go another time.'

Kate wiped her hands with a tea towel and smiled at her. 'That's very thoughtful of you, love,' she said. 'But you shouldn't have to worry about money at your age. Things aren't that bad and we can certainly afford a nice outfit for you for the disco.'

Christina squirmed under her gaze. She felt guilty for accepting praise when the real reason for refusing was entirely selfish.

'We'll go shopping on Saturday,' her mother said with an air of finality.

'Hmm, right. I have to go; I have lots of homework to do,' she said, rushing out of the room. Now, she had no choice but to accept her mother's generosity. It was obvious from the sound of her voice that she had decided that Christina should go to the disco and she was determined to make it happen.

On Saturday, Kate took her to Galway to buy an outfit. She picked out a pair of bright pink jeans. She had to lie down on the floor of the dressing room and hold her breath in to get the zip up. She loved them! Her stomach was concave in them and the colour was completely impractical. She couldn't believe her mother was willing to buy them for her but, after reassuring herself that Christina could still breathe while wearing them, she agreed to get them. Getting a top to match was a bit more problematic. Everything she tried on had enormous shoulder pads and she was afraid she looked even broader and more flat-chested than normal. Both the shop assistant and her mother convinced her that the large white shirt with the puffed sleeves and the belt that cinched her waist looked great on her so, with slight reservations, she took it.

It was only on the night of the disco, when she was fully dressed in her new outfit and standing in front of the full-length mirror in her parents' bedroom, that she became convinced that her outfit was far too flashy and conspicuous. It had been a bad choice. She would stand out, a target for derision. It was so unlike anything she wore or had ever worn before that she was tempted to dash back to her bedroom and change back into her shabby black jeans with her old red and grey jumper. Or better still, she wanted to forget about the whole idea and stay at home, but she didn't know how she could explain that to her mother after all the bother she had gone to. She tried to tell herself that she looked stylish but a little voice in her head sneered at her and told her she looked ridiculous. In any case, it was too late to back out.

After her father dropped her off at the disco, she kept her coat on over her outfit. She noticed Helen and Cliona with all the others from the class on the far side of the dance floor. A Human League song was playing but it was too early in the night for many to be out dancing and she didn't dare venture across that wide open space so she pretended not to have seen them. She decided to wander around the edge and pretend to bump into them. Lynn was standing at a table with a drink in her hand, surrounded by admirers. She looked great. She was wearing a dark purple rah-rah skirt and an off-the-shoulder cream top with a loosely tied rope belt. Christina instantly regretted her own choice. She felt stiff and overdressed while Lynn looked cool and relaxed.

She casually wandered over towards the group pretending to be examining the decor while looking out for other people she might recognise. She hoped Helen and Cliona would see her and call her over but they seemed to be deep in conversation with a couple of boys from the all-boys school in Oughterard. She glanced at Lynn and saw her throw her head back to laugh at something hilarious Jim Ryan was saying. She approached the group. A gang of five girls she didn't know moved onto the dance floor and started to dance to 'A Town Called Malice'. She focused her attention on them.

'Hey, Christina, you made it. You're not cold, are you?' Lynn said loudly as if she had only just spotted her.

'Hi,' she said and unbuttoned her coat.

'You managed to tear yourself away from the swotting. Imagine that.'

'I never study on a Saturday anyway.' The words sounded very prim and proper even to her own ears and she hoped the dim lights would hide her embarrassment.

'Anyway, I hope you're going to be nice to poor Brendan tonight. You have the poor guy's heart broken.' Everyone laughed, even Cliona and Helen.

Lynn clapped her hands together to catch everyone's attention which was already on her anyway. 'So, whose turn is it to go to the bar?' She looked around. 'Christina, you're elected. A tonic water for me, thanks. Anyone else?'

At the bar, she worried that her five pounds wouldn't be enough and when she needed an extra fifty pence she didn't know how to tell the barman who had already poured the drinks. Jim Ryan was standing nearby and noticed her confusion. 'Is everything OK?' he asked.

'Sorry but I'm fifty pence short. Could you watch the drinks while I go and ask one of the girls for more money?'

He laughed. It was a nice laugh. 'There's no need. Here.' He handed her a fifty pence coin from his pocket.

'Thanks,' she said and smiled at him. He had left the school the year before and was now in college in Galway. She had seen him around the school the previous year but had never had the occasion or the courage to talk to him before. Now that she was up close, she liked what she saw.

'I'll help you with those,' he said and picked up two of the drinks.

'But you'll lose your place in the queue.' She took the remaining two Cokes.

'I'll come back.'

He put the glasses on the table. 'See you later. Christina, isn't it?' he said before he left.

Helen nudged her and gave a whoop of approval when he left but was soon silenced by a glare from Lynn. A warning bell rang in her head. She remembered that Lynn had been talking to Jim when she arrived. It might not be the best idea to step on her toes.

'Cover me,' Lynn said, glancing over her shoulder. She took a 7-up bottle of clear liquid out of her bag. Christina guessed it was gin or vodka. They all drank some of their soft drinks to make room and then Lynn topped up their glasses from her bottle. 'Here, pass your glass,' she said to Christina.

'No, thanks,' Christina said.

'Oh come on, be sociable for once. Have one with us.' Lynn shook the bottle at her.

'Just a little bit then.'

She had gulped back quite a bit of her Coke but Lynn filled it up almost to the brim with vodka. She didn't protest. Furtively, she looked at her watch. It was only half past ten. Another two hours before her father came to pick her up. Maybe, if she stayed on the side-lines, at the edge of the dance floor, time would pass quietly and uneventfully until she could go home. She held her glass tightly in front of her, raising it in front of her face as she would a mask while she sipped from it. Cliona and Helen didn't make much of an effort to talk to her and she started to think that it might have been part of the set-up, that it might have been on Lynn's request that they'd invited her.

'Love the jeans, Christina,' Lynn said. 'Where did you get them?'

Christina frowned, no longer able to take anything she said at face value. She told her. One of Lynn's eyebrows raised in surprise as if to imply that she didn't think anyone shopped there. Under the influence of that single expressive eyebrow, the shop took on an old-fashioned and shabby look in her mind's eye. She hated how much Lynn's opinion could influence her.

'Hey, I'd never have guessed they had anything remotely trendy in there. Goes to show, doesn't it?' she said.

Christina nodded, although she wasn't sure what it showed at all. Lynn poured more vodka into her glass before she could put her hand over it to stop her. Her head was already spinning and she would have liked to sit down.

The DJ put on Come On, Eileen and Lynn jumped up as though stung. 'I love this one. Let's dance.' The alcohol was making Christina's head fuzzy and she was finding it hard to walk, never mind dance. She almost tripped over the two steps down to the dance floor. She glanced around to see if anyone had seen her. The alcohol had not yet eliminated her self-consciousness. She caught Jim Ryan looking at her. He smiled and raised his glass in acknowledgement. She looked away, pleased but mortified, as she joined the group. Lynn was in flying form.

After the song, the music switched to a slow set and she found Brendan in front of her asking her to dance. From the side, Lynn winked at her. She didn't know how to say no without creating a fuss so she accepted. The song would soon be over.

But when one of Brendan's hands slid downwards over her bum, she stopped moving. 'Don't do that,' she said.

'Loosen up, Christina. We're here to enjoy ourselves.'

'Well, I don't enjoy that.'

'Fine, have it your way. Frigid bitch,' he said and walked away leaving her alone on the floor. She wasn't sure what frigid meant but the way he said it gave her the shivers. She slipped between the dancing couples to the edge of the dance floor and made her way back to the others.

Lynn was laughing when she got to the table. 'Now, what did you do to poor Brendan?'

'Nothing,' she said and took her jacket. 'I'm going home.' She stormed away, anywhere had to be better than there.

Jim Ryan appeared in front of her. 'Hey there,' he said. Her eyes were sore and on the verge of tears, her cheeks were blazing with anger and her stomach was heaving in a very frightening way. She avoided his eyes, sidestepped him and dashed outside. The cool air hit her face. She closed her eyes but quickly opened them again as her head spun dangerously out of control and the ground became unstable under her feet. She managed to get around the corner before vomiting. A little bit splashed up on her new jeans. She stared down at them and at the pool of sick by her feet and tears of self-pity rolled down her face.

Steve looked at her back on the other side of the bed, an invisible but impenetrable wall between him and her. Maybe coming here hadn't been a very good idea. At first, he'd thought it might be a breakthrough for them. Most of the time they seemed to live their lives in parallel lines, neither coming together nor diverging from each other. This might be fine by Chris but it wasn't what he wanted. He was prepared to wait to see if time would change things, but he wouldn't wait forever. For the first time, she had reached out to him and asked him for help. He'd seen it as a new departure but nothing was ever quite so simple with Chris. She was a labyrinth of a woman. And he couldn't figure out why. From what he could see, her family seemed nice and normal. Or, at least, as normal as any large family you'd meet. When you had that many people in one family, there were bound to be some issues or problems. Her sister was deaf and her brother looked as if he might have a bit of a problem with alcohol but these problems didn't look insurmountable to him and the people most concerned seemed to be coping.

Although she was the one who had asked him to come here, ever since he had arrived, she had given him the impression that he was intruding. He wasn't a great believer in talking things to death. People talked far too much about stuff instead of getting on with it, in his opinion. Wounds healed better for not being poked. This time though, he wondered if it might be a good thing to ask her upfront what she wanted from him. But he'd wait a while, he didn't want to make this about him and their relationship. She had a lot going on at the moment, what with her mother's illness and her family's problems. He wouldn't add to it. There would be time later to talk about the two of them. At least, he hoped there would. How long could he wait before knowing if this had a future? Was there a formula for this kind of thing? He could only say that he wasn't prepared to give up just yet. But he wasn't a masochist either. Sometime soon, he'd need to feel that she could give him a chance, that there was a possibility of a future for them. He'd made that same mistake before with Abby, he didn't want to make it again.

Abby was the reason he'd left Birmingham and moved to Ireland. She was almost ten years older than he was and in the middle of a messy divorce when he'd met her. She had two kids and felt guilty as hell about the break-up and how that was affecting them. The kids hated him and blamed him for their father not coming back. Eventually, she gave in to them and they'd both decided to let it go. He'd been upset at the time but he'd known somehow that it was probably for the best. Now he found he was asking himself the same questions again.

He looked over at her. There was a subtle change in the line of her back. Some of the tenseness had left it. He leaned up on one elbow to look at her face. She was asleep. Gently, he pulled her shoulder towards him so that she wouldn't fall out of the bed. In her sleep, she turned over and slid down into the hollow in the centre of the bed towards him. He gazed at her. Why wouldn't she give them a proper chance? Just maybe if she did, they could have something special. They were very different, but maybe that was a good thing. He never considered himself a romantic man but he had to admit that there was something about Chris that fascinated him. She was like a chestnut. While the prickly casing on the outside might be hard to get through, the conker inside was beautiful, smooth, rich in colour and irresistible to the touch. He loved her but she drove him crazy too. He pushed away a few strands of hair that had fallen across her face. She flinched and moved away and sank back into sleep again. Finally, he closed his eyes and fell asleep too.

Chapter 18

'So are you saying you don't want me to go with you to the hospital then?' Steve said. It was morning and they were facing each other over coffee at the kitchen table.

Christina shrugged. 'I'd rather go on my own but if you really want to, then come.'

'Of course I don't really want to go.' The note of impatience in his usually even voice gave her a pang of apprehension, even though she could understand it and was expecting it. 'The reason I came here is to be with you. There's not much point in me taking time off work if I end up hanging around here while you're at the hospital, is there?'

'Fine, then come, if that's the way you want it.'

'But the way I want it isn't the point.' He broke off before starting again. 'Chris, you can be so unbelievably infuriating. Have it your own way. Go on your own.'

His order was sharp.

'Steve, I'm only going in for a short while. I want to catch the doctor when he's doing his rounds. I'll be back before lunch. We can do whatever you like this afternoon.'

He stared at her, his brown eyes boring into her as if he was trying to say something with them, now that words had failed. Steve so very rarely got annoyed that it was disturbing when he did.

'As soon as I know what to expect with Mam and have a rough idea of what's happening

I can make a plan for the next couple of weeks. I'll feel better then. If you need anything, Louise is around and it's Nuala's day off.'

A beam of sunlight shone through the window and showed up a breadcrumb in his beard, a white speck trapped in a dark brown web. She would have liked to reach across and brush it away, but it was too intimate a gesture for them right then. Instead, she stood up.

'I'd better get ready and go then,' she said.

In front of the door of the ICU, she paused took a deep breath and pushed it open. Who knew what she would find on the other side? No matter what she had to face, she preferred to be alone when she came to see Kate.

Slowly and meticulously, she performed the hygiene protocol but finally, there was nothing else to do but leave the washroom. From a distance, she could see four or five people in white coats standing around at the end of her mother's bed, blocking her view. As she got closer, an older man who seemed to be the most senior, hooked a clipboard onto the end of Kate's bed and spoke to the others in a low voice. She couldn't hear what he was saying because of the pounding noise in her ears. Lynn was one of those he was talking to. She noticed Christina arriving and took a step towards her.

Christina sidestepped the group to get a look at her mother's face. Kate's eyes were closed but her position in the bed wasn't the same and her hair had been brushed. She looked better: not as pale as she had on other days, her cheeks had a pink glow. Her breathing was audible. Christina let out a sigh of relief.

'This is the patient's daughter,' Lynn explained.

Christina addressed the man who had spoken. 'Can you tell me how my mother is doing? Do you expect her to come out of the coma soon?'

The doctor paused before replying.

'I'm afraid your mother isn't doing as well as we might have hoped.' His voice was calm and professionally detached.

Inexplicably, she felt angry; she had been caught unaware. The tiny rush of optimism she had felt on seeing her mother's warm complexion had been unfounded. Out of the corner of her eye, she could see an expression of sympathy on Lynn's face but she avoided looking at her directly. She waited for the doctor to continue, unable to speak.

'She appears to have developed an infection. Her temperature is up and we're not sure exactly what's causing it. We'll start treatment with antibiotics immediately but when we get the blood test results back, we'll be able to put a more targeted approach into place.'

'What do you mean, an infection? How did that happen? Was it something she caught here?' She glanced down at the bed and the tubes leading from it with new suspicion. 'Or did she catch something from one of us?'

'It's impossible to say. She's weakened by what she's been through so her body is bound to be susceptible to any possible infection she might encounter. We should see an improvement once the antibiotics start to take effect. We'll know better tomorrow. Don't worry, we're doing our best.'

'So when do you expect her to come out of this?'

'I'm afraid I can't say at this stage. At the moment, it's not absolutely clear why she has not regained consciousness. She's certainly not receiving any treatment that's preventing it. I know this probably doesn't help but we'll just have to wait and hope for the best. Now, if you have no more questions, we need to move on.' He was already walking towards the next patient.

But that's not enough, she wanted to say, not nearly enough. She didn't trust herself to speak anymore.

He led the group of junior doctors and students to the next bed. He turned to Lynn. 'If you could take those blood samples from her and send them up to the lab as soon as you can. And tell them it's urgent.'

Urgent. The word hit her like a punch in the chest.

'Will do,' Lynn said.

Lynn took an elastic band from a metal dish beside the bed. She picked up Kate's inert arms one after the other and examined her veins. She tied the band around her right arm above the elbow and tapped, searching closely for a vein. She frowned.

'Christina, would you like to step outside for a couple of minutes? Her veins are very sunken. It might take me a while.'

‘I’d rather stay,’ she said.

Lynn prodded and tapped the vein in the crook of Kate’s elbow again. She took the disposable syringe from the tray and peeled back the plastic packaging. She stuck the needle into Kate’s arm but failed to connect with a vein. After two or three attempts, she paused and took off the elastic band to put it on the other arm.

Christina felt faint. She turned away to leave. ‘Christina, are you all right?’ Lynn called after her.

‘I’ll come back,’ she said, without looking around.

The waiting room was empty of people; a fact she was grateful for. She wanted to get out of the hospital and walk away, never stopping so that no one could catch up with her. But equally, something was holding her here, something grim and determined. Despite everything that had happened between them, the link with her mother was just as strong as ever. Instead of breaking, it was pulling her apart. The past twenty-five years telescoped down to nothing while the days of her childhood and adolescence moved into focus.

She remembered the first time she had realised her mother was a person who existed in her own right, who wasn’t just an extension of her and her brothers and sisters. She had been around eleven or twelve.

She and Dad had come home from a wedding. It must have been Uncle Shay’s. It was late, nearly two in the morning, but she heard them come in. She sneaked to the top of the stairs and peered down, curious for titbits of news. Her mother was still giddy and excited, her father looked uncomfortable in his suit and shirt. He was pulling off his tie with relief. Kate was hanging up her coat.

'Go on, you're jealous, admit it.' Her mother was teasing her father.

'I am not,' he said.

'Well, it's all right if you are. A little bit. And maybe you're right to be.'

'Don't be ridiculous,' he said but there was an edge of annoyance in his voice.

Then, her mother spotted her through the bannisters. 'What are you doing up?' she said but she wasn't cross and Christina knew it would be OK to come downstairs. 'Back to bed, miss. We'll be up shortly after a cup of tea.'

'I'm not tired and there's no school tomorrow. Let me stay up for a few minutes. I want to know how the wedding went.'

'Well, all right then, just a few minutes,' her mother said. She hummed a tune to herself as she prepared the tea and seemed to be almost dancing as she moved around the kitchen. They went into the sitting room where her father was stirring the embers of the dying fire. The other children and Auntie Breda were asleep upstairs and there was an unusual quietness in the house. They sat close together around the fire to absorb the lingering heat and she was thrilled at being allowed to stay up alone with the adults, at being active while the rest of the world slept, oblivious.

After a few minutes, her father hauled himself up and declared that he was going to bed, even if they weren't.

'I'll tidy up here and then I'll be right up,' her mother said.

'So was the wedding good then? What happened?' she asked.

'I had a great time. I danced all night long. I couldn't get your father out on the dance floor, but that didn't stop me, I found another partner.'

'Who was that?'

'Oh, I had a good few dances with a cousin of Bernie's. A very nice young fellow.

And a great dancer although he is a good bit younger than me.' There was something almost flirtatious in the way she said it. Christina was surprised. She'd never seen her mother like this before. Kate leaned towards her and laughed. 'He even asked me if I'd consider marrying him.'

'What?' she said.

Her mother laughed at her shocked face. 'Oh, he didn't say it in a bad way. I don't think he noticed my wedding ring. All he said was that he was ready to meet someone and settle down and would I be interested in getting to know him better with a view to marriage.'

'What did you say?' This kind of talk was scary.

'Oh, silly billy, of course I told him I was already married and that I had all of you. What do you think, that I'd up and leave you?' Her mother ruffled her hair affectionately. 'But still it was flattering to think that a young man like that could be interested in an old married woman like me. I told him he was sure to meet a very nice girl and she'd be very lucky to have him for a husband. He was a little bit embarrassed at having asked me but there was nothing much to it really.'

'Oh,' she said but she had caught a glimpse of a side of her mother she didn't even know existed and it was disconcerting.

'Don't worry, sweetheart, I'm just being silly. I had a couple of glasses of wine over the course of this evening and that always makes me giddy. Your father was getting a bit cross with me, but I was thinking that I was there to have a good time. It's not often I get out to enjoy myself.'

'Mmm,' she said. 'I think I'll go to bed. I'll take the tray into the kitchen on my way.'

'Thank you, love, good night,' her mother said and kissed her.

'Christina?'

The voice cut through her memories and drew her back to the hospital.

'Christina, you can go back to your mother now if you like. I got the blood samples in the end and they've gone up to the lab for analysis. Sorry about earlier but your mother's veins are quite sunken and particularly difficult to get blood from.'

'I'll go back in in a minute.' She didn't move from her chair. She could feel Lynn standing over her, watching her, but she refused to look up.

'Can you tell me what's wrong, Christina?' Lynn said quietly.

'I'd have thought that was fairly obvious.' She lifted her chin and looked at her. Lynn's hands were stuffed into the pockets of her white uniform, her face determined.

'Of course I'm not talking about your mother. I think there's something else. Ever since we met last week you've been crabby with me and I'd like to know why.'

She stood up. 'It's been a long time, Lynn.' As she said it she realised it was the first time she'd said her name out loud for a long, long time. 'We have very little in common anymore and I don't see why I should discuss my life with you or confide in you.'

Lynn crossed her arms. 'I'm not asking you to confide in me or tell me about your personal affairs. I just get the impression that you're mad with me and I was wondering why. I can only imagine it's something that happened in the past'

A white wave of anger swept over Christina and she had to wait until it subsided before she spoke. In an attempt to look cool and unruffled, she raised an eyebrow. 'I think you're making a big deal out of nothing. You are the least of my worries at the moment. I have a lot going on in my life right now so I'm not really in the mood for old school reunions.'

Lynn's cheeks reddened and she opened her mouth to speak but then closed it again. 'Fine,' she said. 'If that's the way you want it. I'd better get back on duty.' She swung around and walked away.

After a moment's wait, she followed her to the ICU but stopped at the door and, instead of going in, she turned around and strode towards the stairs and the outside world.

Chapter 19

There was nobody around when she got home and drove into the yard. Even Archie, her Dad's dog, didn't appear and bark at her. It was colder today than any other day since she'd arrived and a hazy mist of rain drifted down around her. She opened the back door and slipped into the kitchen. Nuala and Steve were there. They didn't notice her arrival at first. Steve was playing a guitar. It wasn't his own; he must have found Matthew's old one from when he used to play. He was singing softly in muffled words she couldn't distinguish. Nuala was sitting on a chair in front of him leaning forward, one palm flat on the smooth part of the guitar. There was something calm and intimate about the scene and her instinct was to step back. She wondered if the pang she felt was jealousy but it couldn't possibly be. Nuala looked up at her, smiled and withdrew her hand. Steve stopped playing and placed the guitar flat across his knees.

'How's Mam?' Nuala signed.

'Not great. She has an infection. They're treating it with antibiotics,' she signed and said clearly for both Steve's and Nuala's sake. Nuala's smile disappeared. Steve put the guitar against the wall behind him. 'Are the doctors worried?' he asked.

'I'm sure they are. They didn't say that directly though. It's hard to get concrete information from anyone.'

'What about Lynn? Was she there today?' Nuala said, using her voice. Christina was surprised. It was obvious that she was making the effort for Steve. He must have made an impression.

'She was but she doesn't know any more than anyone else.'

'Do you want to go back this afternoon?' Steve spoke clearly and made sure that he was turned towards Nuala.

'I don't know. Maybe not. Maybe this evening.' Lynn's shift would be over by then.

'I'm planning to go in to see her this afternoon.' Nuala said.

Christina nodded. Speech felt dangerous now. She left the kitchen to put away her coat in the hall.

Nuala's phone vibrated in her pocket as a message arrived. She checked who it was from and went outside into the yard. It was her doctor confirming an appointment for Saturday. A shiver of fear ran through her. Although her decision was made, until she told someone else about it, the possibility of turning back was always there. She looked down at her hands and made the signs for 'my baby'. Then her hands formed the sentence: 'I'm going to have a baby.' Her nose tingled as she watched her empty hands rock to and fro for the last word. What would they say when she told them? They would probably be nervous and protective over her as they always were, but in the centre of her being she believed that she could cope. All she had to do was convince them. She knew well it wouldn't be easy. For a start, she was terrified of the idea of allowing her baby to cry unheard and uncared for in the night but she would find a solution somehow. She had a lot of love to give a baby and that had to be the main thing. Occasionally, a little voice in her head mocked her and told her that there was a lot more to raising a child than kisses and hugs but she managed to push it away to a corner of her brain.

The first person she would tell was her mother. She owed her that. She would go this afternoon. She would find a way to tell her. She saw the others by her bedside speaking to her, hoping that she could hear them through her coma but even that possibility was closed to her. She wanted to push open her mother's eyelids and look into her eyes. Even if she wasn't able to reply, it would already be a huge comfort if she knew. She hoped desperately that her mother would come through to help her raise this child but if she didn't, then she'd manage. Her mother had coped. If this was a hearing child, then she would find a way to help him or her just as her mother had helped her. The child might resent her just as she had resented her mother at times but they'd muddle through all the same.

She went outside to look for her father and tell him that she was going to the hospital. He looked at her closely and hesitated. 'I'll be OK, Dad,' she signed.

Her confidence convinced him. 'Take care, drive carefully,' he said. He had never become as at ease in sign language as her mother, brothers and sisters had but she didn't hold it against him. He did his best. That was another thing: she'd have to get her full driver's licence as soon as possible. Until now she'd been putting it off, nervous of how the examiner might react to her but now she'd have to go for it.

At the hospital, as she sat by her mother's bed, she watched Kate breathing, a visible thing that showed in the rise and fall of her chest with each breath. A nurse was taking her temperature, frowning slightly as she examined the result. She jotted it down on a chart and looked up. Nuala smiled. She didn't ask for any information. It wouldn't change anything.

After the nurse left, she pulled the stool in closer until she was only centimetres away from her mother. She was helpless in front of the closed shutters of her mother's eyes. For a while, she sat quietly, rubbing her mother's arm. She pulled Kate's two lifeless hands together and wrapped them around her own. She paused, unsure of how to talk. Her language was much more complex than just the movement of hands. So much had to do with the position of the rest of her body, how it interacted with her hands, her facial expressions. She stumbled on the first, the simplest of words: me. Usually she'd point to herself but this wouldn't work here. She took a deep breath and, inside the nest of her mother's hands, she made the sign for cat. It was her nickname in sign language. Her mother would know. Then she signed the letters I, L and Y. It was not how she would usually sign 'I love you' but she hoped her mother would understand anyway. She paused. There was no response but she could feel a sense of life that gave her the courage to keep going. She had to choose her words carefully. She made the sign for 'baby' and 'future' and then the sign for 'cat' again, just to be clear. Even though she knew there would be none, she waited for an answer. Then, she made the sign for 'happy' and as she did, she realised that she really was happy about this baby to come.

Now she could tell the rest of the family and already she felt better about it. She picked up her mother's hands and put them back in place before kissing her and leaving.

'I need to make a call to the office first before we go,' Christina said. 'There are a few things I need to sort out with Frank.' Deirdre, Mark's wife had phoned and invited herself and Steve over. It would be good to get out of the house and her nieces would be an entertaining distraction. They were planning to walk there; the rain had stopped even though the sky was still an unremitting blanket of cloud.

She took her mobile phone and notebook with her to the sitting-room, not because she wanted to keep anything from Steve but she needed to be alone to switch to business mode. Frank was in his office and took her call straightaway.

'How are you, Christina? I hope your mother's getting better.' It was a polite prelude to the more serious questions. Frank liked to think of himself as a considerate, accommodating boss but, when Russell was around, his thoughts didn't stray far from the company's bottom-line.

‘She’s reasonably stable at the moment, Frank, thank you for asking.’

‘Good, good, good, glad to hear it.’ Frank moved swiftly on. ‘So do you think you’ll be back before the board meeting next week? I’d like to present some simulations of the CCM takeover before we get board approval for the funding. The sales guys feel that a twenty per cent increase in the first year is doable. And then that sales will stabilise out to a ten per cent increase per annum for the following couple of years. I think that’s a reasonable estimate. Do you think you could do something up along those lines?’

She paused. ‘I wouldn’t call a ten per cent increase ‘stable’. And I can’t help but feel that Sales are being overly optimistic there.’

‘I’m not so sure about that. I leaked the word to Jim Dowd of Symbiotic Technologies and he thinks it’s a great idea. He said we should get a bigger share of their business if it goes ahead.’

She shook her head slightly at the phone. Frank was always willing to listen to even the most tenuous stories, as long as they were positive ones.

‘In any case, we can talk about this on Monday, Frank. I’ll be back in the office next week. In the meantime, I’ll talk to Donal and Aoife and ask them to start work on getting the figures.’

‘Great stuff, Christina, I knew you wouldn’t let me down. One last thing. Russell asked if he could to talk to you the next time you rang in, he’s flying back tomorrow morning, but I don’t have to tell him you rang, if you’d rather not talk now.’

She glanced at her watch. It was hard to have a short conversation with Russell, but once he went back to the head office it would be impossible to catch him between meetings. 'No, go ahead, put me through. Thanks, Frank.'

Russell's warm twang rumbled down the phone at her. 'Christina, how are you? Good to hear from you. I believe you're having a hard time there at the moment.'

'My mother's not well but we're hoping she'll pull through. The doctors are doing their best.' The platitudes rolled easily off her tongue. They all wanted to ask the right questions but no one really wanted to hear the answers.

'As soon as possible, I hope. The reason I wanted to talk to you, Christina, is that we have an opening coming up in Pittsburgh. We'll be looking for a VP of finance next year. Ted Hingle is retiring and I think you could be the right person for the job. What do you say?'

'VP?' she said, disconcerted.

'Yes, ma'am. Vice President. With all the attendant benefits. I won't go into the details of the package now but I don't think you'll be disappointed. I just wanted to put the proposition to you and see if you were open to it. I would have preferred to talk to you face-to-face about this but unfortunately, circumstances have prevented that.'

'Well, I'm flattered, Russell, I don't know what to say.'

'Oh, I have to say we'd be more than delighted to have you with us on board the US team. You're very well considered. Just think about it and we'll talk about it again soon. You have time to decide, although from what I understand, it wouldn't be too difficult for you to uproot.'

For a reason she couldn't define, this comment hurt. She wondered who his informant was. Probably Frank.

'Thank you very much, Russell. I'm sure you can understand that I'm not in a good position right now to make a decision like that but I'll certainly be thinking very seriously about your offer.'

'Do that but I hope you'll give us a chance to do what it takes to persuade you to come.'

'Of course. Leave it with me. Have a good flight back tomorrow, Russell. I'll be back in the office next week. We'll be in touch then.'

'Best of luck to you, Christina.'

She hung up. The slim mobile phone was heavy in her hand. She looked around at the comfortable, slightly shabby sitting room, at the armchair her mother habitually sat in, at the yellow and brown ashes that had tumbled over the edge of the fireplace, at the photos over the mantelpiece capturing their various communions, confirmations, graduations, at the aerial photo of the house and farm that her father had been so proud of. It was a very different place from the high-flying corporate world Russell was asking her to join. The words 'not difficult to uproot' echoed in her ears. She put her phone in her pocket and returned to the kitchen.

Steve was picking at the chords of the guitar in an absent-minded way. 'Ready?' he asked as he looked up. 'Are they coping without you?'

She laughed. 'I don't know, Steve. They're up to no good; spending money, taking over companies, making wild sales projections. I'll have to go back soon before they get carried away.'

He looked surprised. 'Do you mean that? Are you going back soon?'

'They need me back there. There's a board meeting next week that I don't want to miss. There are important decisions for the business that are going to be made at the meeting. I should be there to try to talk some sense into them about the new takeover'

'Do you honestly think they are going to listen to you? I thought they had their minds made up.'

'I know, they probably have. Still, it's my job. I don't want to let the company down.'

'Chris, when was the last time you took all your holidays? I think if there was ever a time when you needed to take time out, it's now.'

'Let's talk about this on our way to Mark's house.' She wanted to discuss the job offer with him but it would be easier outside the house. The past had a way of creeping up on her and seeping into her present. She didn't want it to contaminate her life with Steve too much. 'Come on, Deirdre will be wondering what's keeping us.'

The grass was whitened with frost and made a slight crunch as they walked through it. It was nice to walk along together, her gloved hand in Steve's, without needing to talk. She tried to bring up the subject of the Pittsburgh job but she couldn't find the right words. Steve wasn't a big talker at the best of times but he seemed quieter than usual. Before she could get around to it, they arrived at Deirdre and Mark's, red-cheeked from the cold. The house was warm and perfectly tidy. Deirdre had made dinner for them and it was only when she smelled the lasagne coming out of the oven that she realised that she had hardly eaten that day. She got no pleasure from food anymore; it was merely a fuel source to keep going. Afterwards, Mark offered to drive them back but they refused. She liked the companionable silence in the cold. She didn't want to break the spell. There was plenty of time; she would talk to Steve later about the job, when there weren't so many other things clamouring for her attention.

Chapter 20

1988

She first got wind of the house party Lynn was organising for the end of school when she stumbled on Maura Sheehan, Helen Spollen and Geraldine Fitzpatrick in a huddle in the cloakroom giggling about it. She knew she wasn't invited when they stopped talking as soon as they noticed she was there. She pretended to be busy looking for something in her school bag. She took out her homework notebook and examined an exercise in it, frowning to show that she was thinking deeply about it and oblivious to what was happening around her. Their quick return to laughter and chattiness as soon as she left made her burn up inside with embarrassment.

She was desperately looking forward to leaving school. She wrote the number of days left until the last day of school on the inside back page of her notebook and every evening before going to bed, she crossed out the figure and replaced it with the new one underneath. She worked as hard as she could, convinced that the better her results were, the better her chances of escape. Once she got her jobs done around the house and spent half an hour or so on her sign language lessons, she would sit at the small table she had wedged between the wall and her side of the bed and attempt to get a couple of hours of study done before she had to vacate the room to let Louise go to bed. Knowing that her study time at home was more limited than she'd like, she focused intently in class in an effort to absorb as much as possible on the first hearing. She didn't care anymore what the others thought or at least she managed to care a bit less.

Although Lynn was still dismissive of her and never bothered to speak to her any more, she was much less the target of her mockery.

From scraps of conversations and hints dropped, she found out that Lynn's party was to happen on the Saturday night after the last exam. Neither of her parents would be there; they had agreed to leave the house to her and her friends. There were plans to get in plenty of alcohol and Jimmy Keegan had organised to get a consignment of weed from his older brother who was in college in Galway. Lynn had persuaded Kieran Colton from two years ahead to do the music. He already did part-time DJ work and had the biggest collection of records of anyone they knew. She suspected that she was the only one in the class who was not invited, although there was no one she could ask directly. Not that she would have wanted to even if she could. As the end of the school year approached, talk about it became more open and excited.

One day, she was in the science lab early. It was her week to set up the equipment for the experiments. She was on her own, taking the Bunsen burners out of the cupboards under the benches when Lynn and Cliona came in. As usual, Lynn's hair was perfectly curled back from her face in a good imitation of Farah Faucett-Majors' hairstyle. She was wearing very shiny, pale pink lip-gloss and immediately Christina became conscious of her worn uniform and hair that stuck out in all directions no matter how she tried to slick it down with water in the mornings.

'Oh, hi Christina,' Lynn said in a perfectly friendly voice as if they greeted each other this way every day. 'I've been meaning to say this for ages but I'm having a party at my house on the 27th of June – it's the Saturday night after the exams – and I was wondering if you'd like to come.'

Christina stopped and looked at her suspiciously. She glanced at Cliona to see if she could see any sign of a trap there. 'I'll see,' she said warily. 'I might have something planned for that night, a family thing.' She knew she didn't sound very convincing but it was the best she could come up with on the spur of the moment.

'Oh, come on.' Lynn laughed outright. 'What could you possibly have on that night? You should come, it'll be fun.'

Christina blushed, partly from embarrassment and partly from annoyance. Lynn's casual dismissal of the possibility of her having an alternative social life made her feel even more mundane and insignificant. 'I'm not sure, I'll think about it.' Far from being the nonchalant brush-off that she had intended it to be, her response sounded surly and ungrateful even to her own ears. 'Thanks for the invitation, though,' she added.

'No problem, see if you can make it. Come along for eight o'clock if you are coming,' Lynn said.

She nodded and turned back to the cupboard for the petri dishes, conversation concluded. While Cliona walked to her desk, Lynn stopped suddenly as if she had forgotten something and turned back to her. She spoke in a quiet, confidential voice.

'Oh Christina, I have a favour to ask of you. I'm in big trouble for biology and maths. I just can't seem to get a grip on those two subjects.' She laughed and her incompetence was transformed into an appealing quirk. 'I really don't want to get a bad mark in them so I was wondering if you could help me out.'

Christina was torn; she wouldn't mind explaining some of the stuff to Lynn who wasn't at all stupid, just not interested enough to make an effort, but on the other hand, her time was precious and she couldn't afford to waste it during the last few weeks. 'Well, OK, if you want but…'

'Oh, Christina, I knew I could rely on you. Here's what I was hoping for. The seating in the exams is by alphabetical order so I'm pretty sure we'll be close together. If you could let me know some of the answers by pushing your paper over to let me look at it then I'm sure I'd be able to copy enough to get a decent mark.'

She made it sound so easy. Christina's ears buzzed. So this why Lynn had invited her to the party! A sneery voice inside told her of course it was. She didn't care if

Lynn cheated, but she didn't want to ruin her own future by taking risks like this.

'What if we get caught?' she said, for a lack of something else to say. She wanted to be more forceful and tell her to get lost but these were the only words she could find. Lynn had that effect on her; her words and thoughts got tangled up and tripped up over each other.

'Oh, we won't get caught.' Lynn was confident. 'We'd just have to be clever about it. And hope that Mr Dempsey is invigilating.' She said this last with a cheeky grin.

The rest of the class crowded into the lab and noisily took their places. 'Thanks, Christina,' Lynn said and gave her arm a quick punch before taking her seat. The conversation niggled at her for the rest of the day so that she found it hard to concentrate. That evening, she was distracted when her mother asked her to practice her latest signs with Nuala. Nuala was learning the signs much faster than any of them, even than her mother who was able to practise during the day.

After mulling over it for a while, she thought that the problem wouldn't arise. She hoped that she'd be seated too far from Lynn to be of any use, or that the supervisor would be Mrs Higgins, who everyone knew had eyes in the front, back and sides of her head, or even that one of them would catch a highly contagious disease and have to be isolated from the rest of the class during the exams. Eventually, when nothing more was said about it over the next few days and she continued to be ignored by the class, she managed to convince herself that Lynn had forgotten about the request and it sank slowly below the surface of her consciousness.

During the final few weeks before the Leaving Cert, Lynn kept her distance from her and she started to think that her wish had been granted.

On the first day of the exams, she discovered that Lynn was sitting right behind her. It was English, Lynn's best subject, and one of the ones she was less good at. She was nervous, nervous of making a mess of the exam, nervous of Lynn and conscious of her presence behind her. She read the paper, found a question she could answer reasonably well and started writing. Soon, her anxiety evaporated and adrenaline made her pen fly across the pages. As the words flowed out, she gained in confidence and knew that she was doing a good job.

Lynn was with a group of her friends, hanging around in the corridor after the second English exam in the afternoon. She gave Christina a secret look but didn't speak to her as she passed by. On the bus home, Christina felt a warm glow smouldering inside her. Everything would sort itself out, she had done well in her exam, the finishing line was in sight, she'd been worrying about nothing.

The next morning was Maths. She was looking forward to this subject. It was one where she should do well. She liked the way it had clear rules and boundaries, and that to each question, there was one right answer even though it could be arrived at in different ways, each one a path paved with a step-by-step series of logical deductions and calculations. There was something satisfying about finding that answer and knowing that that was the end of the problem.

She was sitting at her desk waiting for the room to settle down so that the invigilator could distribute the papers when Lynn passed by and whispered to her, 'Make sure you let me see. Just stick it over to the right once you're finished with the page and I'll be able to see it.' She made a funny face as if this was a practical joke they were planning together.

All Christina's excited expectations for the exam melted away. A knot appeared in her stomach. The invigilator was an outside teacher; someone she didn't know. He didn't look as if he was watching them very closely but you never knew. He was a messy-looking, middle-aged man, wearing a waistcoat that barely met over his belly. His hair grew in long wisps that he tried to smooth over his balding head but they managed to break free after a while. He wore glasses that looked as if the top half had been cut off them and he peered out over the top of them whenever he heard a noise from the room.

About half an hour into the exam, she felt a steady pressure against the leg of her chair. She understood it was a signal from Lynn to let her see what she had done. She considered ignoring her; after all, in a little more than a week she would be finished with school and a few short weeks later she would be going to college, or so she hoped. She had deliberately applied for courses in Dublin so that she could get as far away as she could. As for money, she'd cope; she was entitled to a grant and she could find a part-time job.

Lynn increased the pressure on her chair so that it almost moved under her and she knew that it was impossible to refuse. She hated herself for it. Why couldn't she stand up to her? She wanted to get on with her exam and get the thing over with. A rush of anger suddenly flooded through her. Fine, let her have the answers, what did she care? It was Lynn's problem. All she wanted was to be left alone and if that's what it took, well then…

As soon as she had finished the first problem she turned her stapled exam book back to the first page and pushed it to the side of her desk so that Lynn could easily read it. She took another page and started on the next question. She couldn't see what Lynn was doing from behind but she could sense her stretching forward to read the page. A light tap on the leg of her chair was an indication to turn the page.

She had almost finished the paper when she looked up instinctively. The invigilator was watching her and not in a distracted, scanning-the-room sort of way. Although he didn't move from his chair and looked just as dishevelled, he was attentive to her reaction. She quickly bent her head and continued writing. She resisted the temptation to check if he was still looking at her and forced herself to finish the question before glancing up. By then, he had picked up the exam paper and was reading it.

When Lynn next pushed against the leg of her chair, she moved her chair forwards, away from her. She wouldn't take any more chances, no matter what Lynn said or did afterwards. When the exam was over, she braced herself for either an onslaught from Lynn or an indication that her guerrilla war against her was about to resume. She told herself that it didn't matter, that she could cope with anything for the few days that remained and her resolution made her feel strong but, instead, when she caught her eye, Lynn gave her a complicit wink.

For the next couple of days, Lynn was careful and didn't ask her for anything but on Thursday, it was biology. She stopped at her desk that morning. 'Are you planning on doing the question on circulation if it comes up?' she asked.

'Not sure,' Christina mumbled. 'It depends on what else there is.'

'If it does come up, do that one. Make sure to let me see it.'

'I'm not sure if that's a good idea.' She shot a look at the invigilator who was calling order in the room.

'I heard someone say that circulation is coming up and I haven't covered it at all. Oh come on, Christina, don't be so mean!'

She was amazed that she could still ask but even more amazed that she herself was considering complying. Sure enough, circulation came up and it was one of the top questions with the most marks. Her heart sank. Lynn softly tapped out an SOS against the leg of her chair. She panicked and glanced up at the invigilator. He was gazing out the window, deep in thought, twirling his glasses in his hand. She slowly pushed her exam sheet to the edge of her desk and moved her body to the left so that Lynn could see.

She had almost finished her third question when the examiner stood up and wandered down the aisle. He stopped near both of the girls' desks and looked at them. He had one hand in a pocket and, in the other, he held his glasses by one stem. Her heart was pounding. She was both hot and cold. She remembered the teachers telling them horror stories of students being caught cheating and being dismissed from the exams, never being accepted in university and spoiling their chances in life. Her world darkened as if a black cloud had halted over her head and the idea of being trapped here forever became a reality. She tried not to look up but she was very conscious of him looming over her. If he looked into her eyes, her guilt would be obvious.

'Be careful with your papers, girls,' he said in a low voice. 'Keep them out of sight.' He continued his stroll. For a second, the relief took her breath away. She lifted her eyes from the desk sufficiently to watch the baggy tweed trousers moving away from her.

After the exam, Lynn was in a good mood. She seemed to be immune to the fear that had paralysed Christina for a few minutes and still left her shaky. She had two more exams after that but they weren't subjects Lynn took so she was safe from now on. There would be no more cheating and no more risks.

'God, I'll be so glad when this is all over,' Lynn said. 'I swear I am going to get so pissed next Saturday. And I hope none of you are going to show me up by staying sober.' Her gaze encompassed them all, even Christina, who was hovering near the door. Everyone laughed. Christina, who still hadn't made her mind up if she would go, wavered. Maybe she would go along for a little while, just to show up. She didn't want them to think her even more of a weirdo than they already did.

Chapter 21

Christina and Steve arrived back, glad to get out of the cold and into the warm house. It was bustling with all the family members around. Even Mark arrived in shortly after them. Jim, Matthew and Aidan were in the sitting room watching a hurling match on television. Steve joined them. Louise and Nuala were talking earnestly in the kitchen.

Christina was about to go upstairs to return a call from work when Nuala stopped her. 'Please come into the sitting room,' she signed. 'There's something I want to tell you. It won't take long.' She noticed Louise's serious face behind her and her heart thumped. She went back into the sitting room and perched on the edge of the armchair where Steve was sitting and waited for her sister to speak.

Nuala had their attention now. She stood beside Jim's armchair and glanced at him nervously. 'I'm glad you are all here,' she signed. 'There's something I need to tell you.' Steve glanced at Christina for explanation. She whispered what Nuala had said in his ear. Nuala took a deep breath and signed quickly. 'I'm going to have a baby.'

'What?' Matthew exploded. Jim looked as if he hadn't fully understood what she had signed. The others glanced around waiting for someone else to react first. She told Steve quickly what she had said but he seemed to have understood already.

Nuala shot a look at Louise who spoke up. 'Nuala just told me about this a few minutes ago so I don't know much more than you. All I can tell you is that she got pregnant accidentally but she's not seeing the father any more. I don't think she wants to talk about that at the moment.'

'Nuala,' Jim said with a note of reproach.

'I'm sorry, Dad. This isn't how I wanted it but it's how it is,' Nuala said out loud. Despite her apology, there was no contriteness. Instead, there was a steely determination that Christina had not seen in her before.

'You're crazy, Nuala. Are you sure you've thought this through? There are other alternatives, you know,' Matthew said and signed simultaneously. He looked around at his siblings for support. 'Like not going ahead with it?'

'Matthew, stop it.' Jim was even more shocked by his son's suggestion than he was at his daughter's announcement.

'Oh, come off it, Dad, people go to England all the time. Nuala's not ready for this. Of all people to have a baby on her own.'

'I think she can manage, especially if we all chip in,' Louise said, trying to sound more confident than she was.

'Sure she can,' Aidan echoed.

'It won't be easy though,' Christina said. 'I mean it's all very well to say we'll help out but you do a lot of travelling with your job, Louise, and it's not sure that we can bank on Mam being able to support them.'

'Well, if that's the way everyone is going to react, then yeah, she's going to have it tougher than I thought,' Louise said.

'How do you feel, Nuala?' Jim took his glasses off his nose and folded them away.

'I'm sorry if I disappointed you but I think I can cope. I'll have to,' Nuala signed. Jim frowned as he tried to comprehend her gestures. He put his hand on top of hers when they came to rest.

'I still think you don't have to go through with this.' Matthew signed furiously. 'I say wait until you're in a stable situation. When things will be easier.'

'When will things be easier? They might never get easier.' Nuala signed back with large annoyed gestures. 'I'm going to do my best to make this work.'

There was an awkward silence during which Christina caught Steve's eye. She wondered if he had understood but, before she could whisper anything, he shook his head slightly to let her know that he didn't need an explanation. He looked at Nuala. 'I know I'm not really part of this family, Nuala, but I'd like to say congratulations. I'm sure you'll make a great mother.' Nuala hesitated and looked to Louise. Steve's beard made it difficult for her to lip-read. As soon as Louise had interpreted, she turned to Steve with a big smile.

'Thank you,' she said and simultaneously put her fingers to her chin to make the sign for thanks.

'Yes. Congratulations!' Mark said. He grasped his two hands together to make the sign for that word. He stood up and put his arms around Nuala. His move towards her changed something in the mood in the room. Aidan, Matthew and Louise also approached Nuala to hug and kiss her. Even Jim stood up and patted her on the back. Christina held back. Lots of people were talking now, and finally, when the buzz calmed down, Mark announced that he was going to the hospital. Jim and Louise said they would go with him.

'Not me, I was there this afternoon,' Nuala signed. 'I'm tired.'

'I don't know if I should go,' Christina said. 'Maybe it would be too many people for her.'

'We won't stay too long', Louise said. 'And I think it does her good to have us around her. I'm sure it'll help her make it through.'

'Well, all right then. I have to go back to Dublin soon anyway,' Christina said.

'Already?' Mark said. 'When are you going?'

'Probably tomorrow afternoon. I have a lot going on at the office. It's not that far away, I can come back quickly enough if I have to.'

'I hope you find the journey a bit shorter than you have for the past few years,' Matthew said.

'Stop it, Matthew,' Mark said. He turned back to her. 'I do hope we'll see more of you. If Mam makes a recovery, I know she'd be glad to see more of you.'

'Of course she'll make a recovery,' Louise snapped. 'And anyway Nuala is going to need all of us too.'

'Well, don't count on me.' The words left Christina's mouth as if she had no control over them. 'I won't be in Ireland for very much longer. I'm moving to the States next year.'

She felt like she was a helpless observer watching an accident unfold in front of her. She didn't want this to happen but there was nothing she could do to make it stop. Everyone stared at her. She sensed rather than saw Steve's eyes on her but she avoided looking directly at him.

'What do you mean? Are you leaving your job?' Mark asked.

'Not exactly,' she said. 'I'll still be with the same company but based in the head office in Pittsburgh.' Now, she was seized by a crazy recklessness that made her light-headed. It was like the illusion of flight in the split-second after leaping off the edge of a cliff. 'It's a major promotion they're offering. Vice-president of finance. I'm looking forward to it.' They looked baffled; she might as well have said she was going to specialise in nanotechnology.

'How come you didn't tell us about this before?' Louise asked.

'The time wasn't right,' she said.

'And it is now?' Steve asked quietly.

Her heart thumped painfully. She forced herself to laugh it off. 'Oh, it's not until next year. It's ages away, there's no point in talking about it now. I only mentioned it because I didn't want you to rely on me being here.'

'Don't worry, we won't rely on you for anything,' Louise said heavily.

Steve left the room. She could hear his steps as he climbed the stairs. A fluttering in her chest was making it hard for her to focus on what was being said or even on what she was thinking.

'We'd better go now if we're going,' Mark was saying. 'Hurry up, everyone, we can talk in the car.'

'Go ahead, Mark, don't wait for us. I'll take my own car,' she said. She was anxious to get out of the room and see Steve. She should explain this to him. Still, she delayed going to him and went into the bathroom and locked the door behind her. She looked at herself in the mirror but the image that looked back had changed in minute but significant ways so that it was almost unrecognisable. There was a hardness in the eyes and face that frightened her. She remembered a horror story she'd read as a child where the character had put on a mask that had become grafted to his face so that it could no longer be removed and it became his face. She covered her eyes with her hands. It would have been a relief to cry but there were no tears: the well was dry. She fixed her hair and straightened her collar, although she wasn't sure why.

Beyond the door, she could hear no noise so she assumed those who were going to the hospital had already left. She eased open the door and went downstairs. Steve was standing in the kitchen, his hands in the pockets of his jeans. She was relieved to see him.

'Steve,' she started in a soft voice. 'I'm sorry about that. I didn't mean to say it like that.'

He turned around to look at her. 'But you're not saying it's not true?'

She took a deep breath. 'No. It's true. I've been offered a job in Pittsburgh.'

'And you couldn't have talked to me about it?'

'I meant to. I wanted to talk to you about it earlier but I didn't know how to.'

'That doesn't say much for our relationship.' He was quiet and spoke as if he had little hope of diverting the inevitable course of their conversation.

'Maybe I'm no good at relationships.'

'That's a little too easy to say, Chris. Nobody is any good at anything they make no effort with.'

She had no answer for that. They stood staring at each other in silence until Steve walked out of the kitchen. She heard rummaging noises upstairs and then after a few minutes, he came back down. He stood at the bottom of the stairs with his bag in his hand.

'What are you doing?' she asked.

He looked down at the bag in his hand. 'I'm leaving. I'm going back to Dublin.'

'Now?'

'Yes, could you bring me to the train station, or would you like me to call a taxi?' He had never spoken to her so coldly before. He didn't even seem angry, just as though he felt nothing for her any more. It was worse than anger.

'Do you have to go now? Can we talk more?' she said.

'Chris, I don't think there's any point. We've reached the end of the road. I'll move out of the flat as soon as I can get something else sorted. I could stay in the spare bedroom or, if you want, I'm sure Alan would put me up for a while.'

'No. Stay as long as you want.' She examined his face for a crack in his resolve but there was none. 'So now you've got exactly what you wanted, haven't you?' a vicious little voice said, in a corner of her brain. 'It was always a question of time and now is probably as good a moment as any. It could never have worked out between you,' it continued. She would have liked to tell the voice to shut up. She wanted to ask Steve why he had stopped loving her but she knew the answer; it was blindingly obvious. It hurt that he was leaving but it had a rightness about it, like something slotting into place. At least, she could hold on to her dignity. She would not beg.

'I can drive you to the station. I'll check train times. Maybe we can talk more when I get back to Dublin.' There was a glimmer of hope that maybe in the flat, away from Kilnalough, they might find their way back to each other.

'Maybe. I won't stay any longer than I can help.'

She had no doubt that he would quickly find a new place to stay, just as he would easily find a new person to be with. A needle of pain ran through her. It was for the best, though. Why put off the anguish when she could get it over with now?

He looked steadily into her eyes without flinching but they were no longer the warm brown eyes she was used to. All humour had been drained out of them. It was as if the light of love that illuminated them from behind, the warm light that shone through and made him extraordinary to her, had been extinguished. It was terrifying. She took out her phone to check for train times, unable to keep looking at him.

'Don't worry about the timetable. There's a train every hour or so and I don't mind hanging around the station if I have time to spare. Tell everyone I said goodbye.'

She hesitated. She put on her jacket and took her handbag from under the hall table. 'We can go now then.'

Nuala appeared from the kitchen and gave her a significant look that said she knew what was going on. How had she come to understand so much? For a second, she wondered if she should discuss things with her when she got back and ask for her advice.

'I'm taking Steve to Galway to take the train. See you later,' she signed brusquely.

Nuala nodded.

She was on her way to the door but on impulse she turned back to her sister. 'Congratulations. I'm sorry about earlier. I hope everything works out well for both of you,' she signed.

Nuala nodded again. 'And for you too.' She followed her to the front door and held it as they left. 'Good luck, Nuala,' Steve said a little loudly. He shook hands with her and squeezed her arm in parting. 'Look after yourself and the baby.' She smiled at him inscrutably.

It was dark and cold outside. Christina opened the boot of the car so that Steve could put his bag in it.

The silence between them was as heavy as the darkness that crowded in from outside the car. As she watched the miles increasing on the clock, she was struck with a sudden doubt that maybe she could do something to avert this.

'You can leave all your things in the flat until you have a place of your own, you know. It won't bother me, you can always come and pick it up later.'

'Thanks,' he said. 'But I don't have that much stuff. And I'm not sure it'd be a very good idea.'

'Maybe not,' she said and concentrated on counting the telegraph poles.

'Do you want to put on some music?' she asked. 'They're all your CDs anyway.'

He glanced quickly at her. 'No, I gave them to you. They're yours,' he said. 'But in any case, the radio will do fine.' He flicked around the channels until he fell upon an Alicia Keys song and let it play.

It was already completely dark when they arrived at the train station in Galway. She got out of the car and watched Steve pull his holdall from the boot. He stood for a moment looking at her. She tried to imagine what he might be thinking.

He hitched up the bag on his shoulder and took his set of keys to the apartment from his pocket. They both looked at them as he held them out in the palm of his hand.

'I'll leave them behind in the apartment when I go,' he said. He was making it sound very official and real. Every word he said was making it harder to go back to how things were before.

'Whatever you want. I don't mind,' she said and her voice sounded surprisingly steady. Or maybe it wasn't so surprising; this was the calm in the eye of the storm. What good would panic do?

'Well then, I suppose it's time to say goodbye.' Steve shuffled on his feet, looking uncomfortable for the first time.

'Do you want me to come in and see if there's a train soon?' She looked at her watch.

'No, it doesn't matter if I have to hang around for a while. You go on to the hospital.' Steve leaned towards her and kissed her cheek quickly. His beard brushed against her skin. She suppressed an urge to press her hand to her own cheek to hold on to that feeling for a little while longer.

'Goodbye, Christina, I really hope your mother pulls through.' He said it as though he would never know for sure. She tried to swallow the lump in her throat.

He turned and walked off towards the platform, his long strides taking him rapidly away.

'Goodbye,' she managed to say belatedly, but the word croaked out of her mouth and she didn't think he heard her. Should she run after him? Try and explain? She smiled bitterly at the notion. What was there to explain? And in any case, at least she now had the cold comfort of knowing where she stood.

She sat in the car, numb and disorientated, until a taxi driver beeped at her to move along. She drove aimlessly from the station, going with the flow of the one-way streets and taking turns seemingly at random until she ended up at Salthill. She pulled in. She stared out over the water. Further along the seafront, the lights of the hotels and restaurants were the centre of activity but she didn't approach them. She walked down to the beach and continued on towards the water's edge. She stopped and sat on a rock until the cold seeped into her and she started to shiver. Finally, she walked back to her car. Instead of going home, she found herself driving through the gates of the hospital car park. She sat behind the steering wheel, wondering if this was the right place to be. A few people gave her strange glances when they noticed her sitting motionless in her car, staring straight ahead through the windscreen. She didn't care. She'd made a mess of the situation with Steve but her biggest mistake had been to allow herself to believe, even for the shortest while, that it could have turned out any other way.

From the platform, Steve watched her car drive slowly away. As far as he could see, she didn't look back. He turned on his heel and stormed away to the platform. Had Chris really no idea how much she had hurt him? Despite their struggles, he had believed that they were slowly, very slowly, building a life together. He never thought she would go off and build an entirely other one without including him in any way in the plans. Now that he was excluded he wouldn't stay where he wasn't wanted. On the journey to Galway, he harboured a tiny hope that she would back down but she held firm. Maybe he had misjudged their relationship all along. He had convinced himself that they could be good for each other, once Chris let him past the barriers she had erected between her and the world. But Chris had higher barriers than most. Love was not a game she was prepared to gamble on; the stakes were too high for her and he couldn't force her. He prided himself on his practical approach to life, he didn't expect people to change for him and he knew only too well that being fair in life didn't mean life would be fair with him. He would move on, make a new life and let Chris live hers.

Still, knowing a thing didn't always make it easier to absorb. His heart ached. He stood on the platform staring across the rails. The wind whooshed down the corridor of the tracks but he stood firmly in place while it swirled around him. He would go back to the apartment and pack up most of his stuff. Maybe this time, he'd get his own place. He was a bit old to be sharing a house with a bunch of other lads as he had done since he'd arrived in Ireland. He shrivelled up a little bit at the thought of living alone. He would miss living with Chris; he liked her calm, self-contained presence around the place; he liked the droll comments she made when they were watching television, they told him a lot about her. He had learned over time that although other people might think her standoffish on first appearances, she was deeply kind. Everyone thought Chris was sophisticated and composed, almost to the point of being cynical, but he had caught glimpses of a raw, naive innocence she tried her best to hide. It made him feel that she needed him and it brought out a primitive, protective instinct in him. He smiled to himself, who did he think he was, some kind of old-fashioned manly hero? The world had moved on a long way from that.

Chapter 22

1988

On the night of the party, she almost turned back as she walked in the gates to Lynn's house. She could hear the music from the road. Red, blue and yellow lights were flashing in the sitting room and through the bay windows she could see people dancing. She would have gone home if there was any way she could have done so without her mother noticing. Her mother had insisted on her going, saying it would be good for her to get out, that she had worked hard enough for the exams and that she was entitled to have a bit of fun. She didn't feel like discussing with her mother why she didn't want to go; the whole thing seemed so complicated now and she was finding it hard to separate out what had really happened from the interpretations that her imagination had woven into it. In any case, it was all over now: by the end of the summer she would leave Kilnalough and she could start a new life in college, in a new place where nobody knew her.

Maura Sheehan and Vincent Delaney were pressed up against the wall beside the front porch engaged in a passionate kiss. She hurried past although there was no fear of them noticing her. The door was open and she stepped inside. Her eardrums were immediately assaulted by the noise. She could see that the guest list had been extended far beyond their own class. Kieran Colton must have invited most of his friends and she saw a few people from last year's Leaving Cert class. About ten people were talking to each other in the hall at a volume that was more like shouting, holding glasses or bottles in their hands. She wasn't sure what to do and hovered for a moment between the dancing in the sitting room and the sounds of drinking and laughing coming from the kitchen. In the end, she wandered into the kitchen where Lynn was holding court. She looked supremely glamorous in a colourful, embroidered gypsy top, tight, black jeans and long, dangly earrings.

'Aha, here comes the class swot,' she shouted when Christina entered the room. 'Go and put your coat in the spare bedroom. It's the last one on the right in the corridor.' She waved her in a general direction and continued whatever story she was telling.

Nobody passed any remarks of her and Christina turned to leave the room. On her way out, she noticed Jim Ryan in a small group. She could feel her face getting red as she remembered the last time they'd met. He looked up and caught her looking at him. He smiled and gave her a little wave. She was mortified; she hoped he didn't think she was keeping track of him.

She took off her jacket and went looking for the spare bedroom. It was easy to find: the bed was already lost in a sea of coats, jackets and jumpers. She added hers to the lot and returned to the party. She avoided the kitchen and went to the sitting room. Three or four couples were occupying the armchairs or sitting on the floor in a corner, lost to the rest of the world. Most of the others were dancing, alcohol having removed both inhibitions and elegance. Another large group was standing inside the door, joking and laughing. She stood nearby hoping to be noticed and drawn into the circle but after a while she gave up and went back into the hall.

'Well, Christina, come over here and talk to us.' Brendan Duffy shouted at her and she was almost glad to hear a familiar voice, even if it was his. He was talking to Colm and Tom. 'Do you not have a drink?' he asked when she joined them. The incident on the bus seemed to be forgotten. Nobody had referred to it for months and she was working hard on telling herself it had never happened.

'Not yet,' she said. 'I'll go and get one in a minute.'

'Here, have this,' he said and thrust a plastic glass with some kind of punch in it at her. 'No thanks, it's all right,' she said.

'Go on, I haven't touched it, I'd prefer a beer and I want to smoke a fag anyway.'

Asked like that, she didn't like to refuse and took the glass.

Brendan passed his cigarettes around and lit up. 'Guys, it's fuckin' great to be finished with school, isn't it?' he said. She nodded in agreement although she wasn't sure they had the same reasons. 'I'll never have to set foot in that place ever again, never have to look at McFadden's ugly mug again.' Ash from Brendan's cigarette fell on the carpet but he didn't notice or, if he did, it didn't bother him.

Cliona and Deirdre approached them. 'What are you doing out here? Come on, there's a drinking game going on in the kitchen. This year's class against last year's class. We'll need you for this one, Brendan,' They pulled the boys by the arms as if they were resisting. Unsure of what else to do, Christina followed them.

In the kitchen, they were forming teams on either side of the kitchen table. The idea was to have ten members on a team, each with a pint glass of beer or cider. They could only drink when the person before them had finished everything in their glass and thumped it down on the table. The winning team was the one who reached the end of the line first. Lynn counted Christina in for their team and she went along with the plan, not wanting to be a spoilsport by opting out. All the pint glasses were filled up to the brim. She looked at her own nervously. She was sixth. As each drinker raised their glass, the others chanted encouragement to speed them up. When it was her turn, she picked up her glass and tried to drink it down but she gagged and spluttered all over the floor and down her top.

'Ugh, Christina!' Lynn said. 'How useless a drinker are you?' Everyone else laughed.

She put her glass down, still half-full and stepped back from the table.

'Let's get someone else, someone who can drink,' Lynn said, looking around for a replacement.

'Anyway, I'll go and clean up,' she said but nobody was listening. On her way out the door, she saw Lynn give Brendan a push. 'You should go for it,' she said.

She rushed to the bathroom to avoid being cornered by Brendan and locked the door behind her. It was a luxurious feminine room, full of cotton wool balls and mirror lights and oodles of lotions and bottles and magnifying mirrors and fluffy dressing gowns. It was nothing like the basic functional bathroom they had at home. Her face was hot and her eye-makeup was bleeding towards her cheeks. She never knew how to put it on properly anyway. Her white top had splatters on it where she had coughed out her drink. She picked up a hand towel, wet the corner of it and tried to rub out the worst of the patches. Her top looked even worse than before. All her careful efforts to look good for this party seemed pointless. She was fed-up; maybe it was time to go home. She picked up a sponge and wiped off the black streaks under her eyes. The cold water invigorated her and she decided to prolong the pain no longer and to go home.

Brendan was leaning against the wall, smoking, when she came out. 'So?' he said. 'Feeling better?'

'I'm fine,' she said. 'No big deal.' She knew very well that his concern didn't run deep. As she walked past him, he caught her arm to stop her. 'What's the rush? Stay for a chat.'

She looked at him. His eyes were bloodshot and she suspected that it wasn't just due to beer. 'No thanks, Brendan. Why don't you go back to the party?'

'Oh, not good enough to talk to now, am I? You were happy enough to see me earlier on.' He stood closer to her and leaned against the wall, one hand beside her head.

'I don't want to talk to anyone right now. It's not just you. I'm going home.' She ducked under his arm and went to the spare bedroom to find her coat. She was searching for it among the piles of clothes, when he followed her into the room.

'Come on, Christina, stay another while, the party's just getting good now. We can have a bit of fun, the two of us.' His voice was a low cajoling rumble.

'No, Brendan, I mean it, I'm going home.'

He came closer. She was one of the tallest girls in the class but still her eyes only reached the level of his neck. Clumsily, he put his arms around her and pulled her towards him. His mouth landed on hers. She was so shocked that she didn't react immediately. Then, his hot breath, stinking of alcohol and cigarette smoke, made her stomach heave. She turned her head away and pushed him in the chest.

He kissed her on the neck, his hands running up and down her back.

'Stop,' she said but she didn't think he heard her. They were at the end of the bed, in a narrow space between bed, wardrobe and wall.

'Come on, Christina, don't be like that.' His voice was different this time. It sounded as if his tongue was covered in fur. A tingle of fear ran through her now. His hand slipped below her top and across the skin of her back, travelling upwards. She recoiled from his touch.

'Let me go, Brendan,' she said nervously. His lips covered hers and he pushed his tongue inside. It was large, slippery and invasive. She tried to pull away but they both stepped backwards and the unyielding hardness of the wall at her back hemmed her in. His hand moved along her back until it reached her bra. He fumbled with it and it pinged open. She gasped, feeling as if he had torn her open and exposed her. He moved to grab her breast roughly. She tried to jerk away. But he just groaned and pushed up even closer against her. There was something hard pressing against the bottom of her stomach. It took her a second to realise what it was.

She panicked: she had to stop this right now. 'Stop it, stop it, leave me alone.' She was shouting but the door was closed and noise in the corridor trapped her voice in the room. She struggled to get her hands between them and push him away but he was holding her too tightly.

One of Brendan's hands was now under her skirt, one finger worming its way under the elastic of her pants. 'Oh yes,' he moaned. As soon as his fingers touched her vagina, she felt as if an electric current ran through her. He must have taken this as a sign of approval because he moaned even more and removed one hand to unzip his jeans. She wanted to scream but her voice failed her and the sound that left her lips sounded muffled and subdued to her ears.

'No! Stop!' she called out and tried to hit him with her fists but she was no match for his boxer's strength. They stumbled and fell to the floor at the end of the bed, their fall cushioned by the coats and jackets that had fallen off. Brendan was on top of her, breathing heavily. One of his hands was under her top, kneading her breast. He arched up his hips to push down his jeans. He used his knee to wedge her legs apart. She could feel his penis blindly thrusting and butting against the barrier of her pants. He lost patience and grabbed at them to pull them off. She was suffocating among the clothes on either side of her and Brendan on top of her. For a second, she even wondered if she was going to die. He smothered her mouth with his in an impersonation of a kiss and his penis, a hard and smooth battering ram, shoved against her. His eagerness to gain entrance as he tried forcing himself into her evaporated suddenly. She felt a change in him. He tensed, moaned and froze for an instant. She felt the heat of a sticky, wet liquid as it dripped across her bare legs. He lay on top of her without moving. She realised it was over and pushed him away. He rolled over surprisingly easily. She stared at him with hatred. He reached a hand out to her but she slapped it away. She stood up.

'Hey, Christina…' he said but she found her scream: a low-pitched, out-of-control one. 'Get away, get away from me.'

At first, he looked surprised and scared, but it didn't last long. He ran his fingers through his hair. 'I didn't mean to…I didn't think for that to happen.' It wasn't an apology; he was making an excuse for himself.

'Get away,' she repeated. She couldn't think with him in the same room. She was like a caged animal, a rat or a ferret, defenceless but willing to attack and risk all in the attempt.

He stood up, zipped up his jeans and backed out the door, staring at her all the time. He was trying to say something but no words came out. She glared at him. He walked away leaving the door open.

She pulled up her pants and started tugging at the coats around her, throwing them in armfuls behind her. She couldn't go home until she found her jacket. What would her mother say if she came home without it? And there was no way she would ever come back here later to get it. She couldn't find it anywhere; the colours were starting to blur together. Just as she thought she would scream in frustration, she spotted a familiar olive-green sleeve poking out from under a pile. She grabbed it with relief, pulled it out and put it on.

Through the open slit of the door she could hear the party still going on. One of the girls let out a high-pitched squeal of excitement as Tina Turner started to sing 'What's love got to do with it'. She took a deep breath and left the room. Out in the hall, everything looked the same as before: the same groups were still standing around, beer bottles in hand, Lucy Dwyer and Paul McIntyre were still snogging on the stairs as if nothing had changed. Except that everything had.

From the sitting room, she heard Lynn say, 'You're crazy!' followed by a peal of laughter. She flinched. She pushed her way through the bodies to get to the front door and opened it on the cool night air.

She rushed past two entwined couples and, even though they were oblivious to her presence, she waited until she reached the road before breaking into a run. The pounding of her shoes against the tarmac was dull and loud in the silence. She counted her steps, the numbers filling up the spaces in her head so that other thoughts couldn't get in. But whatever she was running from kept up with her, breathing down her neck. She ran past the deserted primary school, its empty playground eerie at midnight. Once she turned the next corner, she would be on the last straight stretch to home.

She was breathless and her throat was sore when she reached the back door. Her mother had told her that she would leave a key under the mat. The house was dark and quiet. She didn't want to wake anyone up. She took off her shoes and tiptoed up the stairs, avoiding the second stair from the top that creaked when you stood on it, but her mother heard her anyway.

'Is that you, Christina?' her mother called out in a loud whisper. 'Are you home already?'

She put her head around the door. Her father was snoring gently. Her mother pulled herself up a bit in the bed. 'Was it a good party?' she whispered.

'No, it wasn't,' Christina said.

'Oh no, that's a pity. Well, go to bed now and you can tell me about it in the morning.'

There was a touch of disappointment in Kate's voice and it made Christina shrivel up inside. She closed over the door and went to the bathroom. The water was only lukewarm: the fire had gone out hours earlier and there was hardly any hot water left but it didn't matter. She took off her clothes and stepped into the bath. She took an old, scratchy, well-worn face cloth and scrubbed her skin viciously while the water filled up. Her thighs, where they were sticky with his semen, burned as if with radioactive matter. She continued to rub until her whole body was stinging and sore. Eventually, she got tired and dropped the facecloth. She got out and sat on the side of the bath, shivering. She took the plastic bag lining the bin and put her skirt and pants in it. She would find a way to get rid of them the next day. Wrapped in a towel, she crept towards her bedroom.

Her mother called out again. 'Is everything all right, love? Are you ok?'

'Yeah, go back to sleep, Mam.' She couldn't say anything. Putting words on it would make it even more real. She feared her mother's reaction. Maybe she would even be disappointed with her and think it was her fault. She had to push that Jack-in-the-box back down and close the lid. The best thing was to not touch the handle at all in case he would leap out at her with a scream.

She put on her pyjamas and then a woolly jumper on top. She realised that her teeth were chattering and she was freezing cold. Louise's little body had drifted into the middle of the bed. She pushed her back over to her side and crawled in. Digging into her back, she could feel the hard plastic of that red-haired doll with the wonky eye that Louise adored. She reached behind her to grab it by an arm and threw it on the floor beside the bed. She curled up in a ball and went over in her head the question on differential calculus from the Leaving Cert that she wasn't sure if she had got right. Images and memories from the night intruded: Brendan's hand on her arm; the smell of beer on his breath; the feeling of being crushed into the pile of coats; the embarrassment of spluttering out the beer in the kitchen; the sound of Lynn's laugh. They swarmed into her brain pell-mell but she did her best to push them away. She refocused on her calculation with all her determination until finally she fell asleep.

The next morning, when she woke up, she wondered if it had been a bad dream. But too many tiny intense details came to her for her to be able to dismiss the reality of it. No matter how she tried to ignore each one, another reappeared. Louise tried to talk to her but she buried herself under the duvet. She didn't come down for breakfast despite being called several times by her mother from the bottom of the stairs. Finally, her mother came up to see what was wrong.

She stood in the doorway. 'Why aren't you getting up, Christina? I have an appointment for Nuala with her deaf group this afternoon and then I have to take Enda to Spiddal for a match. I could really do with a hand.'

'Yeah, all right. I'm getting up now.' She mumbled from under the duvet.

'Why are you talking like that? Did something happen last night?'

She poked her face out. 'Hmm. It was something to do with one of the guys at the party.'

'What do you mean?' Her mother waited for further explanation.

How could she explain it? How to put words on what had happened? 'He asked me out a while ago but it was just a set-up. He was doing it just to make a laugh of me if I said yes.'

'Oh, love, that's awful. So did you say yes?'

'No. I don't like him. I never did.'

'Good. Then the stupid joke didn't work.' Kate was turning to leave.

Christina spoke up. 'But then last night…He was there and…' She trailed off. What train of events would she trigger if she actually said out loud what had happened? Would her mother insist on confronting someone about it? She hesitated.

'Don't pass any remarks of him, love. Boys are silly at that age. If you ignore him, he'll soon move on to someone else.'

‘I hate him. He’s a bastard, a fucking bastard.’ Underneath the duvet she clenched her fists so that her nails dug into her palms.

‘That’s enough, Christina. There’s no need for that kind of talk. I don’t like it. Now, I want you to get up and light the fire for me. I have a lot to do today. If you change your attitude and want to talk about it properly, we can do that later. Right now, I have too much going on.’

As Kate went down the stairs, hot, bitter tears squeezed out of Christina’s eyes and she punched her pillow.

Chapter 23

It was almost midnight when she entered the hospital. The atmosphere was hushed and the corridors were empty. Visiting hours were long over but the intensive care unit didn't apply the same visiting times as the rest of the hospital. They tended to allow close family to come and go throughout the day.

She made her way quickly to where her mother was, the path all too familiar by now. After scrubbing her hands and putting on a blue disposable bonnet and face mask, she entered the unit proper and looked around to check if Lynn was on duty. She saw other familiar faces but it looked as if Lynn wasn't there.

At the nurses' station just inside the entrance, two nurses were talking in low voices. They gave her a nod of acknowledgement as she passed by but said nothing.

It was different in the intensive care unit at night. Lights were dimmed. The machines still hummed, hissed, and bleeped but they were no longer the same background noises that they were during the day. They dominated the night and reminded those who could hear them that it was they who ensured the continuity of life. Occasionally, a murmured conversation drifted through the warm, heavy, chemical-laden air but voices were lowered and no words could be distinguished.

She pushed her mask to one side and kissed the soft, loose skin of her mother's cheek. 'How are you, Mam?' she said. 'It's late. Everyone's gone home but I wanted to see you.' Through the window, the night was patched with rectangles of light created by the windows of the houses. Galway had grown. It was a real city now. Years before, she used to laugh when people called it a city when it was just a town, and not even a very big one at that. Now, the title 'city' fitted better.

She found a stool and pulled it in close to Kate so that she could talk to her in a low voice. She had no idea if her mother could hear her, as Lynn had suggested she might, but it felt good to talk to her.

'Please get better, Mam. Come back to us.' It was more of an incantation than a request.

A young doctor doing the evening rounds came to Kate's bed. He seemed surprised to see her there but didn't challenge her presence.

'I won't be long,' he said. 'I'll just check on her and then I'll leave you in peace.'

'How is she doing, doctor?' she asked while he examined the output from a machine.

'It's hard to tell. At least she's stable at the moment.' She didn't like the sound of that 'at least'. Was there an underlying message in what he was saying? As she examined his soft, young face, she realised that he didn't know what was happening behind the wall of silence either but he didn't want to admit that.

'What about the antibiotics? Are they working?'

'We changed her antibiotic today so we'll monitor that and see if it does a better job fighting the infection than the previous one.'

'Thank you,' she said. He left quietly, moving on to the next patient.

Kate's cheeks were rosy but she no longer saw this as a good sign. A sudden wave of exhaustion washed over her. She slumped on the edge of the bed. She moved in closer to Kate so that she could feel the comforting warmth of her body.

She closed her eyes and drifted away to the sound of the machines around the bed as they ticked out their version of time.

Something was dragging her out of her sleep to break the surface of wakefulness. In that in-between moment, she became conscious of a trickle of drool spilling out of the side of her mouth. Her body was stiff and sore from sitting in this awkward position on the stool. She looked up to see if there was anyone around but the unit looked empty. She felt a twitch in her mother's hand underneath her own. The lights had been dimmed even further. She glanced out the window; there was no sign yet of any natural light in the sky, just the glow of streetlights. According to her watch it was three am. She rubbed her eyes to shake off the cobwebs of sleep that still clouded her mind, and stretched her neck and shoulders. Kate's hand moved. As she registered the movement, all traces of sleepiness dissipated. She looked at her mother's face. Kate's eyes were open. Was this her coming out of the coma or was this just a reflex?

'Mam?' she said tentatively. 'Can you hear me?'

Kate turned her head more towards her. She made an attempt at a smile. 'Hello, sweetheart,' Kate said in a barely audible voice. She made a slight cough to ease the passage of the words. 'I'm in hospital, amn't I?'

'You are, Mam. After your stroke, you had a heart attack, then you got an infection and you were in a coma. But you're getting better now. We've been so worried about you. It's great that you're awake.' She was overwhelmed to the point of choking.

'I was watching you sleep. What time is it? How long have I been here?'

'It's the middle of the night. You've been here almost five days.' She took her mother's hand and held it tightly. 'How are you feeling? I'm so happy. That's just great that you are here. That I can talk to you.' She was gabbling incoherently. She wanted to jump up and shout out with excitement but three in the morning in an intensive care unit wasn't the time or place.

Kate closed her eyes. She squeezed her mother's hand, terrified that this was just a brief respite before Kate submerged again. Kate opened her eyes again. 'I'm thirsty.'

She grabbed the tumbler with the water sponge in it and held it to her mother's lips. Kate sucked in the water eagerly.

Christina moved closer so that Kate wouldn't have to raise her voice. 'You must be tired, Mam.'

Kate smiled a faint smile. 'A little bit. Don't worry about that. How are you?'

She gave a little laugh. 'Me? I'm fine. It's you that counts. Should I call a nurse or a doctor? Are you in any pain?'

Kate shook her head. 'No, stay here. Talk to me.'

'Everyone will be so happy to know that you are awake. I should call them.'

'Don't wake them in the middle of the night. Let them sleep.'

The two women looked at each other. Christina picked up Kate's hand and held it to her cheek. 'I've missed you. I haven't been around as much as I should have been.'

'Don't worry about that. You were living your life and it's a great life. You are doing so well in your career and I'm delighted that you're with that lovely man, Steve.' Her mother was looking at her with tenderness.

'Actually, I'm not with Steve anymore.' Christina stopped talking.

'Why? What happened?'

'I'm not sure. I messed up. I'm a disaster.'

'We all make mistakes, lovey, that's human. We just have to try to fix them.'

'I think it might be too late for that.'

Kate nodded in acceptance but then said, 'Is it ever too late?'

She had a sudden notion that what Kate was saying could also apply to them. 'Mam, I know we haven't been as close as we used to be. And that's my fault.'

'Don't worry. You've been busy.'

'No, it's not just that.' If there was ever a time to be honest, it was now. 'I kind of threw myself into my work in an attempt to get away from something.'

'What do you mean?' Kate said.

'Something that happened back when I was in school. For a long time, I was bullied. One girl was the ringleader. She got the whole class to block me out. I was miserable for ages and ended up thinking I deserved no better.'

'Oh, that's awful, lovey. I didn't know about that.' Kate said.

'I did try. Honestly. But you were so busy. Anyway, that's not all. There was something else that happened just after the Leaving Cert.' She paused on the precipice. She had never told anyone before. Kate waited for her to go on.

'I was at a party for the end of the exams. It was in Lynn's house. A boy who had been teasing me before that got me in a bedroom and assaulted me. He pinned me down and forced himself on me.'

Kate put her hand to her mouth.

Christina tried to find the right words but none of them were powerful enough to capture the horror of that moment. 'He pulled off my clothes and… Touched me. He tried to rape me. The only reason he didn't is because he ejaculated before he could.'

Kate winced as if the pain was hers.

'I suppose legally you couldn't call it a rape but it felt like one to me,' she continued.

'Oh, my poor girl. You should have told me,' Kate said.

'I couldn't. I wanted to at first but the words wouldn't come out. Then, I thought that if I didn't talk about it, it would fade away and not be real. After a while, not talking about it became a habit that was hard to break.' She stared down at the folds in the sheet of the bed, unable to keep eye contact any longer with her mother.

'He made me feel like a worthless disposable tissue that had been used to clean up a mess and then thrown away. I couldn't bear the thought that anyone might agree with that or ask what I had done to deserve that treatment.'

'Of course you didn't deserve that. How could you even think such a thing? I know you, I know how wonderful you are.'

'I ran away. I was scared. I was so scared to seeing him again or the others who egged him on. I thought the best thing was to leave and stay away.' As she said it, she realised that the shadowy feeling that had been following her around was fear.

'I wondered why we didn't see so much of you. I should have guessed that something happened.'

'It wasn't your fault. It was me. Maybe I should have faced up to it instead of blocking it out for so long.'

'Who did this?'

'It was a boy in my class. I saw him the other day. It set me right back. I felt as if any progress I've made was totally wiped out.'

'I wish I could have helped you. If only you'd told me.' Kate said.

'I couldn't. I was the good girl. The one who didn't cause trouble.' Her nose tingled with unshed tears. She looked down so that her mother wouldn't see her damp eyes. Kate tapped her hand to make her look up.

'You were. You were my rock but that's no excuse. Maybe I leaned too heavily on you.'

'Mam, don't say that. For a long time, I blamed everyone: you, the others in the class, the teachers. It was a way of lashing out around me but I've realised that it was he who did it, not anyone else. I didn't want to think about it so flinging blame around was a way of focusing on something else. I thought maybe that if I didn't think about it or say anything, the feelings would go away and then it wouldn't affect me. But that's not how it worked. I'm sorry.' Tears flowed freely now and her face was wet. She stood up and leaned down to put her head into the crook of her mother's neck. Weirdly and unexpectedly, although she felt awful, it was a right kind of awful, as if awful was exactly how she was supposed to feel. It was a survivable sort of awful. Maybe telling people what had happened wouldn't tear her apart as she had always feared it might. Maybe, in the end, she would be OK. Kate stroked her hair gently.

'You've nothing to be sorry for. You were doing your best to cope. That's all any of us can do. Don't cry.'

'It's OK. You'll think I'm odd but it feels better to cry.'

'Don't be so hard on yourself.'

'We shouldn't talk too much. You should rest. I didn't mean to upset you with all this. I just needed to tell you everything when I could.'

'I'm glad you did, love. I only want you to find happiness. If you do find it, then make sure to hold on to it tightly with both hands.'

Kate closed her eyes. 'Thank you, Mam. I love you,' she whispered. Her mother's hand on her head became still and her breathing deepened.

'Mam? Are you falling asleep?' she said.

Kate made a sleepy sound and then said no more. Christina glanced up and saw that she had fallen asleep. She nuzzled her head in beside her mother on the bed, still sitting on the stool. She didn't want to be anywhere else and after a few minutes, she felt herself falling asleep too.

She woke up when she felt a hand on her shoulder. She looked up. It was Lynn. It took her an instant to recall where she was. Then, she remembered what had happened, their conversation. The sun was rising. The sky was brightening and the roofs of the hospital buildings below the window were coming into focus.

She jumped up, excited. 'My mother woke up during the night. She's getting better. I'm so relieved.'

Lynn said nothing, just continued looking at her. She didn't react the way Christina expected her to and her passivity was irritating.

'How is she now?' Christina rushed on. She leaned in close to her mother and spoke softly. 'Mam. Mam. It's me. Are you still asleep?'

'Christina, I think she's gone deeper into the coma,' Lynn said. 'Her oxygen stats have disimproved. Her temperature is up from when I left last night. It's not looking good.'

'Deeper into the coma? That's not possible. We talked last night. She woke up. She definitely wasn't still in the coma.' She took a step back. Her head was light, drifting upwards.

Lynn didn't contradict her but it was obvious that she didn't believe her. It was as if she was waiting for Christina to come to her senses. Was she implying that she had imagined it? 'I've called the doctors to come to see her immediately. She should be here any minute.' Her voice left no room for hope.

Christina stepped back, dizzy and confused. She tried to mentally retrace her steps and go back over every moment since she had entered the hospital. She tried to recall the precise words they had said to each other, the exact expression her mother had when she looked at her. She tried to capture the sensation in her fingers when she had held her mother's hand; how the ache in her shoulders had felt after she had woken up, as if that would confirm the reality of their conversation.

She returned to her mother's bedside. It was still early but several medical people had arrived and were discussing the situation with Lynn as they stood around Kate's bed. They all wore serious expressions.

'I think we need to call the family,' one of the doctors said. 'Call the priest too, if that's what she would like.'

'What's going on?' Christina asked.

'I'm afraid your mother's condition has deteriorated.' One of the doctors said. 'I'm so sorry but you may need to prepare yourself for the worst.'

Although she was used to protecting herself by anticipating disaster in most situations, this time, she had been blindsided. She brought her hand to her mouth to prevent a moan from escaping.

'It's probably a matter of hours now. You may like to ask your family to come as soon as they can to see her. I think the news would be better coming from you.'

'I'll call them,' she said and turned to her mother. Kate's breathing was laboured now and she could see that she had slipped further away from them than ever before. 'Just one question,' she said. 'I was here earlier, and during the night she woke up and talked to me. Is it possible that happened?'

The doctor exchanged a glance with Lynn. They had obviously spoken about this already. 'Given her condition, I think it's unlikely.' He was cautious in his opinion. 'But she may have made some noises that sounded like words to you.'

'No, this was a real conversation.' She was emphatic.

'Hmm.' He was dubious but didn't want to contradict her. 'We'll leave you with your mother now but we're here to help you in any way we can. If you have any questions or if you need anything, please ask.' As they walked away, Lynn gave her a look of sympathy.

She bent down to whisper in her mother's ear. 'I'll be back in a few minutes, Mam.'

She went outside to the front steps. It was drizzling lightly. She rang Mark first to tell him the news. He was silent for a long moment before he could speak again. They divided up the calls they had to make. She was brief and efficient. There wasn't much to say. Louise said that she would tell their father and bring him to the hospital.

She hesitated to call Steve but decided not to.

Jim, Louise, Nuala and Matthew arrived at the hospital first, followed, one after the other, by Enda, Mark and Aidan. Lynn arranged to move Kate to a separate room at one end of the intensive care unit. She told them that they would no longer be limited to two visitors at a time and that they were welcome to spend as much time as they wanted with Kate. The nurses were discreet and helpful. They quietly entered the room to check on Kate without interfering with the family's mourning. At one point in the afternoon, Lynn came into the room to tell them that she was off-duty but that she would be back early the next morning. She offered them her phone number in case they needed anything. Mark thanked her but told her that they would manage.

Kate was weakening with each hour that passed. She was still hanging on to the life she loved so much by a thread but it was taking more energy to continue to draw in each breath and expel it. Twice, even that effort was too much and everyone in the room waited for the final silence, but then, she mustered up her final reserves of energy and the monitor resumed its charting of her struggle. Jim sat by her side, pale and shrunken. It looked to her as if a part of him was dying with her.

She thought about Steve and imagined him in the flat, playing his guitar or watching a match. It would have been good to have him here with her, but she was fooling herself if she thought his presence would take away or even reduce the pain and loss. She just had to face up to it and wait until it passed. She hadn't told her family about her conversation with Kate during the night, partly because each one was too wrapped up in dealing with their own individual loss but also, because she hadn't quite figured out what had happened.

The day wore on. They stayed in her room listening in silence to her raspy breathing and wandering the corridors when they couldn't take it anymore and needed a break. It grew dark outside. Sometime after midnight, to her surprise, Jim took a piece of paper from his pocket and read out a prayer thanking God for the gift of love and asking for strength to bear the loss to come. It showed an emotional side of her father that she had never seen before. She was glad that he had a means of putting words on his bereavement and she hoped that it would help him to cope.

Finally, in the depths of the night, before the sky brightened, Kate's breathing stopped and she died. Louise burst out in noisy sobs. Mark, Enda and Aidan shed silent tears. Matthew was red-eyed and angry. Only Nuala and Christina remained composed. Nuala rubbed her mother's hair and kissed her cheek. Christina left the room.

Chapter 24

1988

Eight weeks after the party, the Leaving Cert results came out. Kate drove her to the school to pick them up but when they got there, Christina refused to go in. She insisted on staying in the car while Kate got them for her. After a few minutes, Kate returned, carrying an envelope and accompanied by Mr Halpin, the principal. He walked up to her side of the car and opened the door.

'Well done, young lady. You've done exceptionally well. We're all very proud of you. I hope you put these excellent results to good use.' He grinned and held out his hand. She shook it reluctantly and said nothing.

She turned to her mother. 'So how did I do?'

Kate handed over the envelope. Christina slid out the piece of paper inside so that she could read what was on it without fully removing it from the envelope. The results were even better than she'd hoped. There was no doubt now: she would be accepted on the actuarial and financial studies degree course in Dublin. She had refused to put anything in Galway on her list of choices: it wasn't far enough away.

'That's what a combination of good teaching and a good student achieves,' Mr Halpin said. 'All the staff are delighted for you, Christina.'

She stared up into his grinning face and thought about how much she wanted to leave him, the school and everyone in it behind and never see them again. 'Thanks,' she said and then turned to her mother. 'Can we go now?'

Mr. Halpin stepped back. 'Well, I'd better get back. Goodbye, Mrs. Cavanagh. Congratulations again, Christina.' He shut the car door.

'Was there any need to be so rude?' Kate said, when they were driving home. 'He was only trying to be nice.'

She gave a snort of disbelief. 'All he wants is the good publicity for the school. He doesn't give a damn about me.'

'That's not true, Christina. Why do you have to be so cynical?'

They drove the rest of the way home in silence.

Three weeks later, she was indeed offered a place on the course she wanted. At long last, she was leaving Kilnalough.

As her departure became imminent, it was as if Kate had only now realised that her going to college meant moving away from home. In the two weeks before, Christina caught her gazing at her as if her face had become unfamiliar. Every time Kate went shopping, she picked up some little thing for her new flat. She bought her a cookbook and signed the inside flap with 'Eat well! With much love, from Mam.'

One day, while Kate was cooking the dinner and Christina was playing with Matthew, she stopped and folded her arms. 'It'll be strange here after you go,' she said. 'It's great that you got the course you wanted but it won't be the same without you.'

Christina, on the other hand, could hardly wait to go: life could start properly once she was gone. The contrasting attitudes of the two meant that her last weeks at home were painful for both. When Kate said that she couldn't find anyone to mind the little ones and that she couldn't take her all the way to Dublin, Christina said that she didn't mind, that she was quite happy to take the train anyway. When Kate apologised for not being able to give her more money, she told her not to worry, she would get a weekend job in Dublin to help pay for her studies.

On the day she left, Kate took her to the station in Galway with her bags and helped her to board the train. She was bright and cheerful but Christina knew her mother well enough to see that it was a brittle enthusiasm. The stationmaster paraded along the platform and blew his whistle: the train was about to leave. Kate hugged her tightly and held on for longer than usual, reluctant to let go. Christina hugged her back and, for the first time, felt a twinge of anxiety about this big move. She broke away from Kate's embrace to lean down to kiss Louise and Nuala who had come too. She waved at them from the train for as long as she could see them. Her mother's face was a contradiction, with its combination of a wide smile and eyes that were full of heavy, unspilled tears.

Christina stood on the steps at the main entrance. The bare branches of the trees around the hospital were stark black silhouettes against the brightening sky full of a jumble of cloud shapes in different hues of red and yellow, becoming dark blue and black at the highest point of the sky. The street lights were still on, spots of light losing their power as the sunlight grew. The road through the hospital grounds was quiet and abandoned. The sunrise made even this urban setting beautiful. It was her first day in the world without her mother.

She watched a woman approach the entrance. As she got closer, she could see that it was Lynn, returning to work. She was wearing a black coat with a tartan scarf and carried a large bag on her shoulder. She stopped in front of her. 'Hi, Christina,' she said. 'How is your mother?'

'She died,' she said. 'About an hour ago.'

'I'm so sorry. She was a lovely woman. You were lucky to have had her as your mother.'

Christina looked at her in surprise. 'I'm not sure that I appreciated my own luck.'

'Sometimes we don't. Not until we see what it's like to be without.' Lynn stepped up beside her and turned around so that they were both observing the new day. 'Was that your husband who came with you the other day?' she asked after a moment's pause.

'No. I'm not married.' She was too exhausted to be on guard anymore. Nothing mattered. 'Are you?' she asked.

'I was,' Lynn said. 'We divorced two years ago.'

'I'm sorry. Do you have kids?'

'I have a daughter and a son. Nine and seven.'

She found it hard to imagine Lynn as a mother.

Lynn prepared to leave. 'I should get inside. I'm on duty in a few minutes. If there's anything I can do…'

'Thank you. I should get back too. They'll be wondering where I've gone.'

'How are they all coping?'

'I don't know. She was the heart of our family. I think everyone's afraid the family will fall apart without her.'

'I hope that doesn't happen. She'd have hated that.'

She shot a look at Lynn. She had put distance between herself and her family when even Lynn knew how important family was to her mother.

Inside, Christina found everyone congregated in the waiting room. Jim was sitting in a chair with his head in his hands. Nuala was sitting beside him, one hand on his shoulder. Matthew was pale and had his hands thrust into the depths of his pockets. At the far end of the room, Mark was on the phone making arrangements with the undertaker. Louise was sobbing quietly, being comforted by Aidan and Enda who were themselves red-eyed.

'They asked us to leave so they could deal with the body,' Enda told her when she entered. 'Are you OK?'

She nodded. The body. The words were strange. This was no longer their mother, no longer Kate. She no longer belonged to them. All they had were her remains.

She sat on the other side of Jim and exchanged a glance with Nuala. Nuala was the one who surprised her the most. Of all of them, she had been closest to Kate. She had always relied on Kate who had been her champion. And yet here she was, coping better than any of them with the loss of her. She looked strong and capable, able to support others rather than leaning on anyone. She wondered if it was delayed shock or if, as a result of her pregnancy, her focus had been diverted elsewhere.

'You look OK, like you are dealing very well with this,' she signed at Nuala.

'Yes. I would have loved to have had her for longer but not any differently. It must be hard for you,' Nuala signed back. She was looking at Christina with compassion in her eyes and she could see a part of her mother in her. When did her little sister grow up and become so wise? Sign language was sometimes so economical and went directly to the core meaning. Nuala was right: Christina's grief was magnified by regret. Now, her relationship with her mother was frozen in time, fossilised in her memory so that it couldn't evolve or change. It was now what it would always be, and she had to live with the knowledge of the lost years when she had avoided going home, when she had allowed fear to crowd out love.

'You'll be a great mother, Nuala. Even if Mam is not here to help you, I'm not worried.' She gave her a rueful smile.

Nuala smiled back. 'I'm not worried either, at least, not really. I'm lucky in that I know very well what a good mother looks like.'

Christina stood up and hunched down in front of Nuala. She hugged her.

Mark hung up and addressed them all. 'So the arrangements are made. Dad wants to wake Mam at home so we'll do that tomorrow evening. The removal will be on Friday and the funeral is on Saturday morning.'

It was all terribly final. She, who prided herself on her logical brain, realised that she had been holding onto a sliver of hope that maybe all this was a mistake, a gigantic diagnostic error that could be corrected. But the cogs of time turned in one direction only and they were forcing them all forwards, leaving Kate behind.

'There's something I'd like to talk to you all about. It happened the night before last,' she said suddenly. 'I came here late to see Mam. I was sitting at her bedside and then, at some point, I fell asleep. During the night, I woke up to see Mam with her eyes open, fully alert. We talked and then after a while we both fell asleep again.'

Everyone was listening to her.

'Did you call a nurse?' Aidan asked and she could hear the doubt in his voice.

'No, she said she wasn't in any pain. We just talked. For a good few minutes.'

'What did she say?' Louise was curious.

'She said she was glad to see me.' She hesitated to recount the detail of what they had said to each other. 'She said she loved me. She asked me about Steve. She was very peaceful, and then she just drifted off to sleep. And so did I. When I woke up a couple of hours later they told me that she was worse and that she was dying.'

'Did she have difficulty speaking?' Matthew piped up.

She hadn't thought of that before. She remembered how her mother's words had been perfectly clear, although spoken in a low voice. She had been tired but there had been no slurring because of the stroke. 'No, she didn't,' she said slowly as the realisation dawned on her.

'Are you sure you didn't dream it?' Louise said. 'We've all put in a rough few days. It could have been your mind playing tricks with you.'

'No, it did happen. I remember the details very clearly,' she said but she was no longer quite as sure as she had been.

'Did you talk to any of the doctors or nurses about it afterwards?' Mark asked.

'Yes, I asked them about it. One of them said that it was unlikely although they didn't say that it couldn't have happened. But I can't believe I could have imagined all that.' Her faith in her own senses was diminishing by the minute.

Lynn arrived at the door of the waiting room. 'Excuse me,' she said. 'Kate has been transferred to the mortuary. Please let me know if there's anything I can do.'

'You've been great, Lynn,' Mark said. 'It's been a huge help to have you here. We really appreciate it.'

'Indeed we do.' Jim roused himself. "Thank you on behalf of all of us.'

This was Jim's first reaction since Kate's death and she was pleased to see that he was speaking for the family. It gave her hope for the future.

They drove home. Everyone was subdued, each absorbed in their own memories. Everywhere she turned, she encountered reminders of her mother's presence that caused darting needles of pain in the face of her now everlasting absence. She found Kate's belongings left around the house as if she might, at any moment, arrive and continue using them. She found her fountain pen beside the phone in the hall. She was the only person she knew who still used a fountain pen.

Even the kitchen floor tiles reminded her of how proud she had been years before when her mother had asked for her opinion the day they went to buy them and had chosen the ones she preferred. For years, she had hopped between the randomly placed flowered tiles to the extent that even to this day, she felt a silly twinge of transgression when she walked heedlessly on the plain ones. Her heart constricted when she watched Mark's little girls laughing as they played a game of knocking each other off the poof. They would not have strong memories of having Kate as their grandmother although she had loved them dearly.

She welcomed being ambushed by this pain as signs of how much her mother had meant to her. She also welcomed it as her punishment for all the time she had stayed away from the family home even when she knew that it hurt her mother. Luckily, there wasn't much time to dwell on things as there was a lot to do to prepare for all the neighbours, family and friends who would descend on them that evening for the wake.

It was strange but the one thing that didn't trigger a profound sadness in her was the sight of her mother's body laid out in the sitting room. Her still features and yellow-tinged skin looked nothing like her at all. Her spirit, that spark of life, when it had left her body, had taken with it everything important about her so that this shell of her body was unrecognisable to her. As people came, they stood by the coffin and held Kate's dead hand or even kissed her waxy cheek but she couldn't do it.

The house became a hive of activity, every room downstairs filling up with people. Kate had been popular, not only with her own family and friends, but with the friends of all her children and the many people the vagaries of life brought her into contact with. Christina kept busy serving tea, coffee, whiskey and food. She listened to stories of her mother's kindness and consideration for others and it was a bittersweet comfort to hear how others had benefited from her company when she had missed out on it for so long.

In a lull, she stepped outside the back door to phone Frank and tell him that she would not be back at work that week after all. He was full of sympathy, encouraging her to take all the time she needed.

Above her was a clear sky where the moon was clearly visible. She turned her face up to it, appreciating the chill night air on her skin. As she turned back to go inside, she caught a glimpse of the reddening glow of a cigarette being stretched. She approached. It was Matthew. His face was twisted with sadness and she could see the shine of tears on his cheeks.

'Matthew,' she said quietly. 'Are you all right?' This was not the young, smart-alecky brother she knew.

He looked up, a flash of anger on his face at being found and she expected him to lash out with a sharp comment but the anger faded as quickly as it came. He looked away from her. He threw his cigarette butt on the ground and crushed it with a heavy foot. He mumbled something she couldn't hear. She put her hand on his shoulder and squeezed.

'I fucked up,' he said, staring straight ahead.

For a lack of something to say, she said nothing.

'She worried about me. I hate that. I know I disappointed her.'

'I don't think you did disappoint her, Matthew,' she said. 'She loved you. If she did worry, it's just because she wanted what was best for you.'

'Well, it's too late now. All she'll ever know now is that I was a fucking failure.' Matthew's voice was infused with bitterness. He refused to look at her.

'I messed up too,' she said quietly.

He glanced at her. 'You?'

'I left a long time ago and I didn't come back as often as I should have.'

'You were a big success. She boasted about you. I tried, but no matter what I did, things went wrong.'

'Don't be so hard on yourself. All she wanted was for you, for all of us, to be happy. You're young, Matthew. So you've hit a few bumps on the road. You can get back on track. She invested too much of herself in each of us to give up on that.'

The back door opened. Light flooded out. Louise walked towards them. 'I was wondering where you two were. Come inside. Uncle Pat is after telling the story of Mam and the 'antique' lamps she inherited from Auntie Ita. I know I shouldn't but I laughed so hard. I'd forgotten all about that story but it was the funniest thing.' Suddenly, her voice changed and the remaining warmth from her laughing leaked away. 'I'm really going to miss her,' she said. She could hear a reflection of Kate's humour and resilience in Louise's voice.

'Hey, come on. We'd better get back inside.' Louise was already picking herself up again. 'Let's go. The whole lot of the MacNamaras just arrived and the place is already jam-packed.' She linked an arm through each of Christina's and Matthew's and they made their way back into the house.

The rest of the evening passed in a whirl of tea and stories and buns and laughter and tears. She was glad that she hadn't a minute to think about anything. Over the course of the evening, Jim had been revived and had taken a step back from the brink of sadness towards the warmth of human company but when it was time to climb the stairs to go to bed, his buoyancy deserted him.

Chapter 25

The morning of the funeral, she knocked on the door of Nuala's bedroom before opening it. It was a pointless piece of etiquette since Nuala couldn't hear it but nevertheless she did it for herself to assuage a sense that she might be intruding. Nuala was sitting at her dressing table with her back towards her. She was motionless as though she was looking into the mirror but her gaze was fixed on a point far beyond the mirror. From the doorway, she reached her hand in to the light switch and flashed the light on and off. Nuala turned quickly to look at her.

'Are you all right?' Christina signed.

Nuala's hands swirled to make the sign for confusion. 'Everything happened so fast,' she signed. She took a deep breath. She clenched her fists against her chest under her chin and then exploded her fingers outwards. It was the sign for afraid.

Christina shook her head. She pointed at Nuala and then clenched her own two fists, holding them in a position of triumph on either side of her head. It was the sign for brave.

Nuala smiled. Christina was proud of her little sister. She would cope with whatever life threw at her.

'I came to ask if I could borrow something black from you to wear. I didn't bring enough clothes,' she signed.

'Of course.' Nuala opened the door of her wardrobe and motioned Christina to choose whatever she liked before taking out a black dress on a hanger. Ruefully, she patted her stomach. 'Maybe you could wear this. It's a bit tight on me already.'

'Oh wow, Nuala. You already have a bump. That makes it so…' She struggled to find the sign for 'real' and just mimed happy amazement.

'I know,' Nuala signed back. 'I'm just sad that my baby will never know Mam.'

'They will.' Christina nodded confidently. 'You'll pass on all the things she taught you and they'll know her through you.'

'Thanks. I hope so.' Nuala put her hands on her stomach possessively.

'I'll take this then and try it on. Thanks a lot.' She took the dress and left.

Mark arrived with his family, followed by Aidan with his girlfriend, Saoirse, and Enda. Louise had stayed in the house that night but her boyfriend John called to the house to go to the church with them. They had decided before that they would all go to the church together. Christina was dressed and ready in good time before everybody came. She put on the kettle to make tea in the kitchen for them as they arrived. Despite the circumstances, the sadness was punctuated with instances of laughter and warmth. Jim was struggling with his unaccustomed tie and Louise had to take it from him and make the knot around her own neck before transferring it to his.

Finally, everyone bundled into the cars and drove away to say the final goodbye to the woman who had united them all in the first place. Christina and Nuala travelled together. Nuala always had a knack of seeming self-contained as if the silence that surrounded her cushioned her against the stresses and everyday irritations that bothered everyone else. She never felt the need to fill up empty spaces with meaningless words or sounds and Christina was in admiration of her composure. Conversation was not possible with Nuala in the car because of the lack of eye contact so they sat quietly in the hum of the car engine as she drove over the narrow bridge and past the local shop-cum-pub on their way to the church. One of the local farmers had opened the gate to one of his fields so that people could park in it. There were cars parked everywhere. Kate had been well-liked and lots of people had come to pay their respects.

As she switched off the engine, she looked across at Nuala and could see that she was not quite as composed as Christina had assumed her to be. She was staring down into her lap before she looked up with red, tear-filled eyes. Christina, who had managed to remain steady all morning, felt her own eyes fill up. Nuala squeezed her hand and she squeezed back. Nuala took a deep breath and let go. She was glad that they didn't need to say anything. She thought about all the times her mother had worried about Nuala, anxious to do the right thing, how she had fretted about her future but now she sent out a silent message to her: 'You have nothing to worry about, Mam. She'll be fine.' She felt a surge of warmth as if her mother was answering that she knew. This was ridiculous: grief was making her imagine crazy things. She blinked her tears back and put her hand on the door handle, waiting for a second to see if Nuala was ready to leave too. Nuala nodded and they both got out of the car.

It was a sunny, crisp day. The grounds of the church were full of people, talking in low voices. Why don't they go inside, she thought, it's cold, they should get in out of the cold. She and Nuala entered and she could see then why so many of them had stayed outside. The church was already full to the brim. All of the seats were occupied and people were standing everywhere they could. The first two pews had been left empty for the family and the two women walked to the top of the aisle through the ranks of friends and neighbours Kate had known over the years. A kaleidoscope of faces swirled in front of her as she linked Nuala's arm. Some of them were people she hadn't seen for a long time and many of them she didn't recognise at all. Then, out of the tide of faces, she was jolted to see familiar ones, ones that were totally out of context. She was amazed to recognise Frank, Aoife, Peter and Noel, her colleagues, in one of the pews. She hadn't expected to see them there. Aoife gave her a little wave and a grimace of compassion while Frank nodded at her. It was a Saturday. They had travelled on their day off to her mother's funeral. The tears that she was holding back threatened to return. She nodded back at them and made her way to the top of the church and took her place beside her father.

After the mass, hundreds of people queued up to pass in front of the family to shake their hands and express their condolences. Jim was dizzy from the unaccustomed contact and had to sit down.

At one point, for a reason she couldn't explain, she turned away from the flow of people to look down through the church and she spotted Steve near the entrance. It felt as if it had been ages since she had seen his familiar face but it had only been days. She hadn't expected him to be there but of course she should have known he would come if he knew about it. He held her gaze, looking at her steadily with very little expression. She wanted him to react, to reach out to her even if with just a half-smile or a raised eyebrow but instead, his expression was blank. They had exchanged positions; now, he was the one whose emotions were unfathomable while she tried to understand him. Louise glanced around to see what Christina was looking at. Christina winced at her.

Louise leaned in. 'I rang him,' she whispered. 'Maybe I shouldn't have interfered but I thought he should know. I rang your apartment and got him there. He's a nice guy.'

'I know he is,' she whispered back 'Thanks, Louise.'

'You should hold on to him,' Louise said. Her words and the way she said them reminded her of what her mother had said to her that night in the hospital.

She took Louise's hand and held it tightly. 'I think it might be too late. But thanks, Louise. I really appreciate that.'

Louise looked surprised. 'You know me. Never say die.'

'Sometimes you remind me so much of Mam.'

'Thanks. I'll take that as a compliment.' Louise winked at her and turned back to greet the people passing by.

Frank was in the line of mourners coming to pay their respects. When he got to her, he leaned across the pew and kissed her cheek. 'I was so sorry to hear about your mother, Christina,' he said and she could tell that he meant it. 'You take your time and do whatever is best for you. I know about the offer from Russell. If you take it, I'll miss you but I'll understand.' She was touched.

'Thank you, Frank. I appreciate it.'

Peter and Noel shook her hand and told her that they were thinking of her in her loss. She hadn't expected them to care.

Aoife was red-eyed as she shuffled her way forward. 'It must have been such a shock. If there's anything I can do, let me know.' There was a lump in Christina's throat. She swallowed and looked upwards towards the ceiling to prevent the tears from flowing.

Outside, there was a cold wind that made people huddle together in groups before they hurried away to their cars. People milled around the family and she was drawn into conversations reminiscing about her mother. Louise cried at each story and Enda was almost as emotional. Jim still seemed stunned by the events of the past few days. She suspected that he wasn't sleeping. He was shaken and old-looking. Over and over, he recounted the details of the first night of Kate's stroke repeating the same phrases to each person who stopped to talk to him. As much as she could, she looked around for Steve. He should have been easy to spot with his height and beard but she could see him nowhere. Finally, the crowd thinned out and the hearse prepared to leave. Nuala wanted to travel with Jim so Christina ended up on her own. She was about to leave the church grounds when she heard a low, familiar voice beside her.

'Hello, Christina. I'm so very sorry for your loss.' She turned towards Lynn. It was the first time she had seen her out of uniform since her mother had fallen ill. In black and grey, she still had that same sense of style that she had when she could make her school uniform look like something she might have voluntarily have chosen to wear.

'Hello, Lynn. Thank you for coming.'

'I wanted to. I liked your mother.' She was preparing to move on.

'Can I ask you something?' Christina asked.

'Of course.'

'That last night before my mother died, just before you woke me up, when I fell asleep on her bed…'

Lynn waited for her to go on.

She hesitated to expose herself again to Lynn's ridicule, especially for something so important to her and yet she wanted to know.

'I thought she spoke to me that night.'

'I remember. You told me that you thought she had woken out of the coma.' Lynn didn't seem at all fazed by what she was telling her.

'I was so sure we talked. Except that everyone in the family seems to think I might have dreamt it or imagined it or something. But it felt so real. She seemed perfectly coherent to me, not slurring or anything. Is that possible?'

'This is my ninth year working in intensive care and I've seen a lot of people die there,' Lynn said slowly. 'I'm not surprised by anything anymore. I think people can find an unexpected energy when they are close to death. I've known people to reach out and grab someone firmly or even jump out of bed shortly before they died. It often happens that a patient who was totally muddled beforehand will have a lucid period before moving into the phase of active dying. I don't know if that's what happened with your mother but I think it's totally possible. I certainly wouldn't rule it out.' Lynn pulled her scarf tighter around her neck as a gust of wind whistled past them.

Christina was silent for a moment as she absorbed what Lynn was saying. 'So it could have happened?' she said slowly, as much to herself as to Lynn.

'Another thing I've learned is that there is still a lot that medicine can't account for. We think it's all an exact science but then, stuff happens that even the most experienced doctors can't explain. Sometimes, we just have to accept that there are things we'll never know for sure.'

'Thank you for that. I really appreciate it. I'd better go now. The hearse left ages ago.' When she turned around, she could see that most of the people had left.

'I won't go to the graveyard but I really hope that everything goes OK for you and your family,' Lynn said, holding out her hand.

'Thank you.' She took her hand and shook it.

She walked to her car, her step a little lighter than before.

Lynn glanced at her watch. She was on the evening shift so she had just about enough time to get some shopping done before picking Sam up from soccer practice. He'd be delighted to see her.

It had been a strange week. She hadn't thought about Christina Cavanagh for years and then this week she had occupied her thoughts a lot. If truth be told, she wasn't terribly proud of how she had behaved towards her when they'd known each other at school. They had started off as friends but then, it had been all too easy to make fun of Christina. She had to admit, jealousy probably played a part in it. Christina had a great family, where everyone got on and her mother made a proper dinner every evening. She had seen how Christina's mother loved her and made even Lynn feel welcome and special when she came to visit. In her own house, it was as if her mother didn't even notice her or, if she did, it was with exasperation because she created more work for her. She felt as if her mother couldn't care less if she dropped off the face of the earth. With hindsight, as an adult, she could see that her mother had been struggling to come to terms with her father's infidelities and had looked for answers on the inside of a bottle but, at the time, she hadn't seen it like that.

Christina had been an easy target. She hadn't set out to hurt her but when Lynn had arrived first in that new school where everyone had been friends for years before she got there, she was so terrified at being excluded and ignored, that she got the notion that if she got in first and did the ignoring and excluding then it wouldn't happen to her. It was a crazy logic, she knew.

So why did she do it? Probably because she could. It reminded her of something Andy, her ex-husband, had said a few years earlier. She had been annoyed and cross with Sam for being destructive and careless. All he wanted to do was smash up the towers of Lego and wooden blocks they had spent ages building up, sending them flying everywhere in the playroom. 'It's because that's all he knows how to do,' Andy had said calmly. 'He hasn't learned how to build yet so he just breaks them down.'

In any case, it wasn't as if that time at school had been all that bad. It was a relatively innocent time, just teenagers acting silly. The stuff that happened nowadays with social media and self-harming was far, far worse. Still, when she had first seen Christina a week or so ago, her first thought had been if Christina still remembered the incidents that had happened between them at school. And then, when she was so cool and distant with her, she supposed that she was still annoyed with her. That she was still harbouring a grudge had come as a surprise to Lynn. She'd have thought that compared with the success Christina had made of her life that the stupid little rows of their teenage years would have faded away into nothing.

Even at school, Christina had seemed a bit aloof, like she was better than everyone else, but now it was as if she belonged to a different, more cosmopolitan world. She looked elegant and refined and wore designer labels while Lynn struggled to pay the normal bills, especially since she was on her own. Being a single mum and racing from work to home to school meetings to matches or dance practice didn't leave her much time for the gym or beauty salon. Face to face with Christina, she felt the lack even more acutely. Why would

Christina even care about a silly tiff that had happened a thousand years before in Kilnalough Community School?

Still, she'd been glad this week had given her an opportunity to pay her back for old slights. She had always liked Kate Cavanagh. As a teenager, she had even daydreamed sometimes about how it would be if she were her mother so it had been a pleasure to look after her and she hoped that she had contributed even a teeny bit to making her last days easier for her and her family.

Christina had seemed so relieved just now when she had told her that she thought it was possible that her mother had emerged from her coma for a short while before succumbing to the final sleep. She wondered what that conversation had been about, for it to strike Christina as so important. Even if she had come out of the coma, you couldn't bank on anything a person might say in those conditions, especially with the amount of morphine Kate had been on, but she hadn't mentioned that to Christina. There was something about the anxious way she had spoken that made her hold back. Life was funny; just when you thought you had it sorted, it threw all kinds of new things at you. She probably might not see Christina Cavanagh again, after all, twenty years had passed since their last encounter, and they were certainly not friends but it had been nice to see her after all this time.

Maybe she'd make a shepherd's pie for the kids. They loved that and it might make up for the fact that she wouldn't be there to put them to bed. There were times when she envied people who had no kids. They didn't have to deal with the constant worry of providing for the voracious needs of these demanding little creatures that everyone insisted you had to adore unconditionally every moment of the day, but then, when she looked into their eager little faces telling some story from school or when she sneaked into their bedrooms after a long shift to look at them asleep, all the frustrations and scepticism got wiped away, and she felt like the luckiest woman in the world.

She drove away, one of the last cars to leave, and hurried to get to the supermarket before pickup time.

Chapter 26

There was a little over a mile between the church and the graveyard, the graveyard being closer to home. She knew every inch of the journey, remembered it from all the Sundays she had spent going to mass with her family. They always used to stop at Noonan's shop on the way home to buy the Sunday paper and sometimes, if their parents had the money and if they were in a particularly good mood, they got sweets. Not going to mass any more was her first act of rebellion after she left home to go to college. Her faith, once strong and childlike, had started to disintegrate when she was in her early teens until she stripped off the final tatters and threw them behind her when she went to college.

The graveyard was set back from the road, at the end of a rough path that sheep wandered across at will while they grazed in the fields on either side. There were already lots of cars parked in all the available spots so she left her car at the side of the road and walked down the path. The sun was shining. The cross at the top of the small disused church beside the graveyard stood out, black and obvious against the blue sky. From the distance, she could see four men removing the coffin from the back of the hearse and hoisting it onto their shoulders. She panicked. It was true. It was properly true. Her mother was dead. And she would never see her again. Never again would she have her in her life. She was being stoned by these harsh truths that made her knees buckle.

A single crow flew across the sky, making an ugly sound, before landing in a tree by the graveyard wall. It should be raining, she thought. Raining and bitterly cold, with a sharp wind, a reflection of her feelings inside.

Jim was following the coffin. He looked like an old man, hunched and worn. Age was not a concept that she had ever really associated with her parents. Theoretically, she had known that they were getting older, but she had a hard time imagining that this was something that might actually change them. Her father was sixty-six but he had aged ten years in the last week. Nuala was on one side of him and she hurried up to join them to link Jim on the other side.

'Are you OK, Dad?' she whispered to him.

He glanced up at her. 'I'll be fine,' he said. 'It's just hard to imagine life without her.'

Nuala looked across at her and made a face of compassion.

'You will be fine, Dad. I'm sure. It'll be hard for us all to adjust but we'll get there,' Christina said as she shifted her position so that he could lean on her more heavily as they shuffled forward.

Kate's sisters, Carol, Anne and Breda were in a huddle beside the gaping hole in the ground where they would bury Kate. Their eyes were red from tears and Carol was holding a sodden hankie close to her eyes.

'Oh, Jim.' They pounced on him as soon as he arrived. 'It's so dreadful. Poor Kate. We'll miss her dreadfully. She was far too young to go.'

'She was so enjoying being a grandmother,' Breda said. 'I don't know how many times she insisted that I should become one too. It didn't matter a damn that I kept telling her that the decision wasn't up to me.'

Carol laughed through her tears and Jim smiled.

'She was mad about Mark's two little girls all right,' he said. 'The other day they were fighting over some toy in the sitting room while I was watching a match on the telly. I told them to whisht up and you'd think I was after setting the dogs on them the way Kate jumped to their defence.'

'That was Kate for you,' Anne joined in. 'She had great time for the little ones. A heart as big as a whale. Christina!' She turned her attention to her. 'She was so proud of you. She couldn't be stopped from telling everyone how well you were doing.' She seemed to be bearing no grudge for Christina's snarkiness at the hospital which Christina regretted now. They were doing their best to cope as everyone was and their presence was making things easier for Jim.

The undertaker, in his solemn dark suit and discreet, invisible manner, approached and offered them individual flowers to throw on the coffin once it had been lowered. There was something artificial and staged about the gesture but she took the flower anyway. If all of these rituals helped people to span the newly opened void in their lives, who was she to object.

The priest called them all to order. This time, the ceremony was short, only a few words whisked away on the breeze. The coffin was held over the hole suspended on long straps that the undertaker's men held steady. Slowly, they released the straps so that the coffin descended a little jerkily into the dark earth. She found it hard to imagine that her mother's soft, plump, comforting body was really inside that wooden box. A spasm of pain ran through her. Aidan put his arm around her shoulder and squeezed her. Loss and grief were breaking down, at least temporarily, the invisible, untested barriers in her family that had been there before. The priest dropped a symbolic clump of earth on top of the coffin. It landed with a hollow thump. She flinched.

This was the end of the road. There was nothing more to say. People turned to each other in small groups and then, began to wander back to the gate, towards their cars.

'Come back to the house for a cup of tea,' she could hear Louise saying to everyone. 'We'd be delighted to see you. Do come.' When people demurred, she insisted. 'It's no trouble at all. Sure, it's only a sandwich and a cup of tea. We'll see you there.'

As the crowd thinned out, Jim spoke in a low mumbling voice. He was saying a decade of the rosary. The aunties joined in. Her heart constricted. She understood that he was delaying the moment of departure. It was great that he found consolation in something, even though it had come to mean nothing to her. She remembered how years before, in the summer before she left for college, she had told him that she didn't want to go to mass any more. There had been a huge row, with Kate acting as referee.

'Why do you not want to go? Would it kill you to go to mass with your family?' he had said, finally.

'Because I don't believe in God. I don't believe he or she or it exists. That's why,' she had said.

Jim's face had crumpled and all the anger had disappeared. 'Oh Christina,' he had said as if he had taken a blow to the stomach.

She hadn't realised that her lack of faith could affect him so much but she couldn't take it back or lie to save his feelings.

At the end of the rosary, the aunties fussed over him as they guided him back to the car. She followed behind. The last few cars were leaving. A brand new one, obviously a rental, caught her attention. It was waiting in turn to pull into the line of cars making their way slowly to the main road. With a jolt of recognition, she saw that it was Steve behind the steering wheel. She hadn't been expecting to see him. After catching the glimpse of him at the church and then seeing him no more, she had assumed that he'd just come for the funeral and had gone back to Dublin already. The sight of his familiar profile made her hold her breath. She ran after the car to catch him before he left.

'Steve, Steve' she called out, waving at him. She didn't care what the aunties might think. For a second, she thought that he might drive away without seeing her but then she saw his indicator flashing. He pulled over and switched off the engine. He got out of the car. She had never seen him so formally dressed. He was wearing a suit with a navy tie. She never knew that he owned one. He looked different, handsome but almost inaccessible, so far away from the Steve who always seemed warm and approachable.

All the things she wanted to say to him became a jumble and she found herself tongue-tied.

'How are you, Chris?' he said and she had never been so glad to hear the abbreviation of her name.

'OK,' she said. 'Actually, surprisingly OK. Maybe it'll hit me later.' As she said it, she realised it was true. There was a moment of silence filled with distant cars and noisy crows. A sheep baaed nearby.

'Your mother seems to have been a popular woman.' Now that she was up close, she could see that he had even trimmed his beard.

'She was. You know, any issues that there were between us had much more to do with me than her. It was all my fault.'

'I don't know if that's true. I know you, Chris.'

She looked away and took a deep breath before turning back to him.

'I don't think you do, Steve. I haven't exactly been straight with you all the time.'

He looked steadily at her and his brown eyes made butterflies flutter throughout her body. He leaned forward as if someone could overhear them. 'You don't always have to show me things for me to see them,' he said.

That's exactly what she was afraid of.

As if he could read her thoughts, he added, 'and I like what I see.'

'Do you want to walk for a bit?' she asked.

'That would be nice.'

They continued to walk along the path they were on in the opposite direction to the road, across the fields. It was a simple track where the grass was worn away by the passage of feet that got rougher as they left the graveyard behind them. It was comfortable walking beside him without having to talk or even look at him, just knowing he was there.

'So when are you off to Pittsburgh?' he asked finally.

'I'm not going,' she said. 'I've decided to stay.'

He stopped and looked across at her. 'Why?'

She hesitated and chewed on her thoughts before expressing them. 'I think I might be needed here. There's a lot going on and I can't do much to help from the other side of the world. It's my family, after all.'

He frowned. 'When you say here, do you mean here in Galway or here in Ireland?'

'I haven't really got that far yet. I just know that it doesn't feel right to leave. I'll work something out. That's enough decisions for one day.' She grinned at him.

'How would you feel about a bit of help with working that something out?' Steve continued on walking, looking straight ahead of him as he spoke. She was amazed to hear in his voice that he was nervous of what she might say.

'Steve, are you sure you mean that? I've messed you around. I think you deserve someone a lot easier to be with than me.'

'If I wanted easy, I'd never have fallen in love with you in the first place.'

Her heart sank like a stone dropped in the sea before soaring up, breaking through the surface like a gannet.

The offhand way he said it made it even more real and believable.

'When I saw you first in that pub for Rita and Tommy's engagement party, I could see that you weren't entirely comfortable in the group,' he continued. 'You were talking to a few of the women but I got the impression that you'd have preferred to leave and do your own thing. Then, at one point, despite yourself, you laughed at something someone said and I thought, I want to be the one who makes her smile. And then as I got to know you, I could see the kind, intelligent, thoughtful, prickly, difficult Christina and I thought, that's who I want to be with.'

This was the longest speech she had ever heard from Steve. How had she ever managed to be so lucky as to find him? But was it fair to subject him to a life with her?

'Steve, you are a great guy. I think I don't deserve you.' She tried to say it casually but she didn't know if she succeeded. 'Even my family has a hard time with me and they don't have any choice. You could find someone nicer than me, someone uncomplicated, someone you could have kids with. Why me?'

'We could both play this game but I don't know if it's a great idea. I'm thirty-six, my job doesn't pay very well, I know I'll never earn nearly as much as you. I don't even own a car. I'm starting to think I'll never make it in music.' He patted his tummy. 'I'm overweight. I'm not the best-looking guy that ever lived. I'm not much good at housework. Will I go on?'

She stopped to look squarely at him. She could see how much it had cost him to admit, even to himself, even in the midst of the litany, that he might never succeed with his music.

'I don't care about any of those things,' she said. 'None of those things is you.'

'Well then. Why can't you accept that it's the same for me? I want to try to make it work between us. But only if you want that too. Maybe we won't succeed but maybe we could.'

'Before she died, my mother told me I should hold on to you with both hands.'

'A wise woman.' He smiled before turning serious. 'One thing I am sure of is that I can't make this happen by myself. You have to want this too.'

'I do want it, Steve.' She wanted to throw her arms around him but hesitated. Maybe this was what her mother meant: she had to take the risk of reaching out for what she wanted. She leaned up, put a hand on either side of his face and kissed him.

'I love you,' she said.

THE END

Acknowledgements

In memory of my mother, Annie, who gave me a happy childhood, the luckiest thing that can happen to anyone.

Thanks to all my wonderful family and friends for your support, help and love. Having you is the second luckiest thing to happen to me.

And special thanks to Joan Paul, Marie O'Mahony, Lorraine Fabre and Sean Mahon who encouraged me in my writing over the years whenever I felt like giving up.

Thank you to Mathilde Viret and Fiona Kearns for their talent and patience in illustrating and designing the beautiful cover.

Printed in Great Britain
by Amazon

46795969R00175